TEMPEST OF BRAVOURE

KINGDOM ASCENT

CASTAWAY

* CITY OF THE DEAD

*FORTHCOMING

TEMPEST OF BRAVOURE

CASTAWAY

VALENA D'ANGELIS

Tempest of Bravoure—Castaway by Valena D'Angelis Published by fabled ink.

www.fabled.ink

Cover by 100 Covers.

Maps by Valena D'Angelis.

First Edition, revised on March 10, 2021

The Bankis
Iskala
Crystal Sea
Fallvale
Bravoure
Sea of Khal
Ailura
Galies
Indus-Kali
Teh

Ilia

The Moors

lis

Kanjuuna

Vargna

Kanmvi

Elb

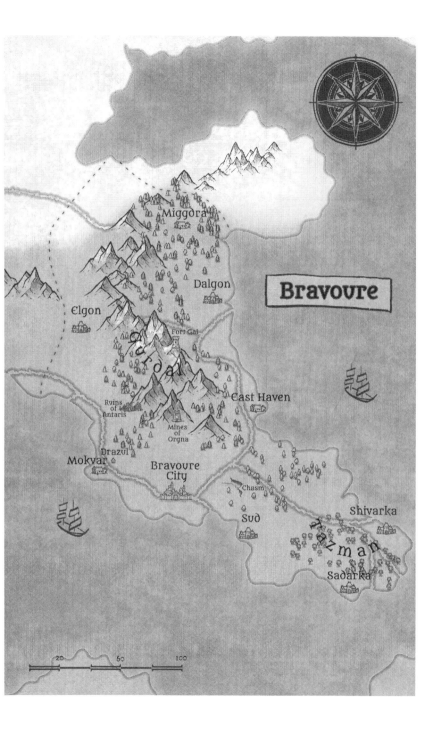

To you, who made it through Kingdom Ascent and joined me here.

1

POLITICS

Slashing through the damp air, the rough leather ripped against her skin and sliced through her flesh. Meriel's eyes snapped open wide. She screamed so loud that her voice died in a broken whisper. She hung by her wrists, stripped of her clothing, bare, and blood trickled down the arch of her back.

One more slash.

Her torturer, a Dwellunder scum with flashy yellow eyes and vicious teeth, came to stand in front of her and gave her the vilest of smiles. Behind him, leaned against the stones of the castle's dungeon, was Xandor Kun Sharr, the dokkalfar prince who had just taken the Golden City under siege.

Meriel screamed again. Blood continued to drip down her legs and slid from her shackled ankles to the floor.

Xandor quietly stared. He crossed his arms, his amber eyes fixated on his sister. With a delicate flick of his hand, he ordered her torturer to stop. The ugly scum dropped his arm, the one that held the bloody knout with bits of Meriel's flesh embedded in the thongs.

Xandor slowly ambled to his sister. Her knees were bent. Her head faced the ground. He saw the tears that flowed among the blood on her face.

"Don't cry, dear sister," Xandor said in a soft tone. "I'm almost done with you."

Meriel slowly raised her head and shuddered. Spasms on her torn back made her flesh bleed more. Her lips trembled, her breathing was hoarse. She could not speak, but her blazing purple eyes said everything. Xandor seized her silver hair from behind and forced her to stand.

The scream that erupted from her almost burst his eardrums.

He passed his arm between her breasts and seized her burning face. He pressed himself against her back and relished the warm feeling of her blood against his clothing. He made her set her gaze ahead, forcing her to look through the tiny window that faced the city of Bravoure.

"See," he uttered as she struggled against his grip. "There is your precious Academy." He held his hand close to her face, revealing something in his palm: a tiny, black marble. "And this is all that will be left of it."

Xandor dropped the marble to the floor. It clinked against the damp stone tiles and clinked again until it rolled into the darkness. Between the locks of silver hair that stuck to the dried blood on her face, Meriel saw a cloud of thick smoke in the distance. Her heart instantly shattered more than it already had. Anger boiled from deep within her. She turned her face slightly and saw the vile embers of her brother's eyes.

She tried to spit at the cursed brother she hated from deep within her gut. She wanted to unleash her bitter wrath upon him. But she could not speak. Something forbade her to.

It was not the mix of blood and saliva that clogged her throat, it was the *quūora* fang, the magic suppressor, the rhodium needle lodged between her vocal cords.

The one that forbade her to fight.

Meriel painfully stared at the window, at the scorched Academy far in the distance. The hurt in her heart overtook anything else she felt. The Academy...burning before her eyes. Her dear Academy.

Luthan.

Meriel yowled as she felt Xandor's hands reach above her wrists. He proceeded to unchain her.

"Brings back memories, doesn't it?" he whispered, caressing her with the touch of a caretaker. "Feeling me so close to you..."

Meriel's gut turned on itself. She could feel his warm breath on her aching shoulders as he held her by the hair again and murmured more destructive words to her. Once she was loose, Xandor let her fall down to the cold ground.

He would come back a few days later to announce the death of Thamias and the destruction of Antaris, as well as the Faculty and everything else around it. More days later, he would tell her the Bravan King had been hanged. Then, on that one bright summer day, he would free her. Meriel would have the opportunity to crawl out the exit of the golden castle, only to see the decaying face of her mother, hanging from the gates, with no body attached.

1365:AV, NOW

Ahna gazed through the window, observing the people marching the dark streets of Bravoure city this evening. Her mind, distracted by memories of a time unforgotten, traveled to images of the Magi Academy of Bravoure burning and collapsing from a fire too grave. That day, she had thought the magi to be dead. All

3

of them, *dead*. Her friends, her husband, gone in the pyre of the Dark Lord. Ahna had decided to flee and never look back. But here she was, fifty years and a decisive battle later. Ahna had discovered the first clue that shattered her reality. The magi may still be alive, and tomorrow, the dark elf would set out to find them.

Two years had passed since the fall of Sharr, and two years since the Rebellion. In the radiance of victory, the capital city of Bravoure was thriving again. The squalor and misery—all put to an end. The corroded bridges, the drought, the stench of the northern sewers restored to their state of prewar Bravoure. Had it not been for the rebels who had rallied the people, Bravoure could have never gotten back on its feet so quickly. Even the land of Galies, Bravoure's most trusted ally, had been there to assist with the revival of the kingdom.

However, despite this glorious rebirth, the Bravan people were wounded, suffering from the terrible scars of a fifty-year trauma. In these times of rehabilitation, they needed to place their hopes in someone who could not only heal the city but also their hearts. And in the light of a new dawn came a familiar shadow. The treacherous veil of politics.

"This new guy, Goshawk, he does have his way with the people," David noted with a sharp tone.

The Resistance commander sipped his wine and went on to enjoy his roasted chicken. His beard had grown, and his coal eyes of Tazman still shone with the light of righteousness. Kairen went to fetch another bowl of soup from the cooking pot by the fire. She glanced at her husband and at Ahna, at the man with a gleaming earth-brown skin tone and the elf with her silver curls, who still focused her attention out the window. A warm smile drew on Kairen's face as she gazed upon her dear family.

"Charles Goshawk," she began. "One of Bravoure's old bankers. He promises to double people's riches with his new five-

Sol recovery plan. Something about introducing a new credit system."

As she went to sit back at the wooden table, Thamias, Ahna's little brother, stepped out of the kitchen. He held a platter of more roasted chicken, which he placed in the middle of the table. He went to sit next to his sister and turned his head to David.

"Why are you not campaigning?" the younger dark elf asked.

David let out a loud laugh. "I'm a soldier, not a leader. But Mother Divine wishes me to be Bravoure's next Great General!"

They ate their roasted chicken, potato corn soup, and glazed momrogis in David and Kairen's new home. A modest wooden house in the center of the capital, where the two lovers had rebuilt their lives. This house used to belong to David's aunt, who had passed away shortly after the Rebellion. She had no children and no family other than her beloved nephew. She had taken her last breath knowing he and his army had led the Resistance to victory.

Ahna's attention returned to the table, and she poured herself an extra glass of red wine while clearing her throat. "Charles Goshawk made a profit of Sharr's reign. Now, he makes a profit out of the people's desperation."

The upcoming elections—the only topic in Bravoure most cared about, almost obsessively. A new leader was to be elected. Not a king, but a regent, the emblem of a new regime. However, not all in Bravoure agreed with this idea of democracy. Some wanted a Resistance leader to govern. Some even believed Mother Divine should be crowned Queen.

"Mother Divine wants a separation of power between the State and the Congregation," David explained. "She is even against the Red Cardinals endorsing anyone in the elections."

"Astea is right!" Kairen reinforced. "Just as the military should not be involved in politics."

"Galies was benevolent so far, but the arrival of their envoy doesn't reassure me. I don't trust this man," her husband warned with a frown.

"We knew their help wouldn't come without debt," Kairen retorted in an evident tone. "They've been very kind, but the people would obviously prefer a Bravan regent."

The couple referred to Malyk Faun, a diplomatic envoy from Galies who oversaw the efforts to rebuild the city. Malyk Faun was now a permanent citizen within Bravoure, and he presented himself at the upcoming elections.

"What do you think of Goldwing?" Ahna inquired.

"He has gold in his name!" David exclaimed with enthusiasm. Everything was about gold in Bravoure. "He would be a great leader, but he is too kind, unfortunately. I believe Zhara, his counterpart, would be a better choice. I am thinking of voting for her—definitely not Goshawk. If Goshawk wins, we'll lose our soul to our worst enemy."

"What would be worse than Sharr?" Kairen queried with a raised brow.

"The Economy, my love." David cheered and finished his wine.

Thamias heard this talk of campaigns and elections without listening. He was more focused on the fistful of delicious mushroom and spinach momrogis in his plate. These dumplings were complemented with gravy-based sauce from the roasted chicken and spices of the Gurdal mounts. This refreshing flavor dissolved in his mouth and the scent even spread from his throat to his nostrils. But as much as he tried, he did not enjoy it.

Thamias was preoccupied, no—anxious about his own role in all of this. All of this talk of rebirth and prosperity. As Dragonborn, he was the Congregation's protégé. But he was not the symbol of hope people had wished for. After all, in his amber eyes, he was the failed prophecy, and for some, he had begun to look too much like Xandor Kun Sharr. Thamias hated this. He hated to be compared with the man who had tormented him, practically all his life.

After the Rebellion, a dark seed of hate had grown in the people's gut. The doubt in Thamias and his sister, and the few *dokkalfar* who remained in Bravoure. Even those born in the capital, those who had not come from the Dwellunder in the first place. There was resentment, distrust, and most of all, hostility toward the dark elf kin.

Fortunately, most citizens kept their composure when in the presence of Ahna and her little brother. Thamias, who mostly assisted David with his work in the castle, had even made a few friends.

"How's the Academy doing, Ahna?" Kairen inquired as she plucked the last piece from the loaf of cloud bread.

"The main tower is finished!" the elf replied, and Kairen immediately applauded. "There is still work to be done in the auditorium, but the lecture halls are just about done! Thanks to the Resistance's efforts to preserve so many scrolls and books, we have the library opening tomorrow." Ahna raised her glass in the air as a sign of celebration.

"And how about Miya?" Kairen lowered her voice playfully and posed this question with a teasing glint apparent in her copper eyes. "Is she going to be your *beautiful* librarian?" She swayed her red hair exaggeratedly behind her shoulders, to suggest something that made Ahna blush.

Ahna kicked her feet underneath the table, and she laughed.

"Miya?" Thamias wondered out loud. "Tailor-Miya, Miya?"

Kairen kept on laughing. "She's not just a tailor. She also helped Ahna with the Academy. I hear she's very good with her hands…"

Ahna interrupted her with another kick to the leg. David joined the laughter and rose to his feet. He stepped closer to his wife and embraced her with his strong swordsman arms.

7

"Alright, my love, you've had too much to drink," he said as he laughed some more.

He kissed her on the neck and motioned for her to help him clear the table. Thamias' gave him a hand with the larger plates, and Ahna collected the empty wine goblets. They brought the plates and cutlery to the kitchen, where a bucket of hot water was ready.

"Leave it, I'll handle it," David said.

"No, you need to hurry," Kairen retorted gently. "Luk Ma will be here soon."

And speaking of the sindur tom, someone knocked on the door.

"Ah!" David exclaimed and signed to Thamias. "That's my favorite councilor. Come, Sonny, let's leave the ladies alone."

He plunged the plates into the hot water and headed toward the door after he kissed his wife on the forehead. Sonny—Thamias by his common name—checked his sister for approval. She gave him a nod and a gentle smile.

"Go, but be careful with the boys!" his sister said with amusement.

"You be careful, *systr*, wherever you're going," Thamias returned with a wistful smile.

Ahna kissed her brother on the forehead, bidding him a sweet goodbye. She held his hand for a bit, then, with hesitation, she let him go. After all, she was leaving tomorrow.

"We're just going into the square," David reassured Ahna. "Don't worry, *bahi*, I'll keep an eye on your little brother!"

David opened the door and greeted Luk Ma, the man-lynx who had led a platoon of a hundred scouts in a different life. Luk Ma's whiskers wiggled when he noticed Ahna and Kairen. He waved at them with his soft paw. Sadly, Luk Ma had lost his other arm to the wounds of war, but it did not make him any less proud. He and David waited for Thamias to collect his belongings before heading outside, on their way to the square. They followed the alley lit by a series of bright torches until they reached the Gold Monk, their favorite tavern.

"So, Ahna, are you really going?" Kairen asked the woman she was proud to call *sister*.

The two sat outside on two stools made of wood. Actually, they were more like simple blocks of wood. The house had a little terrace tiled with Gurdal stones and adorned with beautiful potted orchids. It was dark, only the light of Kairen's lantern and moon lit this side of the stone house. Ahna could see, in the far distance, meanders of silver and purple of the indistinguishable flora that covered the moon. A colored mystery that had eluded the magi for as long as they existed. This astral body, fixed to the Domain of Stars, had looked over Terra for centuries.

"I have a lead," the elf declared. "I think one of the lost magi may still be in Bravoure."

"You're just looking for an excuse to miss the elections," Kairen exclaimed with a light laugh.

Ahna chuckled. *That*, she was. Politics was the beast she preferred to avoid. It started lifetimes ago in the Dwellunder, with her crazed father the Duke of Mal. Then it continued in Bravoure, when treacherous mistakes were made before the war. And now, it was there, at the dawn of democracy.

"Goshawk the Banker. You know what rhymes with banker?" Kairen grinned.

Ahna laughed and lowered her face against her palm. "Too bad David decided not to campaign," she said, a little more serious. "I wonder what creative name you would have come up with for him!"

Kairen exhaled deeply to cover her laugh. "Why should we separate the State and military? David is righteous. He's Tazman, for crying out loud!"

"Because the State serves a party. The military serves the people."

Kairen sighed—Ahna was right. As much as they wanted the State to represent the people, in the end, it could never be fully the case. The State depended on the majority's choice, and the majority does not necessarily speak for the people.

"You should campaign, Ahna," the red-haired woman suggested.

"I am an archmage and a dean now—enough titles!" Ahna chuckled again, but the reality of what she was rang between her pointy ears. "I look too much like Sharr."

Truth. A truth Kairen denied, even to this day. But still, a hard truth that justified the people's apprehension of her kin.

As the elf pondered on her cursed memories, Kairen had poured them a final cup of ruby red wine. She handed it to her sister, and they both remained silent, contemplating the moon.

"Since when do we halt at kinship?" Kairen distantly whispered, remembering an old image of someone she had known. "Something Joshua would say."

Ahna smiled slightly as she joined the red-haired woman in her thoughts of the glorious leader of the Resistance. Joshua Sand, the man who had given his life to protect the cause. In his memory, the rebels had built a gold shrine on the capital's central plaza. A pedestal with his name and a hundred rebels' engraved in the metal.

Cedric's name... Ahna shivered from the distant memory of the captain of the Shrike Wing, the spies of the Resistance. She wished the memories away because remembering *him* was simply too painful, even though it was hard to forget a man like him, who he had been, and what he had become.

"Who's going to manage the Academy while you're away?" Kairen asked after a few beats.

"Mother Divine will oversee the final work, and Miya will

assist the opening. The new magi already have a place that welcomes them."

"Ah, yes! It's impressive how you've been able to find so many still scattered around Bravoure."

Ahna drank more of the wine. "Well, it's just a handful. All that's left." She seemed distant, drifting off at the recollection of another memory.

"Do you think you'll find the rest?" Kairen asked for Ahna's absolute honesty.

Ahna took a deep breath. "I'll start with one."

"The old villager from the west," Kairen inferred with a whisper. Her face turned to her sister and friend. She smiled at her with determined but inebriated eyes. "And then what?"

"I'll find the rest." Ahna's heart leapt in her chest. She thought for but a short moment of the idea of being reunited with those she had lost. Much of this did not make sense, except for one thought. One idea that had kept her going for the past two years, investigating, scouring Bravoure for one single clue.

Luthan.

"What if your husband is still alive?" Kairen asked and pulled Ahna out of her clenching thoughts. "What will you say to him?"

Ahna let out a deep sigh. She passed her nervous hand in her silver hair and looked to the floor. "I have no idea." Her heart pounded too fast. Perhaps it was the alcohol or just the memory of Luthan Hyehn. "Just make sure Goldwing or Zhara win the election," she told Kairen before she stood.

"You've spent fifty Sols mourning him," the red-haired woman said. "I would be angry."

"Whatever his reasons were, I could never be angry at Luthan," Ahna shrugged. She placed her goblet on the block of wood that had served as a modest stool. She went to grab her cloak, which was folded casually on the cedar railing, and she turned to Kairen. "I'll be leaving tomorrow. Make sure you get some sleep, little sister. And don't lose my ballot!"

Kairen stood and embraced the elf. "Good luck, Ahna." She kissed her on the cheek and let go.

Ahna looked deep into her copper eyes and smiled with love. She did not wish to spoil the surprise, but she sensed it. She felt the potential aura of life present in the red-haired woman's belly. Kairen would soon come to bear a child, but not quite yet. The elf simply smiled at her sister and friend, then her eyes dimmed a little.

"Kairen," she began. "I don't know when I'll be back—"

"I know, I know, I'll tell Mother Divine to keep an eye on the Academy and everything will fall into place. Don't worry, I can even be an interim dean!"

Ahna giggled. "Alright, alright."

"You'll be back soon, and then we'll have a party in honor of the Academy!"

The elf cast a dear glance at Kairen. "I love you," she said.

"I love you too."

Ahna went to fetch her satchel from the house and disappeared into the streets of the capital. She made her way through the dim-lit alleys to the southwest, where the restored Academy stood tall. It was in this place, in the edifice below the spire, that she had made a new home.

AHNA STEPPED INTO THE BUILDING, head held high, proud of what she and many of the builders had accomplished. She glanced upon the restored symbol of the Magi Academy of Bravoure, the two intertwined statues that symbolized the Equilibrium Order, the principles every archmage should stand for. A white phoenix and a black one, Balance and Harmony, two sorceresses of legends who had freed the Academy from an old corruption. Ahna halted before the two statues that stood tall at the center of the Great Hall, admiring their detail, especially how much had actually been preserved, even after the war. A warm voice brought her back to reality. She was greeted by the newly appointed concierge, Leo, who had the beard and belly of old wizards.

"Good evening!" he amicably cheered.

Ahna gave him a nod.

Before she passed him, he maintained her attention with a wave. "Someone's here for you. He arrived but a few moments ago. I told him to wait in the antechamber. A very handsome man!"

Ahna raised an eyebrow, curious. She thanked him and headed to the room in question. She followed the corridor until it opened into a larger hall, with chairs, sofas and books from another era. There, seated on a chair in the darkness, she recognized the blond hair of her good friend.

"Jules!" she exclaimed.

He rose to his feet and turned to her. Jules, the spy lieutenant, member of the disbanded Shrike Wing. A beautiful smile drew on his face, one she could see in the silver moon rays that rained into the antechamber. He immediately wrapped his arms around her and lifted her up slightly.

"I haven't seen you in—how many moons? Six?" She laughed as he put her down.

"I just got back from Orgna. It's still my home, you know! I've been busy with the dig."

After the war, Jules had decided to help with the restoration of the mines. He and many other volunteers had started with digging into the tunnels. Those that had collapsed during the Battle of Orgna.

"What are you doing here?" she asked, still smiling.

"I'm taking a break, but then I heard from Lynn and Diego that you were leaving!"

Lynn and Diego... The two Squadron Five lovebirds, the Taz swordswoman and the proud captain, heroes of the Resistance, who lived in the fields outside of the village. Ahna visited them every other day. They had grown even closer, like a small family.

"I'm going to a village near the ruins of Antaris," she explained. "There is someone I must find."

Jules cast a curious glance at her. He was not sure what she had meant, but it sounded essential to her. "Lynn mentioned something, indeed."

Ahna invited her retired shrike friend into the long corridor that led to the highest tower's spiral staircase. They passed the Great Hall again, and Jules took a look at the two statues in turn.

"What is this, Ahnny?" he asked with endearing curiosity.

Ahna smiled. "They are Balance and Harmony, the founders of the current order."

"Are they dragons?" the shrike asked, unaware of phoenixes, which made Ahna hold her smile for just a little while.

"Not quite. But they were children of the gods. One was said to be dokkalfar, which is why my mother picked the Magi Academy of Bravoure as our...safe haven."

Jules and Ahna took one last look at the statues, together, admiring how the white phoenix swirled into the black one and vice versa. The statues joined in perfect unity—a duality of two opposite souls that formed one ultimate being. For Ahna, returning these statues back to their rightful place meant the Magi Academy of Bravoure was ready to stand again.

At the fifth level above ground, Ahna opened the wooden door to another hallway. The two continued until they reached another wooden door, which Ahna opened with a small silver key.

They entered a large room with a table, a few chairs, a sofa, and a hearth with an empty cooking pot. There was a large working table in the middle of what was the kitchenette. Past the workbench was a small bedchamber with two crude cupboards. Large blankets of yak fur covered the wooden bed, and they reminded Jules of the coats that kept them warm in high Gurdal. Behind the sofa, there was a secluded garderobe.

Ahna motioned for Jules to sit on the sofa while she fetched some water to boil. She was still a bit lightheaded from the ruby red wine, and she needed some good old Gurdal tea.

"I will go with you," Jules sternly declared in the silence.

Ahna offered Jules a cup of water, which boiled as she squeezed it, and he was utterly fascinated by this simple cantrip used to make tea.

"Amazing!" he sang with a full note.

"I only have these leaves." Ahna handed him a pinch of Gurdal herbs. "It's good for the mind!" She went to sit beside him and let out a long relaxing sigh. "I have to do this alone," she declared.

"Why?" he innocently asked. "You know, you don't have to do everything alone."

"Now you sound like Kairen!" she exclaimed. "You just got back here. You should get some sleep and enjoy the city."

Jules shrugged. "You know, the work at Orgna helped me get my head straight. After the fight, I needed some time away. Some simple time." He pursed his lips, nervous, perhaps hesitant to show his scars. "But I need something new."

The elf sipped on her cup of Gurdal tea. She examined Jules with soothing eyes. She understood what he had been through after this endless war. What all had been through. Going back to regular life, moving on from the loss, and working toward a brighter future.

"And," Jules continued. "I don't want to be in the same city as this scum Goshawk!"

Ahna sighed. "How can he be so popular if everyone I know hates him?"

"Because everyone you know is Resistance."

Touché. The two let the silence settle naturally in the room. They remained there, on the sofa drinking their tea, in the stillness of the night. Jules's eyes stayed fixed on Ahna, on the dawn blue color of her skin. Her curls followed her shoulders like a thick silver shawl.

"If you keep looking at me like this, I'm going to get the wrong ideas!" she joked.

Jules smiled and winked. "Well, you're not as pretty as your brother."

Ahna laughed and shoved him playfully, and he almost dropped his cup of tea. Her laughter then merged with the silence again.

"You probably have a chance with my brother, actually," she said as she smirked.

"So, when do we leave?" Jules asked, changing the subject.

"I'm not going to change your mind, am I?" As Jules shook his head, she gave him his long-awaited reply: "There is a caravan of horses leaving for Fallvale at dawn. They have six carriages. They'll make a pit stop at Mokvar, that's where I'm headed."

"Mokvar, the town close to Antaris?" Jules frowned, confused. To him, Antaris was just rubble, and there was nothing to seek in the area.

"There's a village east of Mokvar, built on the Azul. There's someone I need to find there," she explained.

Jules acknowledged and finished his cup of tea. The elf rose to her feet and looked at him with expectant eyes. "Well, if you want to come with me, then you need to be ready at dawn!"

The retired shrike opened his arms as a welcoming motion. "I'd better sleep then." He nonchalantly undid his shoes, pushing each boot off with one foot, and went to lie on the sofa. "Good night, Ahnny."

Ahna scoffed with amusement as she headed into the bedroom. She went to fetch one of her yak hides and covered Jules with the warm fur.

He thanked her with a smile. Not a minute later, he was fast asleep. Ahna took one last look at the moon and sunk into her bed in turn. Before shutting her eyes, she opened a little wooden box resting on her nightstand. Inside, she gazed upon a small, round marble with the Academy's symbol encrusted into the black stone. Her eyes watered as her mind recalled a painful moment, her last memory of the Academy. She latched onto that one hope to find the magi again before falling asleep.

2

SHARDS OF THE PAST

1291:AV

*Y*oung Meriel Arkamai had packed a full leather bag of robes, wands, and diverse objects. Linens, patches of wool, a brush, and some unidentified items. A figure entered her dorm, followed by a soft breeze that smelled of bell-flowers. There she stood, by the entrance of the room. A woman, much taller than most dark elves, with long curly hair, black as night, that simply fell perfectly on her shoulders. Her skin was of a lighter blue, with some shades of mauve around her angled cheeks and beautiful smile. She always stood with her head held high and purple eyes that could pierce through the air. But Meriel knew what truly hid behind this perhaps too confident allure. She knew what this woman had been through. Years and years of hardship and pain, in a wretched place beneath the earth.

Skaiel Arkamai, a woman who made heads bow wherever she walked, now stood beside Meriel, her daughter, who packed her belongings before leaving for a new journey. Skaiel passed a loving hand in Meriel's back, caressing her softly.

"I hear you're going to Antaris, *dóttr mi*," she said with her honeyed voice.

Meriel immediately nodded. "Yes. They told me yesterday that I'd be going with them."

Skaiel smiled proudly. "I guess your research hasn't gone unnoticed."

Meriel pursued her vigorous nodding. Skaiel had referred to the extensive research Meriel had done to earn the title of Archmage, about planar rifts and shifts and newfound properties of the Abstract Plane. The Dean had become quite fond of Meriel's efforts. After the latest discovery of the ancient artefact that had shaken the Magi Academy, the Council of Archmagi had deemed it necessary for Meriel to head to Antaris, particularly one archmage.

"Archmage Hyehn insisted I joined," Meriel revealed with a blushing chuckle. Her eyes paused on the item she held in her hands, but she gazed upon it without looking. Her mind was somewhere else, with someone else.

Skaiel noticed and teased her daughter. "Archmage Hyehn," she murmured in a sweet song. "The *ljosalfar*... Isn't he your Elementalism teacher?" She smiled as she spoke, but something in her tone requested Meriel to remain cautious.

Meriel laid her hand on her mother's arm as a sign of peace. "He was. But now that I'm officializing the title, we've started working together," Meriel innocently said, her cheeks still rosy by the thought of this high elf Skaiel had heard about a few times. "But I have no idea how to deal with a—"

"With a male or with a ljosalfar?" Skaiel jocularly interrupted.

Meriel chuckled again. "Maybe both."

A few minutes passed and neither spoke.

"Oh, Mother, what should we do with Thamias?" Meriel asked

with a slight concerned timbre. "He's not really been himself since..."

"Don't worry, I'll watch over Thamias."

Skaiel went to browse through the things Meriel had packed, just to make sure her daughter was ready.

"They made you lead of the research, together with Hyehn and Archmage Dallor," Skaiel said with that proud smile still plastered on her face.

Meriel pursed her lips. "I still wonder why they'd pick a ritualist. You know how they look at us..."

"If it's about planes of existence, it's very clear to me. Whether we deal with the occult more than the arcane is of no importance at the moment."

Meriel acknowledged her mother's words, and a slight lump formed in her throat from the burden that had been entrusted to her. But her mother's sweet caress slowly gave Meriel a sense of confidence again.

Skaiel wrapped her arms around her daughter and looked upon her dearly.

"What will you do while I'm away?" Meriel asked.

"The Dean has requested I join her at the Court, as an advisor to the King," Skaiel replied with a slight shrug. "She believes my knowledge of the dealings of Mal would help. I have the kind of political gift others might envy, if I may say so."

She had said this with the pretty smirk of *dryaae* like her. Meriel welcomed a kiss on her forehead and watched her mother slowly pace away in that long black tunic of hers. She turned to the bag of infinite things beside her, which she closed and laid aside. The young elf came to sit on her bed, mostly to think. She would be heading to the Faculty of Antaris the next day, together with Iedrias Dallor and Luthan Hyehn, one a dear friend and the other, something unknown yet.

THE CARRIAGE HALTED. The squeal of the wheels startled Jules, who awoke from his short slumber. He gasped loudly, as though something else had troubled his dreams. He looked to his right, to the elf next to him. Ahna simply looked at the plains in the distance. She seemed taken by the beautiful sunset light that covered the fields of Bravoure. It was dusk, and the caravan of horses had just reached Mokvar.

Ahna stepped off through the back of the carriage, holding her satchel behind her. She had a quiver strapped to her back with a simple crude bow hooked onto it. Her fir green cloak swirled around her legs as she walked. Jules followed her. She paid the driver with a pouch of gold coins, and she turned to her friend.

"We should spend the night here," she suggested. "We can head to the village tomorrow."

Mokvar was much larger than its eastern counterpart, East Haven. A proper town, with its very famous tavern in the center of a charming square. The two headed into the building topped with a roof of hay. At the entrance, they were greeted by a large man, who wore a smile stretched to his ears. Until he saw Ahna. His heart leapt as he gazed upon the dokkalfar woman. His frown matched his faded smile. The towners around them had begun to stare. Ahna had just noticed.

"Haven't seen one of you in a long time!" the bouncer exclaimed. "Most of your kind vanished with the Dark Lord's army."

"It's alright, she's a friend. She's not from Sharr's horde," Jules intervened quickly.

The bouncer scoffed. "She might as well be." He crossed his arms, defensively, and stared her down.

"I am just a traveler," Ahna disclosed, her hands open before her as a sign of peace. Her voice smoothened. "I was in Bravoure long before Sharr." She wanted to come closer to the large man, but he raised his hand in the air.

"You will regret it if you take one step further," he warned with a hoarse voice.

"*Dai*," Jules began, trying to appease the large man. "She's Resistance." He took her cloak in his hand. "Don't you see?" The man's shoulders slowly lowered, and Jules continued, "We were both Resistance."

Still, the bouncer held his head high. He examined the dark elf and the retired shrike carefully. He was about to say something when he heard a voice behind him.

"Did someone say Resistance?" a man shouted from inside the tavern. The voice was familiar.

Ahna and Jules looked at each other. The door opened slightly. A man who wore a grey tunic stepped outside and addressed the bouncer. He had curled, dark brown hair, *and* a Resistance cloak!

"Let them in, Louis," he said with a musical voice.

"George?" Jules asked with rounded eyes. "Squadron Five George?" His jaw dropped, and he opened his arms to greet his long-lost comrade.

George jumped in Jules's arms and gave him a passionate hug. The two laughed and cried together. They had not seen each other since the victory.

"You've been here, all this time?" Jules eventually asked George.

"Yes, shrike-boy. I'm just a regular fishmonger here, but I still wear my dear old cloak like I wear my pride." George released Jules and turned to Ahna. "The mage. Good to see you again."

The man in the Resistance cloak turned around and motioned for Louis to let them in. Louis reluctantly heeded the order, though he was secretly relieved he did not have to fight a dark elf today. George led Ahna and Jules to the counter, where the old bartender kept himself busy scrubbing iron goblets dry. George knocked on the wooden surface to catch his attention.

"Fetch three jars of ale for me, will you?" he calmly requested.

As the old man went to pour some ale into three cups, George turned to his two companions. "What brings you to Mokvar, rebels?"

"We're traveling to a village nearby," Ahna replied. "Close to the Azul."

George gave her three ample nods. "It must be Drazul, named after the river, itself!"

Ahna mimicked his nods as a confirmation. They were indeed headed to Drazul, the tiny village close to the forest. Ahna had heard of a forgotten house there, where a young man had turned into an old recluse. One whom people of the region had spread many mysterious rumors about.

———

THREE JARS of ale landed on the table where Ahna, Jules, and Squadron-Five swordsman George were seated. The attendant brought them some roasted nuts to chew on, with a loaf of cloud bread and garlic oil. George made himself a savory garlic tartine while he caught up on his friends' lives.

"What do you do now, Jules?" he asked the retired shrike.

"I took work in Orgna. I offered to rebuild the mines, and now, I'm looking for something new! How about you?"

George leaned back in his chair, letting out a long sigh. His eyes fixed his cup of ale, and it was obvious that he was struggling to hide the emotions swarming through him. "After the war, I was a broken man. Everybody went around and about, doing what they had to do. Commander Falco rallied the people, the councilors took everyone under their wing, and Mother Divine, she inspired the city's revival!" He took a large sip before he pursued. "Most of us soldiers, we helped out. And then, just like that"—he drew a rising zigzag with his left hand—"the city was back on its feet."

Ahna searched the swordsman's eyes as he recollected shared

memories. He looked down to his cup, squeezing it as though he protected it. Jules kept his gaze on him. George suddenly seemed concerned, and a dark indistinguishable shadow covered his face.

"What happened, George?" the shrike asked his old friend.

The latter expelled a rapid flow of air through his lips. "Like I said, I was a broken man. Thirteen years I spent fighting. David did his best, but us, those who lost everything, we didn't really have anywhere to go." He nervously took another sip of ale. "I hit the ground hard, man." He had admitted his harshest of truths. He brought his hand to support his forehead, too heavy with the sense of shame.

Jules laid a comforting hand on the swordsman's shoulder. "You're with friends," he reassured.

"The ale—alcohol—became my reason to get up in the morning." He looked deep into his cup, and it stared back at him. "I was one of the lucky ones to find Ol' Jon here." He pointed at the old man behind the counter. "He picked me up and offered me a job in Mokvar."

George sighed deeply again. But then, as a light sparked into the brown of his eyes, he smiled at Ahna and Jules.

"It is good to see you, George," the elf said as she put her hand on his.

He chuckled and blushed a little at the softness of her touch. "So, the Academy lives again, thanks to you!" he remarked. The swordsman clinked his cup against hers, as a toast to her achievement. "How long are you staying here, rebels?"

"It depends," Ahna replied. "I'm looking for someone. Someone I knew from before the war."

George nodded and smirked as though he understood what she meant. "Ah, chasing an old flame, am I right?"

Ahna shook her head. "He should be old by now!" She laughed. She crossed her arms in front of her and leaned over the table, resting her elbows on the surface. "No, I'm just following a lead to a part of my past."

The three joyous heroes finished their jars of ale in peace, with the stillness of the tavern as the last customers left. George went to Ol' Jon and requested a room for the two travelers. Ten gold pieces, the two had just enough for a couple of days. They bid the swordsman goodnight, and he strolled to the exit. Ahna and Jules were led upstairs to a modest room with two separate beds, a simple nightstand, and a bucket of hot water. There was a warm torch on the wall that lit the room. Jules immediately collapsed on one of the beds, exhausted from the two days they had travelled to Mokvar.

AHNA LAID her cloak to rest on the nearest chair and began untying the laces of her woven tunic.

Jules cast a glance at her. "Should I turn around?" he asked cautiously.

"Don't worry, I'll keep these linens on," she retorted with a sly wink.

And so, Jules decided to stare at the ceiling. He undid his black boots his favorite way and let them drop on the floor. Ahna went to the bucket to get her face cleaned. She passed her wet hands on her neck and shoulders. The warm sensation helped her muscles relax, and she even got a bit of water to adjust her messy curls. She joined her palms in the water again and dipped her face. When she was done, the elf came to lie on the bed and joined Jules in the staring contest with the ceiling.

"George made me feel...uncertain," Jules expressed his sentiment of the evening they had just spent with the swordsman. He kept his gaze fixed on the ceiling for a little while. "We freed Bravoure, and now, we are stuck with forlorn soldiers and spooky politics."

"The Resistance united people with hope and the idea of freedom," Ahna began, her eyes to the ceiling as well. "Now that people have their freedom back, they let other things become important. Things like…"

"Political campaigns," Jules completed the sentence for her. "Soldiers like George deserved more than being…discarded. Like a tool that was no longer needed. I can't believe David let that happen."

Ahna sighed deeply. "I don't think David was even aware. He's giving his everything to keep the order in this headless kingdom."

Jules turned on his side and searched for Ahna's purple eyes. She did the same and rolled toward him. The two smiled at each other.

"We've been through so much, Ahnny. I hope this adventure doesn't make us run between East Haven, Orgna, Bravoure, Orgna again, Fort Gal, Orgna!" Jules could not even finish his sentence without taking a breath. He chuckled as he remembered the spring of 1362:AV, then his smile dissipated into the silence of the room. His grey eyes turned darker and met Ahna's again.

"Are we ever going to talk about my captain?" he asked, hesitantly.

Ahna opened her mouth slightly at the mention of…Cedric Rover.

"Where do you think he is?" Jules inquired some more.

Two years without mentioning his name, and Jules had finally said it out loud. Hearing it made Ahna shudder. She pursed her lips as she thought of something to say, but no words came to mind, so she simply answered with a shrug and a blink.

"Did you ever find the Cursed Bow?" Jules came with another question.

"I did," she replied immediately, but she did not let him inquire more. "Let's go to sleep, Jules."

Jules got the message. The two travelers sunk into the linen of their sheets. With a wave of Ahna's hand, the flame of the torch disappeared, and the room was submerged in darkness. Only the light of the gibbous moon helped Ahna distinguish the contours of Jules face in the night. He was smiling. Perhaps he enjoyed being *on the run* again. He had spent almost half his life as a Resistance soldier, three years as a swordsman, nine as a shrike. The rush through his veins as he conquered the unknown was definitely something he had missed. It had been all he had known, and he could not live without it.

Ahna kept her eyes open almost all night. In the bed next to her, Jules slept peacefully. He did not make any noise. For the first time in many full moons, he did not have nightmares. Ahna, on the other hand, could not even close one eye. Her heart pounded in her chest. Her hands were wet with an anxious sweat that irritated her, which did not help with the whole falling asleep effort. She rolled left and right in her bed, trying to rock herself to sleep, nothing worked. She could not use a cantrip—those were for forced naps, which did not provide any rest. Though, at this point, it almost felt like this was her best option.

She tried to close her eyes again and breathed slowly to relax her body, and she focused on her own heartbeat. She cleared her mind and just counted the rises and falls of her chest. No thoughts were allowed to pass, only the incrementing numbers that echoed in her mind. At the stroke of ten, the cyclic series started again.

1295:AV

Meriel sat in the Antaris Faculty's garden, admiring the crystalline petals of a white lily. She was mesmerized by the beauty of this simple yet delicate flower. Next to her sat Archmage Hyehn, the man who had followed her here, to support her with research she would conduct as Archmage Arkamai. The first analyses of an Item of Power said to harness power from the different planes of existence.

"What would you call this one?" Luthan asked to get Meriel's attention. A small, blue winter moth rested on his index finger.

The two elves sat on the stone base of the gallery arch, in the Faculty's garden. The sun shone brightly in the sky above Antaris. Luthan's hair had become almost white from the radiance. His ears pointed to the sky above the two. He wore his favorite Archmage tunic, the black robe embroidered with emerald green threads that matched his eyes. The tunic fitted him perfectly and was joint to the side of his body, unlike other garments that closed in front. Luthan searched for the curious glance Meriel cast on the small moth.

"It's just a blue winter moth," she answered his question.

He laughed. His voice sounded almost like a soothing melody to her ears. "But it's summer," he noted with joy. He let the moth gently fly away. "They are the same, yet this one in high Gurdal prefers to mate in the summer. Why do you think that is?"

Meriel pressed her lips in thought and unconsciously diverted Luthan's gaze to them. When his eyes met hers again, his pupils had dilated. The gold dust in his irises radiated with a certain intensity, one that made her head spin.

She cleared her throat and her mind in the process. "They adapted. High Gurdal is chill in summer and terribly cold in winter. Mating behaviors may be subject to change to fit one's surroundings." Her sentence ended with a suggestive glance at Luthan, perhaps a little too suggestive.

Luthan smirked. "Exactly. Now, tell me. How long do we have to talk about mating moths before I get you in my bed again?"

The dark elf chuckled. She brought her hand to her mouth to repress more laughter. She wanted to hush him. They were not alone. There were at least two young magi in the garden. They greeted Luthan and his companion with the utmost respect as they passed them.

"Luthan, be careful with your requests," Meriel teased.

When the two apprentices passed the gallery entrance, Meriel observed them until they were no longer in sight. When she turned back to the irresistible ljosalfar, his eyes burned with the flame of lust. The one they had consumed a few nights prior, after waiting for so long, resisting the urge to do anything romantic. And now, they could not stop themselves from acting like two elven young.

Luthan led his hand to her cheek and looked deep into the ethereal sea of her eyes. "Will you let *me* kiss you this time?" he softly asked, almost in a whisper.

He referred to their first touch, the first move Meriel had actually initiated. That night was everything he wanted to remember, for the rest of his life. Meriel closed her eyes and let the high elf sway her to the cadence of a kiss.

When their lips met, Luthan lit a luscious flame in Meriel's heart, stomach, and even lower. His fingers intertwined with her silver curls. He was nearly clenching a fist when he firmly gripped onto her hair. Her scent drove him insane. He wanted to melt here, with her, their tongues entwined. He knew so well the effect he had on her, just by how her body bent with his. And he was certain she knew the power she had over him.

It took him all his strength to release his embrace. She was smiling, and so was he.

"I love you," she stuttered.

She instantly blushed, stood and turned away, almost making her way out of the garden when Luthan caught her wrist. It was the first time she had said these three words.

He pulled her in closer and took over her lips again, as though they were entirely his, forever. The two elves lost themselves, engulfed in the flames of a forbidden kiss, and when Meriel opened her eyes, she realized they now stood in Luthan's room.

"A pyrofade?" she murmured. "Interesting mode of transpor—"

He tasted her lips again as he slowly led her to his bed in the Faculty of Antaris.

3

MOHINDRA

*J*ules already stood outside, gasping the fresh morning air, when Ahna joined him. The little harbor town bustled with people performing their everyday work. Some women dragged large carts of hay from the fields, some men carried buckets of water back and forth from the well. The sky was grey, and even a few darker clouds collected above the sea to the west.

"It's going to rain soon," Jules observed as the elf came closer to him.

Ahna looked to the sky. "We should move quickly. Drazul is very close," she said.

The two headed onto the road to the east. They passed multiple houses, all topped by combed roofs of yellow hay, until they reached a narrow dirt road that slithered in the direction of the river. Not a few moments as they walked further, they could see a couple of wooden cabins in the distance, behind high trunks of poplar trees.

"This man we're looking for," Jules said. "What is he to you?"

Ahna looked at him. "He was a student and from time to time, he was my apprentice."

"He's a mage?" The shrike immediately opened his mouth in surprise.

Ahna answered with a single nod.

She seemed distant, as though her thoughts were lingering on something else than the memory of a young mage. Little did Jules know, only the images of her late-night dream danced in her mind. *It's just a blue winter moth.* Luthan's voice chanted between her pointy ears. His smell, the softness of his skin. *Gods be damned!* Since when had she become so inflamed with lust? She needed to distract herself.

"His name is Mohindra," Ahna said. "His family was from the Indus-Kali isles. They sent him to the Magi Academy of Bravoure to study with our renowned magic-users."

"What makes you think he's still here?"

Ahna cleared her throat. "I've heard rumors of an old villager here, in Drazul. They call him the Witch of the Woods." Jules laughed out loud to her words. "I'm serious," she insisted. "He's a recluse behind the village. They say he grows trees with his mind. Mohindra was always fascinated by botany."

They talked on as they strolled toward the collection of wooden houses. Jules was genuinely curious about what the Academy had done in the past and who had studied there. Ahna explained most students had been magi, but some others interested in their research had also attended the numerous lectures and teachings.

The Arts of Arcanis divided the practice of magic into five schools: Elementalism, Illusionism, Conjuration, Mysticism, sometimes referred to as Animalism, and Ritualism. These five schools were split into specializations. Most magi specialized in one branch and practiced a second discipline in a lesser form. For example, some magi practiced general Elementalism next to their own school, like Ahna, but some specialized in one branch, Pyromancy, Hydromancy, Aeromancy, or even Geomancy. Photomancy was a skill between Elementalism and Illusionism.

Active Photomancy, using powerful light in offense, belonged to the former school. Illusionists used passive Photomancy as a disguise or to incur optical illusions. Magi highly skilled in Pyromancy were gifted with near-volcanic powers, and archmagi in this branch could create fires so hot, they could tear through the Fabric of Realms.

Ahna's school was Ritualism, an older form of magic with its own branches. The most ancient rituals could even invoke astral energy from different planes of existence, such as the Abstract Plane, that lies beyond the Fabric. To be a skilled ritualist, one must also practice the elements, and facets of the light that surrounds Terra. Ritualism was sometimes frowned upon, as most magi regarded it as a more…occult form of magic. In truth, it scared some of them. The Magi Academy also offered education in a vast number of natural subjects, such as botany or astronomy.

Jules shook his head in an attempt to process all this information. "That whole different-planes-thing goes way beyond me. I just swing my sword." He pointed at the black scabbard strapped to his back, then he averted his eyes to Ahna's belt. "Speaking of which, where is your sword?"

She pointed at the small scabbard attached to her right boot. "I just brought one dagger with me"—she then flicked her head to sign at her back—"and my bow."

"That bow looks a bit simple to me," the shrike noted.

"Looks can be deceiving."

Eventually, the two reached the wooden cabins of Drazul. There were but a few houses scattered around a little well. Large poplar trees adorned the area with beautiful brown trunks and leaves swayed by the wind. The path continued east toward a bouquet of more trees. Some villagers had looked to the two travelers with cautious eyes. Of course, they noticed Ahna and her skin blue as the dawn. They did not dare to look longer than a glance. Jules smiled and simply nodded at them. As they ventured among the trees, they heard a few raindrops fall gently on the poplar leaves, like a thousand little drums. Ahna and Jules picked up the pace. At the end of the path, they could see the shape of a stone house built by the riverbed.

Ahna knocked on a wooden door. No response. She leaned over to look into the tiny window. She could not see anyone in the house. So, she knocked again.

"I don't think anyone's home," Jules deduced.

Ahna knocked a third time. She peaked through the window again—no one. She turned to the blond shrike and sighed with impatience. She hurried past him, headed toward the river, where she looked left and right of the torrent in search of Mohindra.

Jules heard footsteps behind him while Ahna was away.

"Can I help you?" a young voice queried.

The retired shrike turned around, his firm hand on the pommel of his shortsword. His eyes met the young man's, a black-haired villager who wore an ample shawl. He was cowled to cover himself from the rain. He must have been five or seven Sols younger than Jules, just old enough to hold a sword, the shrike thought. His cloak matched his light bronze skin, but he was not from Tazman—his curls were too wavy and not curly enough.

"Ahna!" Jules called the elf who did not respond.

The young man waited expectantly.

"We're looking for the person who lives here," Jules said with open hands to show he meant no harm.

"That's my grandfather. He's harvesting mushrooms in the forest," the young man said. "You can wait for him inside, so we get away from this rain!"

Jules smiled thankfully. He turned to the river and noticed the elf was back on the path. He waved at her to get her attention and motioned for her to return. When she reached the stone house, the young man had opened the door and was waiting inside.

Upon seeing Ahna, he immediately dashed back. He was so startled that he bumped into the table behind him and almost toppled over. Jules stepped in between them and spread his arms.

"She's not a threat!" he assured. "What's your name?"

"F...Farooq," the boy stuttered.

"Alright, Farooq, this is Ahna." Jules raised his hand toward the elf. "She's a friend."

Farooq hesitated to relax his stance. "I haven't seen her kind in moons."

"She's a citizen of Bravoure, just like you and I."

Ahna took a step forward. "It's nice to meet you, Farooq."

The young man finally noticed her cloak. "You two were Resistance, correct? You killed Lord Sharr?" Jules and Ahna nodded simultaneously, and Farooq immediately bowed to greet them. "It's truly an honor." He cast his wet shawl on a wooden chair and headed toward the stone kitchenette at the end of the room. "I'll get us some tea!"

"Mohindra is his grandfather," Jules whispered to Ahna as Farooq had his back turned.

"I thought so," she whispered back. "He reminds me of him."

"Please, make yourself comfortable," Farooq requested with a warm voice. He pointed to the modest sofa by the tiny window. "I'll get us some sweets!"

The young man was busy lighting a fire in the hearth by the entrance. He went to a cupboard and fetched an iron box full of dried jelly-rogis, the type of baked sweet momrogi filled with yellowberry jam and powdered with goldrain sugar. While the water boiled, he came to sit on a chair in front of them.

"How do you know my grandfather?" he wondered. "Nobody knows him."

Jules looked at Ahna, and she leaned forward. "I knew him when he was young, younger than you," she replied.

Farooq rounded his large brown eyes. "But you're so much younger than him!"

Ahna laughed. "No, I'm really not!" She cleared her throat. "How is Mohindra?"

Farooq's gaze bounced cautiously left to right as though he wanted to hide a secret. "He's fine, I think." The young man looked to his feet. "He's a bit…odd, but he's my only family."

The water finished boiling. Farooq picked three large iron goblets and served his guests cedar tea with a handful of powdered sweets.

1297:AV

Luthan nervously took a bite of a dried jelly-rogi he still held in his hand. He seemed to crave sweet things when he was utterly nervous like this. He paced ferociously outside the Council's chamber. He shuffled back and forth between two columns, around them, retreated and advanced again toward the closed door. He gulped the last bit of sweet when the door suddenly opened.

He had to wipe some sugar off his mouth before he cast a glance into the room. Archmagi with robes of all colors raced to the exit. Some looked worried, perhaps afraid. Others had apprehensive looks on their faces. Luthan stepped aside to let them pass. That is when he heard someone speak, still inside the room. Two voices, one being the Dean's, the other Skaiel Arkamai's.

"There are rumors, Skaiel," the Dean said carefully. "A dokkalfar platoon has climbed through the Chasm."

Skaiel's annoyance was apparent in the sharp way she breathed. "This can't be happening. Has contact been made?" she asked with a sense of urgency that sent shivers down Luthan's spine.

A moment of silence passed. Some inaudible words were exchanged until Luthan caught the final sentence.

"They were from Mal, Skaiel," the Dean pressed. "They weren't hostile, but something tells me this will not be the last we hear of them."

Luthan had perhaps misheard that last part. His patience had faded. He wanted to talk to Skaiel. He *needed* to talk to Skaiel.

He wanted to step into the Council's room but was greeted by the Dean's rounded eyes.

"You missed the gathering, Archmage Hyehn," she said with a jocular severity.

Luthan pursed his lips and smiled awkwardly. The Dean gave him a greeting nod, then headed into the hallway. When Luthan eventually stepped into the room, he saw Skaiel's back toward him. He was frozen into place. He had prepared an entire discourse, a whole declaration, and now, he was speechless. Skaiel had her arms crossed and, despite being aware of Luthan's presence, she did not turn until a minute later.

"What is it, Luthan?" she asked, swallowing something in her throat.

Luthan cleared his. "Skaiel Arkamai, I've come to—"

"Please, spare the formalities and get to the point," she interrupted him, and her purple eyes flared. Something troubled her, and she did not care to hide it.

"Skaiel, I…" Luthan hesitated, and Skaiel's impatience reflected in her glare. "I want to ask for your daughter's hand."

Skaiel spontaneously laughed. The ice-cold mood in the room had instantly changed to a warmer, more relaxed feeling. Skaiel's eyes gleamed again, like sparkling gems of glee.

Luthan's stance relaxed, and he proceeded to clarify his words.

"I would like to ask for your blessing. I love your daughter, and I want our bond to be…undeniable."

Skaiel regained her composure and delicately wiped a lighter tear off her left eye.

"Does she want the same?" she asked with a sly smirk. "And I warn you," her smirk faded. "I hope for your sake you haven't done some sick coercion on her."

Luthan's eyes snapped open, and he had to clear his throat again. "No, for Arcanis' sake, no!"

His interlocutor's eyes pierced right through him. "How much do you love her?" she asked, inquisitively.

"More than I can describe," Luthan admitted.

Skaiel took a step toward him, then looked deep into his green eyes. "You know what we…what she's been through," she said in a more serious tone. "Are you ready to face that yourself?"

Luthan did not quite understand what Skaiel wanted him to say. As though she had read his thoughts, she raised her voice to clarify.

"Are you ready to share her burden?" she insisted. "When you bind yourself to my daughter, it's not only about your love for her. It's about accepting what you love about her, and everything else you might not. It's about welcoming all of her into your life for the rest of it." Because Luthan remained silent but attentive, Skaiel pursued with a challenging smile. "I will give my blessing if you are ready to abide by what I have said."

Luthan chuckled awkwardly. He passed his hand, multiple times, in his long blond hair, before relaxing his stance and facing the mother of his future wife.

"Skaiel." He cleared his throat for the last time. "I have loved your daughter ever since she came into my life. Even before she took notice of me. She has opened her heart to me, and I…I have loved her more and more as each day passes and I certainly, most certainly"—he almost had tears in his eyes—"will never stop loving her. Because she's the best Terra has to offer. The best the Domain of Stars has to offer, and I'm not even sure I believe in the Heavens!" He passed his hand in his hair again and addressed the woman who stood in front of him. "*Je elsker henn' mer enn al anneth,* Skaiel. And I hope you understand what I just said because there's no way to express it otherwise."

Skaiel's posture relaxed, and her ruthless smile turned into the most endearing Luthan had ever seen on her face.

"What will your own family think of this…union?" she asked, referring to the obvious issue at hand.

Luthan was ljosalfar, and her daughter a dark elf. Sworn enemies since the dawn of the world they knew. But Luthan did not bulge.

"They can think what they please," he declared.

Skaiel took a deep breath before speaking again. "Your passion burns like that of dokkalfar," she gently said.

Luthan chuckled. "Well, your carefulness tells me you'd make a good ljosalfar."

Skaiel chuckled, too. "A good dark elf you'd make indeed, Luthan Hyehn," she completed.

Luthan was slightly struck by Skaiel's last words. Unsure of how to react, he simply forced a playful face and nodded. "So…" he began. "Does that mean…"

"Go!" Skaiel ordered with a laugh. "You have my blessing. You'd better not spoil it, or I will personally end you!"

"Never."

* * *

THE DOOR OPENED. Outside, the rain was pouring as though the sky had not wept in centuries. The drops pounded against the wooden roof of the tiny stone house. An old man with a heavy basket entered the room. He folded on himself to undo hit wet boots as water dripped from his woolen coat. He leaned on a simple wooden stick he used as a cane. He took off his soaked leather hat, which he placed on the low cupboard beside the door. That is when he noticed his grandson and his guests. He squinted to analyze the two people on the sofa. His beard had grown until his belly. His long grey hair that used to be black as kohl was all over the place.

Mohindra's eyes snapped open when he saw Ahna.

He gasped; his lips trembled in surprise. "Archmage Arkamai?"

The old man dropped his cane. Farooq immediately rushed to him to help him sit down on a chair. Ahna stood slowly. She sauntered toward the old man. She leaned forward and searched for his dark eyes.

"You've grown old, Apprentice," she said with a smirk.

The old man laughed. His eyes sparkled with tears of joy. "I thought you were gone forever." His voice was croaky as though his throat was sore.

"Gone forever?" Ahna asked, her voice low.

"You have to see all the mushrooms I found!" Mohindra exclaimed, ignoring her inquiry.

Ahna felt the tears rising in her eyes. She laughed for a second, but her laugh turned to a frail, awkward gasp.

Farooq looked as if he had no clue what to make of what he heard. He cast an inquisitive gaze at his grandfather. "Apprentice?" He then turned to Ahna. "Archmage?" he stammered.

The old man motioned for him to hush with his brittle hand. "The past comes knocking hard," he declared.

Farooq handed a cup of tea to his grandfather. The latter took a deep breath and looked at his only family. "The Academy was my home, Farooq," Mohindra revealed to his grandson.

"You were a mage?" Farooq asked, lost for words.

Mohindra simply nodded. "I haven't been a mage in a long time, *betu*." He shifted his attention to Jules who sat silently on the sofa. "And who is this young man?"

"That's Jules. He's Resistance!" Farooq praised.

"Does he want to see my mushrooms?"

Ahna chuckled. Jules squinted with a smirk to try and understand what the old man meant. After this short moment of amusement, Mohindra took on a more serious tone.

"Why have you come here, Archmage?" He paused for a moment to collect his strength. "Where are the others?"

Mohindra used his cane to stand up. He walked away from Ahna, but her voice held him back. "I came to ask you the same thing, Mohindra," she declared.

The old man turned to her. His eyes betrayed his surprise. "I don't understand. You were gone. You went with them…" he stuttered, staring at her like she was some kind of revenant.

Ahna stared back at him, trying to piece together why he looked at her this way. "Where do you think I went?" she challenged.

"You never went with them?" Mohindra checked as he realised he might have been wrong about certain events of the past. Events that still coursed through his mind like a bad memory.

"Where should I have gone, Mohindra?" Ahna pressed. "Where did *they* go?" Her patience faded as did her voice.

The old man still stared, this time at the wall behind Ahna. "I really thought you went with them," he said, his timbre filled with a sense of regret.

Mohindra took a deep breath and lowered his shoulders. He was ready to face the past, the veil that darkened his eyes with shame. "We have a lot to talk about, Archmage." The old man looked at his grandson. The rain had stopped pouring outside. "Boy, go fetch some wood for the fire."

Farooq looked perplexed. "But the wood will be wet."

"It'll dry here."

The young man heeded Mohindra's request. He grabbed his shawl and stepped through the door, closing it behind him.

"Tell me what happened," Ahna commanded. Her purple eyes lit as she looked at the old man who was about to reveal a harsh truth.

"If you never left, then that means…" Mohindra fell silent for a minute. "What I'll tell you is not an absolute certainty," he resumed. "You must understand. What happened was our last resort."

Ahna frowned. She grew more inquisitive. With all her heart and soul, she wanted to know the truth of the magi's fate. Mohindra looked to Jules expectantly.

"Should I also leave?" Jules candidly asked.

"No," Ahna immediately intervened. "Whatever Mohindra has to say, you may hear it."

Mohindra sighed. "I was not on the project…but you were. That's why I thought…I thought you had gone with them."

"What project?" the elf questioned.

"The one that involved the Planar Mask."

Shock.

Ahna gasped. "Don't tell me they made it work." As the old man would not respond immediately, she raised her voice. "Mohindra, I've spent the past decades thinking you were dead…"

The old man motioned for her to stop talking. "Yes, they made it work."

Ahna pulled back. She was torn. Torn between a sudden burst of joy, happiness, relief, and the harsh truth of what Mohindra's words meant. What the magi had done.

They left. They gave up.

There and then, she realised she and Bravoure had been left behind by those she had trusted most.

Ahna spun around and stormed out of the little stone house. Jules rushed behind her as she halted by the path in front of the entrance. She crossed her arms and raised her head to the sky. She inhaled deeply to regain her composure.

"What's all this distress about?" Jules asked.

Ahna shook her head. She bit her lip to hold in tears. She looked to the endless forest of poplars in front of her.

"I have no idea where to start, Jules," the elf admitted with a broken whisper.

He came closer to her. He laid his hands on her shoulders and forced her to turn around.

"What happened to the magi?" he asked.

Ahna pursed her lips together. "They're gone." Her voice almost broke in this schism of emotions. "But they're alive. They saved themselves! They left Bravoure behind and saved themselves." She halted to catch her breath and let out the longest sigh. "Cowards," she whispered to herself.

Behind them, Mohindra strolled out of the stone house, walking with untied shoes and his cane. Farooq, unaware of what was going on, rejoined the group and looked to them in confusion.

"Because that's what happened, right?" Ahna addressed Mohindra with spite in her voice. "The magi saved themselves!"

Mohindra scoffed. "We had no choice. Sharr was persecuting us. He was coming to Antaris with an entire army."

"It was *my* research!" Ahna yelled. "Why wasn't I made aware of this?"

"I don't know!" Mohindra shouted in return. "I thought you were."

"Is it because I'm dokkalfar?" Ahna hissed. She figured blaming it on the struggle she never talked about, the reason why most looked at her today with nothing but disgust, was the most sensible thing to do.

But Mohindra only responded with a shrug. "Even given who you are, Archmage, I can't believe you of all magi would be left behind," he said softly.

"Who I am?" Ahna retorted in affront. "After the twenty-some years I spent in this damned Academy?"

The rage inside her began to boil, but Mohindra bashed her words back at her.

"You were Sharr! You still are!" he roared.

The old man's words fell on Ahna's shoulders. She took it all as a slap to the face.

Noticing her distress, Mohindra regained his calm. "The Council made us...forget!" He began to relive the past. "With Sharr's magefinders and spies everywhere, nobody was allowed to talk about the project. We used *memlocks*—those marbles, we used them to remember."

The elf looked to Jules, who had obviously heard everything, looking for his absent reaction to what Mohindra had revealed about Lord Sharr and who she really was. Jules simply looked back at her and Mohindra, as confused as Farooq, perhaps in search of an explanation. *Those marbles...* Ahna's memory flashed back to the marble she guarded in a wooden box on her night-stand. The only thing she had left from the Academy. The rounded stone she kept close to her and held at night. Thamias had given it to her, expressing Luthan's wish to give it to her before he had...vanished. The answer, the one answer she had been looking for, all this time. The black marble she had kept safe along with her grief.

Her eyes veered back to Mohindra with disbelief. "Memlocks?" she inquired.

Mohindra's shoulders fell. He wanted to explain it all to her, but he himself could not understand, despite her being Sharr, how she could have purposefully been left behind by their own people.

"The Dean," he began with severe hesitation. "She gathered us in groups in the Academy's vaults. We made the plan. Once the Planar Mask was activated, the Council devised a plan of escape and made it secret. We transferred all our memories to the stones and forgot. So even when tortured to death, Sharr would never come to know."

"Why didn't you go with them?" Ahna asked the old man, skipping over the last part he had said.

"I didn't make it in time," Mohindra admitted. "But I was

convinced the rest had, those who survived. And that you went with them."

Jules had enough. "Will someone tell me what's going on?" He looked to Mohindra, who responded with rounded eyes. He turned back to Ahna.

"How many?" the elf asked again. "How many *did* make it?"

Mohindra exhaled deeply. "To be honest, I'm not sure."

"What about Luthan…" She cleared her throat. "Archmage Hyehn?" she raised. "What was his place in all this?"

"As far as I know, he went with them."

Ahna's wounded heart squeezed in on itself. How could Luthan agree to this? She stared Mohindra down for more answers, only to find an aimless nod.

"How did they even get it to work?" she asked, her voice slipping into echoes in the forest.

Mohindra sighed with exhaustion. "That, I really don't know."

Ahna fell silent. After all these years… The rumors, the lies she thought the people of Bravoure spread about the magi's cowardice, they were all true. She had to process the realization that the magi, the brave arcane protectors of Bravoure, had abandoned the city after all.

Mohindra pulled her out of her anger-brewing thoughts. "Sharr killed so many of us. We had to think of our survival," he attempted to justify. Ahna did not say more, so he continued. "I had to rebuild a life. I married Farooq's grandmother. She was killed by Sharr with our daughter. My boy is the only thing I have."

"Aren't you…angry? Angry that they left without you?" Ahna could not help but wonder out loud.

"No. I live with the thought that our brothers and sisters still live somewhere."

The elf scoffed wryly. "And where would that be?" But Mohindra only answered with a shrug. He did not know. She then looked to Farooq, who still stood by the entrance of the stone house, waiting. She flicked her chin in the young man's direction. "Does he even know what he is?"

Mohindra let a long sigh escape. He looked to his boy, to his flesh and blood, blood in which flowed the fragrance of the arcane. The old man closed his eyes and cast a wistful smile at his grandson. "He doesn't know. But I guess he knows now."

Ahna remained here, in the cold air of the morning rain. The sky was still grey, and the wind howled gently through the poplar leaves. Birds were chirping, chanting whatever melody they favored. Mohindra headed back into his house, followed by Farooq, who motioned for the two travelers to join them again. But Ahna remained still.

Jules's gaze landed on the elf. "I'm not sure what to make of all this," he said and shrugged.

Ahna took a deep breath to calm herself. "The Planar Mask is an Item of Power," she began to clarify. "One of the artefacts left behind by the Ancients. It was kept in the Antaris Faculty for centuries, at least." She passed her hand in her wet hair to adjust her frizzy curls. "I conducted research in Antaris on the Planar Mask. I theorized a way to activate it, but we never really understood where it would take us, or if it even was possible to set a destination."

Jules laughed out of the blue. "Ahna, you're only making me more confused here!"

Ahna chuckled awkwardly, and Jules's grey eyes brought her to calm. Her features softened, and she continued to explain. "We always thought it could somehow draw energy from different planes and use it to travel long distances. I even hypothesized there were two. Two ends of one conduit through time and space."

The two headed back inside the stone house. They overheard Farooq's voice increase in pitch.

"What did she mean, *daadu*? What did she mean with *who I am*?" he questioned his grandfather, who sat on the sofa.

"I'll explain, *betu*," Mohindra assured, trying to calm down the agitated young man.

"Am I a mage?" Farooq asked, his incredulous voice resonated in the room.

Mohindra noticed Ahna and Jules walking into the house again. He rose to his feet and ambled toward the elf with his cane.

"Archmage," he began with a regretful tone. "I wish things had gone differently."

Ahna simply nodded. "Me too." She raised her head higher. A particular flame shone in her purple eyes. She gazed at the old man and gave him a forgiving smile. "But there might be a way to find them."

Mohindra's eyes only searched for more of Ahna's plan that came to be. "What will you do?" he asked.

"I have to go to Antaris. Perhaps I missed something the last time I went there. Perhaps I missed a clue. Two years ago, I went back there, but I found nothing."

Mohindra immediately shook his head as Ahna was about to collect her belongings. "No, you won't find anything in Antaris." After a long pause consisting of Ahna's inquiring look, Mohindra pursued. "They took the Planar Mask somewhere else before activating it. I am no longer sure exactly where, but I know it was far below ground."

Ahna frowned. "What if they never made it, and Sharr destroyed the Planar Mask?"

"I like to believe that's impossible." Mohindra drew an elderly smile upon his face.

The elf looked toward Jules, hoping for a suggestion of what to do next but knowing she would not get any from him. He was as confused as a cloudy sky. She turned back to Mohindra and shrugged slightly.

"Then I'll get on with a scrying ritual. If they made it in time, they must be somewhere, somewhere on Terra."

4

MISSING IN ACTION

*L*uthan had to be fast. A caravan of horses was already on the way to Antaris—*he* was the last one, still here. He faced a tide of soldiers, so many soldiers. Each wore bronze steel armor that reflected light like a sea of thousands of suns. He passed them one by one, searching for his love, his wife.

"Meriel!" he called her name.

They had trebuchets, cannons, a battalion of archers with fire arrows. The soldiers were with swords brandished and shields held close.

"Meriel!" he called again. Yet no one responded.

Where is she?

He had no time. The Dean had left him no time. Luthan cast a worried glance in the distance, far ahead, at the contours of the city of gold. There was a fire. A massive cloud of smoke burned into the atmosphere above the capital, above his dear Academy. The Magi Academy of Bravoure being burned to the ground.

He called for Meriel again. A few soldiers looked to him,

47

confused, unaware of what was going on. Luthan marched among them, he was almost at the head of the Bravan army. A few feet from him, he saw the shimmer of the royal claymore.

"General!" he called.

The man turned to him. "Good day, Battlemage," the general greeted. "We are taking the city back from the clutches of the prince!"

"We lost the Academy, sir," Luthan conceded in a desperate tone. "He's destroying it!" He nervously tucked his blond hair behind his shoulders.

"Luthan?" a voice called beside him, a familiar one.

Thamias.

"What are you doing here?" Luthan asked. "Where is Meriel? She's not answering the vox-ring."

"She went into the city," Thamias replied. "We're going to take it back. I'm going to transform. It's time to end this."

"By Arcanis!" Luthan exclaimed. "I need to find your sister." The high elf glanced left and right in search of a solution.

Thamias noticed his concern and came closer to him. "When Xandor brought his horde to the Academy, she immediately went after him. I wanted to stop her—"

"Why didn't you?" Luthan interrupted.

Luthan immediately regained his composure, pressing both his hands against the sides of his forehead. He was doing everything to solve this situation in his mind. Suddenly, his tongue clicked, and he plunged his green eyes into Thamias'.

"There's not much time," Luthan sternly declared. "When you see Meriel, tell her to meet me outside the city. She'll know where."

Thamias, confused, instantly retorted, "What do you mean?"

"Xandor is about to eradicate the magi. There's a chance we might survive, and we have to take it. Just take this"—he handed Thamias a small rounded marble with the Academy's symbol on it—"and give it to her."

He then turned around. His cloak and long hair swayed in the wind with the allure of a powerful battlemage. He was already pacing away, but Thamias went after him.

"Where are you going?" the younger dark elf urged. "And what is this?"

"Just give it to her, she'll know what it means," Luthan replied, his back toward him. "We're taking the survivors to Antaris! She's just the first of many I need to gather together."

"Antaris, where the Faculty is? Why?"

The high elf turned to the Dragonborn. "We're going to save the last magi. We're going to disappear."

Thamias was flabbergasted. He shook his head in confusion. He was about to let him march away, but a question emerged from his lips. "How will you do that, Luthan?"

Luthan stopped and veered back to his brother-in-law. "Just give my wife the symbol!" he shouted. "She'll know what it means."

Thamias called him again, multiple times, but Luthan never looked back.

AHNA KNEELED in the multicolored pebbles by the river. She was further away from the house, on a larger surface near the flowing water. The stream was soft there, as the river gathered in an intermediary pond. She was incredibly focused, so focused that she had not noticed Jules walk up to her. The blond shrike observed her as she drew waves in the water with the palm of her hand. She had tied her messy hair in a silver knot, but a few locks danced around the nape of her blue neck. By her side, her satchel was opened, and an aged tome with torn pages lay on the pebbles. The sheets were of this yellow color, the color of parchments from centuries-old books. She held one page in her hand.

The elf murmured to herself. Jules could not distinguish the words, but it was definitely not a language he spoke. She gazed upon the page she clasped, and with the other hand, she drew a large semi-circle above the water.

"*Vatn s liifsins.* Waters of life…" she whispered. "Mirror of souls. *Speglar solna…*" She swayed her hand, tracing back the same semi-circle in the water. "Images of the lost. *Myndir af tiindum, vatn s solna.*"

Ahna's eyes suddenly opened wide. Her pupils dilated with the colors of the Azul. The inside of her irises whirled around with an ethereal glow. She gripped the page in her hand, clenched it in a fist, then brought it to the water. When she released it, the page turned to sparkles of dust that spread into the river.

"*Myndir af solum,*" the elf murmured.

The sparkles froze into place. They were suspended in the water like lifeless stars in the sea of the Heavens. They were blue, purple, green, yellow, white, and formed clouds that touched, avoided, or merged into each other. Their reflection shimmered in Ahna's eyes. With her index finger, she reached for the surface above the green dust. Her eyes turned green. She then touched the glittering blue, her eyes veered to an ocean whirl. She repeated this motion, swaying through the clouds of dust, her eyes matching the colors she touched. She swept through the pond, looking, searching, scrying for something in the water.

As time passed, she grew more impatient. She frowned, and her eyes darkened with consternation. She leaned back, releasing the water. Her chest heaved. Ahna stared incomprehensibly at the river, as though nothing made sense anymore.

Jules took a step forward. "I gather that this didn't go as you planned?" he cautiously asked. Ahna shook her head slowly. He continued, pointing at the speckles in the water. "What's all this?"

Ahna straightened her posture. Her frown still hid her features. She gazed intensively at the river and her eyes returned to normal.

"This can't be," she simply said.

She then went for the book on the pebbles. She held it open, examined the other pages. She scrolled through them, as though she was on an urgent search for an explanation.

Jules crouched by her side and put his hand on her arm. "What's all this?" he asked again.

The elf sighed and pursed her lips. "This"—she waved the book at Jules—"is a scrying book. It has rituals, spells, and cantrips to locate objects, people, animals!" She chuckled at the last word.

"I mean…what did you do?"

"Oh," she collected her thoughts. "Waters give and retain life. It holds memories, images, captures our thoughts. You see, all water on Terra is connected. The river that flows through Bravoure, the Azul, it carries drops from the north, from Fallvale, rain from Galies it collected. The winds brought particles of the waters of Rallis, Vanhaui, and the many islands, down to the river. Clerics actually think the goddess Sabys, the preserver of life, designed it to be this way." She leaned closer to the water. "Here," she said as her finger rippled through the surface. "This is from Tazman."

Jules squinted a little. "What about the blue sparkles?"

"These are drops from Gurdal." She took a deep breath. "These should show me the entire world. All I need to do is browse the arcane through the waters, through each cloud one by one."

"So, what's wrong?"

"I'm not finding them, Jules. I searched the arcane through each part of the world. There is no sign of them." She took a deep breath. "I thought I missed something the last time I tried this, a year ago. But it looks like they're really…nowhere."

Behind them, ahead in the distance, they saw the figure of Farooq storm out of the little stone house. By the entrance stood his grandfather, Mohindra, who looked at him with a sad face.

Jules stood. "I wonder if those two are going to be alright."

"Farooq just found out the arcane flowed through his veins," Ahna said. "I should talk to him."

She stood, slid the book back in her satchel, and headed on the path to the stone house. Jules followed her, and the glitters in the river disappeared.

"WHERE IS HE GOING?" Ahna asked Mohindra, looking at Farooq stroll off in the distance.

"Back to the village," Mohindra answered distantly. "He says he has other things to do than to talk to an old fool like me."

"He'll come around," the elf reassured the old man.

"I'll get him!" Jules announced as he trotted in the direction of Farooq.

Ahna turned to Mohindra with graver eyes. "I don't think the magi made it out of Antaris after all." Her tone saddened. "I don't think the Planar Mask worked."

Mohindra dismissed her words. "It worked, Archmage."

The two headed back into the stone house. The old man grabbed his mushroom basket and placed it on the small workbench in the back corner. He unpacked his collection of morels and shaggy parasols and went to fetch a giant cauldron. He was about to seize a large potato knife in his hand when someone knocked loudly on the door. They knocked again, this time louder.

"Old witch!" someone shouted outside.

Ahna peered through the window. A large man stood by the door, and by the path, Jules and Farooq both kneeled with their hands behind their head. Mohindra went to open the door.

He was greeted by a tall brute who carried a butcher's hatchet on his shoulder. He seized the collar of the old man and hauled him out of the stone house by force. Ahna immediately raced outside. The large man dragged Mohindra to the path, toward two of his friends who were as big as he was. Mohindra bleated and whelped like a panicked fox.

The two men spotted the elf.

"There she is! Grab her," one of them cast.

Ahna immediately readied her stance.

She seized the dagger from her boot and held it in her fist. The brute released Mohindra and marched straight to her. He pounded the ground, and his shoulders swung left and right. As he was about to go for her, she dodged his hand and dived close to him. She launched the pommel of her dagger into his nose. His head jolted backwards, there was blood on his mouth. The blow made him drop his hatchet.

He took a few steps back and yelled. "You dokkalfar scum. You are not welcome here!"

He headed for a hook punch, but Ahna was much faster. She hooked onto his attacking arm. She used his powerful strength to move all her weight upwards, lifting herself, and she kicked him straight in the chest. He toppled and fell on his back. Ahna landed on hers.

The two other men released Jules and Farooq and ran straight toward her. Before they could come closer, Mohindra staggered up. He held his cane firmly and stared them down. As they almost reached him, he hammered the ground once. The rod, which looked like a simple wooden stick, transformed into something different. The wood around it warped on itself and muted into the contours of a large quarterstaff. When the old man seized the staff with both hands, the weapon glowed with a steady green light.

"Get out of our way, witch!" the man on the left ordered.

Instead, Mohindra slammed the staff on the ground. From the point of impact, the mud and roots began to twirl. The soil amassed together and formed a ferocious vine that sprung out of the earth. It twisted around the one man's leg and muted into more vines that entangled the other's feet. The two men were immobilized. They struggled to keep their balance and eventually fell down in front of Mohindra. Jules unsheathed his sword and headed straight for the two men on the ground. The shrike held his warning blade right above their heads.

Ahna stood back up. Before the third man could move, her hands swirled into the air. She focused the flow of her magic. Two hot flames grew out of her fingers and engulfed her forearms. She clenched her fists and faced the brute, who quickly surrendered.

"We are not the enemy here," Jules declared with a roar.

Mohindra snapped his fingers, and the vines released the two men. They immediately crawled away from the old man on all fours. The brute had already taken off. The others joined him, and they were gone as fast as they had arrived.

"Witch of the Woods?" Ahna joked to her apprentice as she put out her flames.

Mohindra chuckled. "Botany was always my favorite subject!"

The staff morphed into his old cane. The old man strolled back toward his stone house.

"I think we should leave," Ahna declared with concern.

"I was going to offer you some mushroom stew," Mohindra said.

"That would have been nice," the elf said timidly. "But I'm only putting you in danger by being here."

"Nonsense!" Mohindra shouted, but Ahna was right. He turned to his grandson, Farooq, who stood on the path with mouth agape. "Come on, *betu*. I have many things to tell you."

The young man simply heeded the call and followed Mohindra. The two stood by the door when they turned to Jules and Ahna.

"It was nice to see you, Archmage," Mohindra said. "I hope you find what you are looking for."

Ahna gave him a warm nod. She was still bitter, but she thought it best to hide it from the old man and his grandson.

"It was nice to see you, Mohindra," she said. "And you, Farooq."

Farooq simply smiled and headed inside. He was too confused by the events. Mohindra fetched Ahna's cloak and bow from the house and handed the elf the rest of her belongings. Jules greeted Mohindra with a respectful salute and marched onto the path with Ahna.

THE TWO TRAVELERS reached a vast field of pink daisies north of Drazul. The sun pierced through the dissipating clouds and shone bright in the sky. They were on the east side of the river. If they continued their march this way, they could even reach the Ruins of Antaris by the late night.

Jules's stomach growled.

"I really wish you'd have said yes to that mushroom stew!" he complained.

Ahna chuckled. "I still have sandwiches from Ol' Jon! Worry not, shrike."

She handed him a stuffed loaf of cloud bread, and Jules immediately gulped it down his throat.

"Do you get this a lot in the city? This…hate?" he asked between two bites.

Ahna shrugged. "Not much more than a few disapproving looks."

"It's not the way it's supposed to be." Jules sighed.

"I get them, though. I'm dokkalfar, after all."

"But it shouldn't be this way."

The elf smiled. Jules did not know, but his words brought a certain welcoming warmth to her heart.

Up ahead, Ahna spotted two large stones among the green grass. "We should take a break there," she said.

Jules finished his bread. "Where are we going exactly?"

"I'm not sure, but I'm hungry too."

They both went to sit on the rocks that faced each other. Ahna pulled a second stuffed loaf out of her satchel, and she gave the third one to her partner who still starved. She looked far ahead, through the large trees that bordered the field. She seemed distant, as though she pondered on what to do next.

"I've searched everywhere," she pressed out of the silence. "The waters give no sign of them."

Jules swallowed and cleared his throat. "Well, could it be that there's no water from where they are?"

"That's impossible," Ahna replied as she shook her head. "All waters eventually find their way back into the Terran sky."

"Even in the Dwellunder?" the shrike asked.

"Even in the Dwellunder," Ahna confirmed. "That's the circle of life."

Jules acknowledged with a low hum. He sat still for a moment, pondering on this whole story of waters and particles and circle of life. In the midst of his thoughts, Jules finished his second loaf.

He then leaned back and exhaled deeply. "Well…" His tongue clicked. "That can only mean one thing, right?"

Ahna looked at him, perplexed and expectant.

Jules went on. "They're not on Terra."

Ahna let out a loud burst of laughter. "Well, they can't be in the Abstract Plane. I doubt that they're in the Heavens! There's no way in Hell they're…in Hell. And the Hollow Earth? Don't even mention it."

Jules reaffirmed his point. "I don't mean they're on a different plane." He paused for a minute and looked up. His grey eyes seemed distant, as though he scouted the sky for an answer. "I mean they're not on Terra." He shrugged. Ahna remained silent, so he looked to her. "No?"

The elf simply had this calculative look on her face. She fixed an invisible point in the grass with her eyes. And then, it seemed like a thousand falling stars crashed in her mind. A realization that had taken a long, long time to manifest itself. She jumped to her feet. She scoffed, she laughed. She brought her hands to her hair in disbelief.

"You beautiful genius, Jules!" she exclaimed as she marched to the blond shrike. She held his face in her hands and gave him a big kiss on his forehead. She paced away and held her conclusive finger up in the air. "They're not on Terra!"

The blond shrike rushed to her. "Wait! Where are you going?"

Ahna paused. She stared at the woods in front of her while Jules was catching up. "The Planar Mask wouldn't take them that far…"

"So, where would it take them?" the shrike asked when he caught up to her.

Ahna stopped for a second. "We thought it would draw energy from the Abstract Plane to move through space, but that would take too much energy. We also hypothesized there needed to be two—one on each end, but the second was never found in the entire history of magic!"

Ahna raised her eyes to the shrike. She bit her lip as she thought some more. All the books she had read, the history of magic, the Fine Arts of Arcanis, even the parchments of the Ancients, all raced through her head.

And then it hit her again. "You have got to be joking…" She stepped away from the shrike and turned to the field. She stayed there to ponder some more before turning back to Jules. "Luna!" she exclaimed.

Jules raised an eyebrow. "Luna?"

Ahna's eyes rounded incredulously. "The moon," she stuttered. "There are old, *extremely* old texts about the Ancients travelling to the moon. But these are just mere legends." She walked in circles. "If the second end of the Planar Mask is on Luna, then it would explain so much."

Jules sighed very deeply. "You lost me there, Archmage."

"I just have no idea how to verify this." Ahna matched Jules's sigh. "This just gets more complicated the more clues we find!"

"Remember when you did that crazy thing with my captain?" Jules asked out of the blue.

"Which one?" Ahna checked.

"The one where you were supposed to switch places."

The elf confirmed with a nod. She knew what Jules referred to, that time she had bound herself to Cedric Rover. How could she forget...

"Well," he pursued. "Cedric disappeared, and suddenly you two were back."

"Yes, that was a portal."

"How did it work?"

"I bound the soil to the Abstract Plane, so we could move through space. It's similar to how we presumed the Planar Mask to work, but our ritual was on a much smaller scale."

Jules frowned. "Can't you do the same now?"

"I'd need to know where I'm going!" Ahna retorted.

"Well, it's the moon! You can see it."

Ahna's riddle-solving finger was back. "It doesn't work that way." She analyzed the situation in her mind. "And even then, traveling to the moon would require a *tremendous* amount of energy...it's nothing I can provide."

The blond shrike pursed his lips together. He suddenly got the glimpse of an idea. He seized Ahna's satchel and pulled out the torn spell book. He held it in his hands, examined it, he wanted to read it. He opened it and began to sift through the scriptures. After a long pause, he exhaled and his eyes met the elf's.

"I can't read this," he said, waving the book at Ahna.

"That's normal, it's magic." Ahna was quite amused by Jules's attempt at reading the arcane.

Jules held the book by the fore-edge. "You said you needed energy," he recalled.

"Yes, arcane energy."

"Isn't this book full of magic?" he asked with an evident tone.

"Well, sure," Ahna answered, slightly impressed by Jules's cunning conclusions. "But I can't just absorb the book. That would be an insurmountable magical force, and I will risk blowing this entire forest apart!"

At that moment, Jules looked behind them, toward the field. He gazed upon the grass, swayed by the gentle wind. In the distance, he distinguished a young man's running shadow, who dashed in their direction. He recognized the young man. It was Farooq. The shrike then smiled with yet another *genius* idea and turned back to Ahna.

"Well, what if there were two of you?" he said as he pointed at Farooq.

5

FULL MOON

*F*arooq reached the two travelers with haste. He held a wooden baton in one hand, and the cloth of his faded green linen tunic swayed by his belt as he ran. His wavy black hair bounced in the wind. He appeared to be carrying a heavy satchel, which he dragged on his shoulder. He panted—he had walked and run after Ahna and Jules for a long time.

When he reached them, he leaned over to catch his breath.

"Hi!" he said, puffing.

The two waited for him to say something.

He winced as he raised himself up. "I want to come with you," he declared. Before Ahna could retort, he continued. "My whole life, I was a nobody. My *daadu* hid from everyone, and I just worked the fields. I've lived this life aimlessly. Now, I find out I'm a mage, and the only ones who can answer all my questions are castaway!" He looked to the two friends with begging eyes. "Please, let me help you find them!" He held his hands together around his baton. "I need to find my purpose, and I think I can find it with you."

Jules looked to Ahna, who gave Farooq a warning glare.

"This is not going to be simple," she pressed.

"I'll take anything more than this," the young man assured.

"What about your grandfather?" Jules asked, concerned for the old man.

Farooq shook his head. "He'll be just fine without me. I gave him no say in this. I'm a grown man, I need to follow my true calling on my own."

Jules chuckled. Ahna took a deep breath, letting it out slowly.

"Then you'll help us get to the moon," she said.

She marched into the trees and motioned for them to follow. Farooq looked at her, confused about what he had just heard. Jules simply shrugged and walked to Ahna.

"What do you mean, the moon?" Farooq asked as he marched behind them.

"That's where we're going!" Jules answered. There was one big problem, though. "Only the logistics are still under review."

Ahna, too busy in her thoughts, began to stroll away. The elf was headed toward the road beyond the trees, the one that went further up north. She still held the book, reading through it as she walked.

"Where are we going now?" Farooq asked again.

"To think," Ahna announced. "If we're going to the moon, then I need to figure out where to even begin the journey. There might be a clue hidden in Antaris. The Faculty…" Ahna paused again. The grave reality hit her as it had done over fifty years ago. Something that dissuaded her from her adamant march. "But the Faculty is gone." She exhaled desperately. "Sharr destroyed everything…"

The elf leaned against the trunk of a large tree. She closed her eyes, gripped by the idea of giving up. There was no way anything remained from the Faculty, not even the stones of its library walls. And even if there was the slightest possibility some astronomy books were intact, they would have faded or drowned in the rain of half a century's erosion. She had searched the ruins herself two years ago, there was nothing left.

Jules pulled her out of her thoughts. "When Cedric did that whole teleportation thing, you said he just needed to picture his target. You know where the moon is."

Ahna shook her head. "I can't just picture the moon. I would need a specific location, a point in space. Something concrete."

The two fell silent. Even if she had Luna in sight, she could not simply imagine being there! But Jules and his insistent, curious soul always contested Ahna's conclusions. He was not going to let her give up so easily.

"Ahna, you are ten times older than I am!" The elf laughed. This was not true, but sure. "You have studied all your life. You talked to me about astronomy! You must know enough about Luna by now to be able to…calculate a place over there."

"Well…" Ahna laid her hands on her hips. "I know how far it is." She started thinking again, very deeply. "I know what the surface looks like from afar. The clouds and oceans… I thought I even saw a piece of land once, a grey body of soil, through the glass lens of the Academy." Jules nodded furtively as she spoke, but she abruptly stopped. She turned to the two with a concerned look on her face. "We are taking the biggest gamble here," she declared, and the look in her eyes then lit with determination. "Jules," she raised her hand to the blond shrike, "give me the book."

Farooq came beside her to examine the Book of Scrying. Above them, the leaves shivered in the wind. Ahna explained to Farooq, as best as she could, what was to happen next. She had felt the arcane flow through his veins, which was how she had known he was a mage. She was going to use this to divide the spell book's force between them. Alone, the book would destroy her and everything around them. Together, they could balance its power so she could control it. With that power, she could open a rift from the tangible world to the Abstract Plane. He did not need to do much, just let the stream of magic flow freely through him, and let her control it.

"I will be opening a portal, but it won't be a simple gateway," Ahna warned. "Since I cannot picture the place exactly, we'll need to search through the Abstract Plane. It'll be like we know where to dig, but we just have to dig."

Ahna closed the book and checked the sky. No moon. She paused for a second to collect her thoughts. Based on her previous observations, Luna was to rise in the late evening.

"Do you have food?" she asked Farooq.

"I have potted mushroom stew and some bread," he replied as he showed his satchel.

She pointed at the two large stones behind them. "Then let's wait over there until moonrise."

***

JULES CHEWED on a blade of dried grass. It was dark—night had fallen but a few moments ago. The blond shrike waited for Ahna's call, while Farooq scrolled through the elf's book on his own. Unlike Jules, he could read it, and he was utterly fascinated by all he was seeing. The words echoed in his mind with a power he had never felt.

Ahna sat still on the large rock. Her eyes were calm, but her heart betrayed the apprehension of what was to happen next.

Jules's voice interrupted her thoughts. "What will you do if you find them?" he asked, curious of Ahna's intentions.

She exhaled deeply. "If they're on Luna, I have no idea how they've survived. But I have to see it for myself. Then I'll think of what to do."

"Who's Archmage Hyehn?" Jules asked. Since Ahna raised her eyebrows, Jules explained his question. "You mentioned him to Mohindra. I figured he was someone important to you."

"He was much more," Ahna distantly said. She let the silence sink in before speaking again. "I thought him dead for fifty years. Now, I'm not so sure."

Ahna's thoughts lingered on Luthan's memory. For many years, they had lived a peaceful life in Bravoure, together. Until Xandor Kun Sharr came.

"What will you do if you see him again?" Jules asked, feeling Ahna's pain through her voice.

"That, I have no idea," she replied, absolutely clueless.

The silence settled in. Jules's thoughts briefly went to the memories of war. He remembered the end of the fight, the Battle of Orgna and the downfall of Sharr. The Resistance's victory.

"Two Sols since our freedom," he said. "It seems like the fight isn't over."

"How so?" Ahna inquired.

"Well, we had to pick up a kingdom from the bottom of the deepest pit. It seems like we've only just begun our ascent back to the surface."

Jules was right. Bravoure's liberation was no synonym for prosperity. After the Rebellion, after the rebuilding of the kingdom, there was still much work to be done. Especially since darkness lurked at every corner to seize the opportunity to rule over Bravoure.

"The rift I'll open," Ahna began, away from this daunting subject of politics. "It will be a tunnel through space and time." Jules listened to her all ears. Ahna stood and motioned something in the air. "Our world, the tangible world, is bound by rules and laws of how elements move through the continuum. The Abstract Plane lies outside these laws…"

"Ahna, let me stop you right there, I don't understand anything beyond my blade."

Ahna laughed. Jules held an endearing smile on his face. The smile of an eager yet prudent nature, the one that made him look so handsome. He firmly believed too much knowledge would cloud his mind from solid things that lay in front of him.

"It binds the different planes of existence together," Ahna said in an instructive tone. "Or at least, we think it does."

"So, you were some kind of teacher?" Jules presumed.

"Yes," the elf retorted with a longing smile. "As I mentioned before, my specialty was Ritualism, which means I intensively studied the planes." She looked back, over her shoulder, to the south, in the direction of the city of Bravoure. "I hope to be able to teach someday again."

"You will!" Jules rose to his feet and stepped close to her. "And you'll have a hundred more magi to teach."

The shrike sat beside Farooq on the other stone. The young man still browsed furiously through the book. He was in absolute astonishment. Simply the fact that he could read the arcane words ignited a kind of spark in his heart. The kind that revealed he had always been meant to do this. He finally began to comprehend why, all his life, he had felt as though he was destined for something bigger.

"What does it say?" Jules asked Farooq, curious himself of the words in the spell book.

"This one is a spell for finding a lost animal," Farooq answered proudly. "It says you need to hold something that belonged to the animal, like a collar or a toy."

Jules took a look at the words himself, but he still could not read. "And then what?"

"Then you wrap the object in the page. It says the page will wither away and you just have to follow the ashes in the wind."

Ahna observed the two men scanning her book. Each page had been written with magical ink that yielded the power of countless spells. Anchored in the ink was an ethereal energy that gave this book its name: the Book of Scrying. One-time rituals to find lost objects, missing pets and…people.

The blond shrike remained seated by the eager new apprentice, who kept his eyes on the book for the evening. After a long moment of silence, Jules leaned back to relax his eyes. He fell asleep, almost instantly. Ahna still held her gaze to the south, picturing the Magi Academy of Bravoure, the one she had restored with the efforts of the city. The library was open by now. She wondered how many people had rejoined the spire. For longer than a few deep breaths, her mind traveled to her past. Ahna sunk into her own thoughts. Her heart remembered the magi she had held dear, some who had become her closest of friends. Those without prejudice who had seen past her purple eyes and the color of her skin. Of all these welcoming souls, she remembered Archmage Luthan Hyehn, the handsome ljosalfar with his long, pure-blond hair and his high elven allure. Her husband, whom she had believed to be dead for decades, almost a lifetime. She did not dare fuel the spark of hope that she might see him again. Losing him twice would be more than she could handle.

But she could not keep her mind from wandering. She wondered what it would be like to see him again—if he still lived. His death was a possibility, after all. And maybe Ahna would prefer that. She had mourned him. For years. And now, she had learned that he, along with many others, had left her behind. If he still lived, then his apology had better be good, or she would take care of ending his life herself.

The good old dokkalfar way, she thought with a forced chuckle.

Would he even apologize? Would she even want to hear his apology? Was there even anything he could say to make this situation less enraging, less hurting, less of a betrayal? Maybe he was better off dead… Oh, who was she kidding? She wanted him to be alive more than anything else. Despite her anger during the confrontation with Mohindra, she had felt the undeniable hope grow in her heart. They had all betrayed her. They had left like cowards to save themselves. However, in the end, they were her friends. And Luthan was the love of her life.

"THERE'S THE MOON!" Farooq called and pointed to the sky.

The stellar object was large, almost full. Ahna could see it clearly. She contemplated it as it had surged above the trees. Its silver colors, with blue and sometimes purple shades. She rose to her feet. Jules was startled awake—he had been sleeping for a long time!

"What?" he shouted. "Oh, it's night."

Farooq, on the other hand, had been sitting next to Ahna all this time. They had mostly talked about magic. About her. About her time in Bravoure, at the Magi Academy, before all the madness. This talk of the arcane only made Farooq eager to learn more.

"Follow me, Farooq." Ahna requested of the young man.

The elf moved to the center of the daisy field lit by the light of the full moon. Farooq joined her hesitantly. "You're going to hold the book with me. Please, don't let it go. Let me do the incantation and let it flow through you. Don't lose focus and don't panic!" Farooq acknowledged, so she continued. "Know that this is something crazy, and you can still walk away."

Farooq shook his head—he was staying. Magic was already crazy to him, what was one more crazy thing?

"What do I do?" Jules asked from behind them.

"You stay put," Ahna firmly said.

She opened the tome in front of her. She motioned for Farooq to seize both ends of the open pages. They each held a corner of the spell book, rested in the crook between their palms and thumbs.

"I will start," Ahna declared. "Any excess magic will go to you. Please, Farooq, let it happen." The young man nodded assertively. The elf then raised her head to the sky and rested her gaze upon Luna. *"Words of magic,"* she beseeched with a whisper. *"Be one with me."*

Her purple eyes suddenly lit. The words on the torn pages began to fade. Each glyph shone with a buzzing light. They danced around, moved in circles, swirled around and found their way to Ahna's fingers. The inscriptions enveloped her hands and slithered all the way to her shoulders. They disappeared into her skin. Her eyes shone brighter.

As the flow of magic sunk into her veins, the arcane words shifted in Farooq's direction. The tome began to wither away. Farooq felt a sharp shock, a power surge through his blood. The young man pressed his thumbs into the book to strengthen his grip. He felt spasms down his arms, and he gave his everything not to let go. He was about to give up when the surge abruptly stopped. The book had almost disappeared, and Ahna released one of her hands.

She turned around, her eyes still fixed on the full moon. Her purple irises were shimmering with arcane radiance. The elf held her free hand in the air beside her. She focused all of her power into a single point, in which she transferred all the energy she had accumulated. The world seemed to rip open before her eyes. A black tear through the tangible world spread in front of her. It formed a crack, a rift, a rupture absolved of light. It tore open and grew larger as Farooq's own energy began to slip away as well. When Ahna released her hold, the book disappeared, and Farooq fell to his knees. She looked at the rift for a moment, examined it with her head tilted. Then, she turned to the two young men.

"I will step through." Her eyes were black. Her voice was distorted. "I will come back if something's wrong. Wait for my signal."

Before they could argue, she stepped through the rift. Soon after, they heard a distant murmur call to them. Jules hesitated, but the voice became louder, and he recognized Ahna. He helped Farooq up, and the two stepped into the portal.

DAVID PASSED through the door of the Goshawk stone mansion. It was too late for dinner and too early for drinks. He stepped into the large and wealthy home with a reluctant pinch in his stomach. The man still wore his commander's tunic proudly, the one crossed in the middle of his chest with silver epaulettes. He was greeted by two butlers who offered to take his coat, which he politely refused—he was not staying long.

The two butlers led David to the dining room. The wooden tiles of the floors cracked softly with their march. A man sat at the table; a man with long, curled red hair and a finely trimmed beard. He was usually very charming. David had admitted it in the past, despite loathing the man. And Charles most certainly had his ways with the ladies, or so they said. But this time, Goshawk looked gross. Disgusting. He ate a chicken leg like his life depended on it.

"Ah! Good evening, Commander," Charles greeted. "Thank you for coming. Please, have a seat."

David went to sit on the nearest chair, opposite of Goshawk the banker, the man who wished to win the election with a sack of gold coins. There was braised chicken on the table. A pot of spiced lentil soup, momrogis glazed in pine syrup—David could smell it—and a large bowl of roasted apples.

"I haven't come for food," David said.

Goshawk dismissed him. "Then, please. Have a drink."

He signed to his butler to fetch David a goblet of red wine. David thanked the butler but did not take a sip.

"What did you want to talk about?" the commander asked.

Charles cleared his throat. "Straight to the point, I see," he observed. "Well, let me ask you a question. What would you like to do after the elections?"

David answered with a frown. "I'm not sure what you mean, Charles."

The two men had been on a first-name basis for a while now. After countless meetings on the instigation of a new plan for Bravoure, David and Charles had had all the time to get more acquainted.

"Would you like to be Bravoure's official Great General?" the banker asked, as direct as he could be.

The commander was not sure what was expected of him. People regarded him as the Resistance's leader. Mother Divine wanted him to go for the official title and lead the Bravan Army. But David had done his fair share of fighting, all his life. Was he ready to take on this task? And why was Charles Goshawk asking him now, of all times? David wanted to give an answer but first willed to understand what this whole meeting was about.

"David," Charles pulled him out of his thoughts. "What if I told you I had a way to give you an army bigger than you could imagine. I could have housing for your men, stable wages, training plans for new recruits. Bravoure's soldiers will make up the most powerful army on Terra!"

The banker held his arms wide open, proud of what he had just proposed. His rallying voice had echoed in the dining hall. David, though, simply had no words to say. The offer sounded like a shaded dream to him. A proposal of such grandeur could not be denied. But should that be Bravoure's top priority, after fifty years under military oppression? Should the people's well-being not come first?

"I'm not sure what to say, Charles. It's a considerable promise."

"A promise I'm ready to make," Charles declared with a big smile.

David had to take a sip of wine. He looked the banker in the eyes, trying to dissect his exact intent. Something felt wrong. This meeting felt wrong. His Taz sense of righteousness began to ring between his ears. Charles seemed to care a little too much about having David on his side. But perhaps this was not solely about David. As leader of the Resistance, David had the people's hearts rooting for him.

"What is to be expected of me?" David queried, most suspicious of Charles intentions. To him, it sounded like the banker wanted David to sponsor him so the people would follow.

Charles held his smile. His golden eyes shimmered, but the trust they inspired felt...fake—David sensed it.

"I just want your men on my side," he said, simply, without a shred of shame. "Some would find it absurd to refuse such an offer, Commander, perhaps even...insensitive."

David stared at Charles for a little while. He remained steady, silent, until the banker leaned back in his chair and clapped once in his hands. A sign that this meeting had come to an end.

"Please, Commander, consider it, and give my warm regards to your lovely wife!"

David forced a smile. He stood to leave and let the banker finish his copious dinner.

6

SKYSHRINE

*J*ules and Farooq shivered as a slight breeze caressed their bodies. Ahna stood in front of them, facing away, looking into the darkness in the distance. They were in a long and unending pitch-black tunnel, and they couldn't see anything beyond their reach.

"What is this place?" Farooq asked, swiping his head in all directions.

The three stood on a platform, yet they felt no ground. There was no smell. And it was dark. Ahna turned to Farooq and closed her eyes that reflected the darkness. The rift behind them suddenly shut.

"We're in a conduit through the Abstract Plane," Ahna said, and her voice returned to normal. Her eyes opened again. "I couldn't lock a portal on an exact location on Luna, so we will have to follow the tunnel."

Once the rift disappeared completely, the darkness that loomed transitioned. A distorted motion of colors whirled in the walls around them, like the color of a rainbow, only purple and blue were the dominant hues. The colors followed them as they walked. The three sauntered deep into the tunnel of unreal shades until the walls around them muted into light.

IT WAS AN ODD-LOOKING TREE. Purple, marked by the absence of bark. Perhaps it was not even a tree. Ahna looked to the sky—too bright. She searched behind Jules and Farooq who had just passed through the Abstract Plane. More barkless trees. Purplish stems with coiled branches and leaves looked like they were made of cerulean ice. She took a step forward and hit her foot against a white, pearly rock that sprung from the obsidian ground. A moon rock.

The blond shrike adjusted his messy hair. Farooq simply stared at the odd-looking tree. Far in the opposite direction, Ahna could see the dark ground turn into a vast field of lighter grass.

"Did we make it?" Jules asked.

Ahna's face was expressionless. "I don't think I've ever seen such trees on Terra."

She made her way to the grass field that extended toward a hill. The only strange thing was that the grass was silver, as though an ash cloud had given it this color. There was no wind, only echoes of distant creatures. A chill ran down Ahna's spine. During this short break, she finally realized just how severely weakened she was from the arcane overflow, but she could still walk. And fortunately, so could Farooq.

"Come." She signed for them to follow. This whole place gave her the creeps.

They headed onto the grey grass. By the far horizon, among the trees, they heard the faint roar of another kind of animal. They picked up the pace. They marched on the silver hill until they reached a strange structure. It was a set of piled up opalescent stones, much like the odd-looking tree leaves.

"What do you think this is?" Jules wondered out loud.

Farooq squinted. "I don't know, but it looks manmade!"

They searched for the elf, who had already gone up the hill. She stood still, distracted, completely ignoring her traveling companions. Her mouth agape, her eyes were large, and her ears flicked upwards. The two men tried to get her attention, but she remained unmoved. Once they reached her, they noticed what she was looking at. In the distance, down the hill and more silver fields, there stood a massive edifice.

A citadel made of the same material as the previous structure. Stones so translucent, it looked like it was made of glass. The same shimmering castle mentioned in the old texts, those that Ahna remembered, those that mentioned the Ancients exploring the moon. The elf gasped. The building, frozen in time, appeared like a transparent sculpture of centuries old ice. Nothing could be seen inside, yet it was as if they could see right through it. It consisted of symmetrical towers of increasing sizes, distributed as square pillars that met in the middle, each taller than the other. The center tower, the highest of all, watched over the silver fields. This construction made it look like the citadel of glass curved from the ground to the moonsky. The back of the castle extended like an arch of decrescent columns. Around the large edifice was a collection of faraway houses, built with white moon rocks that sparkles in the light of Sol.

"What is it, Ahna?" Jules asked.

She gulped for air and cleared her throat. "That's Skyshrine, the lost city…" Her head shook from left to right. "I don't understand. It's supposed to be a myth."

They strolled downhill. The air was light, much less dense than on Terra. They had to take multiple breaks to catch their breaths. Ahna began to feel weaker and weaker. She leaned on Jules for a moment, to be able to walk at a reasonable pace. The white, windowless houses were just in reach. Now that the three were closer, they could even see moving shapes around the dwelling.

People!

Ahna's heart raced. The bright light, the lightness of the air, she felt dizzier the more she walked. She could no longer breathe! There were people ahead of their march. People she probably knew. She was anxious. She wanted to run to them, but she felt the grasp on her consciousness slowly slip away.

"Help!" Jules called. "Somebody help!"

Farooq shouted with him.

The crowd that simmered in the distance fell silent. All eyes were on Farooq and Jules who carried a lifeless Ahna through the silver grass. Two, maybe three robed people, approached them, cautiously at first. They wore the long tunics of apprentices. A fourth figure surged from beyond the crowd that had begun to gather.

The man, tall, with an earth-brown skin and lighter eyes, rushed to Ahna's help. The rest hurried behind him.

"What in Morxairen..." He could barely speak, because he recognized this dark elf that had landed here.

His voice, warm and honeyed, taunted Ahna to open her eyes slightly. She caught a glimpse of his ears that were too pointy for a human but not enough for an elf.

"How did you get here?" the man asked Farooq and Jules.

"We don't have time for questions now, she's moonstruck!" a woman behind him exclaimed.

Ahna tried to look at their faces. She could only distinguish the blur of their eyes and mouths, and bright and dark colors of indistinguishable robes.

"Get them in the Dome!" another man shouted.

The not-quite elven man carried Ahna toward the white houses. When they were just in reach, they were faced with an invisible wall that rippled when they stepped through. Jules and

Farooq noticed a slight shimmer that drew waves into the air. Once inside the *Dome*, they instantly regained the ability to breathe normally. Farooq exhaled a loud sigh of relief. Ahna was able to stagger up straight, but still had to lean on the man who had rescued her. Shielded from the bright sunlight, her sight was recovering quickly.

When she looked at her rescuer, her eyes snapped open with surprise, and she gasped.

"Iedrias," she could barely say.

"Yes, Meriel!" he exclaimed with a big smile. "How did you… How is this possible?"

He was still flabbergasted by the presence of the three. And he was not the only one. More and more people in robes gathered around the central plaza upon which the travelers stood. They stared at them with eyes open wide. None of them dared make a sound.

Ahna held the human-elf wizard in her arms. Archmage Iedrias Dallor, her dear friend from a lifetime ago, with mossy green eyes that could see through one's very soul. His frizzy hair was well trimmed, and his ebony skin gleamed in the bright light of Sol. He had aged, but not as much as Ahna would have expected.

Someone approached Jules. They wanted to make sure he was real. Others stared at Farooq and his clothes. There were mumbles, multiple, but no one dared to move closer.

"It's good to see you, old friend," Ahna finally managed to say despite his embrace. She then turned to Jules and Farooq. "This is Iedrias. I have known him all my Bravan life."

Iedrias smiled bigger. "Meriel…" He picked up on his earlier inquiry. "How did you get here?"

Ahna released herself and shook her head to center her thoughts. "An augmented rift. I had to absorb a whole Book of Scrying to open a portal, Archmage Dallor."

Iedrias's jaw dropped. He was in absolute awe. "With his help?" he said as he glanced over to Farooq. "He seems very young."

Ahna chuckled. "He has a lot of potential."

She now noticed the larger crowd that had amassed around them. Had they been standing there all along? What time was it? For Ahna it was night, but the sun shone so bright. She examined her surroundings. Behind Iedrias, she saw a tall series of steps that led to Skyshrine's entrance.

More people examined them from over there. They whispered things to each other's ears and headed toward the building. Ahna felt a pinch down her stomach. It was not from the late malaise, but from what she sensed when she gazed upon the gates in the distance. Iedrias saw her looking.

"I know that look," the wizard declared. "Luthan's inside."

Ahna's mind was blank. This could only mean one thing: Luthan was alive. But her brain did not grasp it just yet. It refused to deal with the information it had been so eager to get. She could not think about this now.

Iedrias pursed his lips, understanding her emotions. "Come with me," he requested.

He said many inaudible things to the other magi around them. He wanted to disperse the crowd, but many, many questions followed. An intense feeling of wonder and confusion blanketed the village. Iedrias could sense the vibrations in the air. He wanted to appease everyone, but everyone kept on staring, gasping, or throwing questions that he could not answer immediately. Meriel was here. That was all that was on his mind right now.

"I'm going to need to gather everyone, explain everything," Iedrias declared, making a mental note to himself before leading Ahna, Jules, and Farooq toward the citadel of glass.

Before setting foot on the moonstone stairs, Ahna turned around to contemplate the village. It was beautiful. Each next house, perfectly aligned with the previous one, displayed a pearly schiller in the light. There were potted flowers that adorned the pavement, flowers that did not look like they were from Terra. Long purplish stems that opened in large ruby or cerulean petals that formed a welcoming cluster. Ahna noticed tall poles that grew out of the ground. They ended in a lantern-shaped tip, but with no oil inside.

Iedrias explained that they lit on their own during the night. The people, the apprentice or adept magi that had gathered around, they all wore either robes or simple garments. They followed her with their eyes. She barely recognized any. Some faces, older than the others, perhaps. But the rest—they were all strangers to Archmage Arkamai.

As they stood high on the steps, Iedrias gazed upon the three travelers that had just landed on Luna. He recalled the series of events that had just occurred.

"They are…people!" an apprentice had shouted from the Sky Tower an hour earlier.

His friend had caught a glimpse of three shapes appearing far in the distance, close to the forest, with the telescope atop Skyshrine's highest tower. Iedrias had immediately rushed to the three travelers, his heart pounding in his chest. Now they stood before him, with a crowd of at least thirty magi villagers behind. Yet Iedrias had not yet figured how his ljosalfar friend would react upon hearing the news. What it meant for him. How it would break him, to hear his wife had managed to travel the stars…while he had miserably failed for the last fifty years.

Once they reached the foot of the citadel of glass, Iedrias turned his back to the village below and faced the crowd that ambled by the gates. He motioned for Ahna, Jules, and Farooq to come closer.

He then told his fellow magi of Ahna, Meriel Ahn Arkamai, the archmage some had heard of, and some had not. Most people in the crowd were human, some were elven, ljosalfar. No sindurs, no dokkalfar. Many were young, too young to have known Archmage Arkamai. The older ones vaguely remembered her from their youth, some even as their teacher of the Basics of Elementalism. One, in particular, had a smile until her ears. An elderly woman with silver hair that resembled Ahna's, who remembered the archmage as her teacher, when her much younger self had ventured to the occult and learned a few ritualist tricks.

Many had questions, which they kept to themselves, mostly on how the three travelers had managed to get to Luna. Actually, nobody spoke, none had any idea how to act. The crowd seethed with constant surprise, shock, mixed with a euphoric sense of joy. Or perhaps it was apprehension. None of them really knew. If new people had made it to Luna after all this time, maybe there was a way back, after all.

And then there was the question everybody wished to ask. The question that burned on everyone's tongues. Those who had come to the moon begged for an answer with their eyes. Those who had been born here, and who had only heard the echoes of war, still wanted to ask that same question.

The tension rose, until somebody mustered the courage to ask: "What...happened?"

It was Jules who stepped forward to face the crowd. His grey gaze bounced back and forth between their flabbergasted faces. He had tied his blond hair in a knot at the nape of his neck. Ahna had only noticed it now. It gave him the allure of a Bravan knight, especially with that sword of his. The people kept their gaze fixed on him, and Ahna, for a split second, imagined Jules to be a spokesman addressing a crowd of eager souls.

"Sharr's dead." Jules lowered his voice.

Elders opened their eyes wide, the rest stared in silence.

"He's been dead for two Sols," Jules continued. "After the war, the people united against him. It took us half a century"—he clicked his tongue and shook his head—"but we did it."

Iedrias turn to Ahna. He took a moment to examine his old friend as Jules spoke of Lord Sharr's demise.

"You must have gone through so much, fighting an unending war," he assumed.

"I ran away, Iedrias. Bravoure did it on her own," Ahna immediately cut him off. She raised her hand in the air as a sign of dismissal.

The heavy sound of silence fell upon the pavement. There was the crack of pain in Ahna's voice. Iedrias noticed it, the grief and regret.

"Nonsense, Ahnny," Jules told Ahna softly then pointed at her and veered to the crowd. "Her arrival changed everything."

He had said this in a subtle accusatory tone. Unconsciously, most likely, as though he had desired to make an invisible point. That a mage, one that had stayed behind, had helped change the fate of Bravoure.

Ahna gave him a thankful smile and turned to face Iedrias. "How many of you made it?" she asked, meeting the human-elf's green eyes.

"Almost a hundred," he replied. He paused. "What happened, Meriel, after we left?"

Ahna's purple eyes darkened. "Antaris is gone—it's just ruins now. Sharr had *magefinders* crafted, and he used them to hunt us down to extinction after you...disappeared."

Iedrias listened to Ahna as though she spoke through a glass window. Her voice was clear, but his thoughts were not. He had a lump in his throat that transformed into a boulder in the middle of his stomach. She kept on speaking, and he listened. Yet all he felt was the fifty-year-old guilt he had buried deep within.

"A few even turned on us and joined him, afraid for their lives," Ahna said in an undertone.

"I'm sorry, Meriel," Iedrias said in an inaudible whisper.

Everything rushed back in his mind. All the memories. The

prophecy. Ahna's brother, Thamias, the Dragonborn. She looked to him as though she had deciphered his thoughts.

"Thamias still lives," she answered the silent question. "Xandor had him chained in the Tomb of Ghydra. He was trapped there for half a century. But the prophecy wasn't exactly about Thamias." She hesitated to say the next part. "And we named a second Dragonborn."

Iedrias wanted to hear more, but the crowd simmered again. He addressed the people, more people, who had amassed by the gates of the citadel.

He called for them to gather the others. There would be a speech tonight. He would tell them of the three travelers, of what it meant for the inhabitants of Skyshrine. After fifty years were spent wandering these grounds, underneath a dome of protection against Sol's light, Iedrias had given up on the idea of ever getting home. Now, everything had changed.

Many magi, those in lighter robes, spread out like tiny ants with a duty. Ahna noticed some people did not even wear robes. They wore simple cotton garments of grey and blue. Naturals, who had been born in Skyshrine and had never known anything else. The others, mostly elders in grey linens, remained still, to look at the three travelers. One of them, eager to speak with Farooq, immediately asked him about Mohindra.

"He must be your...grandfather?" this elder said with a soft voice.

Farooq nodded hesitantly. "Did you know him?"

"We took many classes together. It was so long ago..."

Farooq was not sure how to respond, so he smiled and kept his gaze on the elder.

Iedrias came closer to Ahna and spoke softly. "I suspect you need a bit of time."

Ahna swallowed something large in her throat, but it got stuck. She wanted to speak yet could not find words. So, she plunged her purple gaze into Iedrias's, begging for him to make the decision for her.

"Let's go inside," he inferred from her eyes.

Ahna raised her head to the castle of glass, the tall edifice built by the Ancients centuries ago. The sunlight rained onto the building and made it look almost heavenly. Its crystalline walls refracted a thousand colors, like the hues of annealed moonstones.

LUTHAN

*T*he gates opened to the castle of glass. Iedrias said a few words to the men by the entrance, and they led the three travelers inside. They entered a great hall, larger than they had ever seen before. It was oval, captured between circular walls with endless shelves that offered over a million books. The structure rose to the top of the castle. There were two corridors, each leading to the right and left wing.

Ahna explored the oval hall with her dazzled eyes. She saw books of all colors, some with golden engravings, some not even the elf could see from where she stood. She noticed a few apprentices standing on very high ladders, tending to the myriad of books. At least, she thought they were apprentices, as they wore their typical black robes. Finally, in the middle of this majestic display, a massive, incomprehensible structure lit the entire chamber. One hundred lanterns hung from cords of all lengths that sprung from the center of the ceiling. The egg-shaped tips illuminated the area with a radiant arcane light Ahna had never seen. An apprentice held one in his hand to serve as a luminous source while he stood on a ladder, searching through his book.

The large hall led to the higher levels of the citadel through stairs scattered in all directions possible. The one immediately on their right coiled toward the elevated platform above their heads. The one just ahead climbed like an octopus' arm to the back of the hall. There were at least three or four far away on the left that spiraled to the different towers.

Iedrias noticed Ahna stupor as she examined the construction of light. "We named it the Taraxacum because it reminded us of an upside down dandelion seed head."

"How…how does it work?" Ahna said.

"The entire spire is powered by its own stones. Annealed moonstones make it possible to capture Sol's energy and translate it into light." Iedrias smiled. His smile increased the more he explained. "The lanterns in the village work the same way."

Jules was simply astonished. The Taraxacum, that large construction that dominated the room, caught his undivided attention. The blond shrike paced toward one of the shiny tips. He hesitated for a second, and Iedrias motioned for him to touch it. When he held the bright hanging lantern, he giggled loudly. Farooq used his baton to poke one, still cautious of its effects.

A few magi stepped into the hall and greeted Iedrias. They signed something to him, something Ahna did not quite understand. She adjusted her hearing to extract what they were saying. They seemed in a hurry, and were awkward about it, like they had no idea what to do but still needed to do it. Iedrias dismissed them. They gave him a nod of warning and strolled to the gates.

Ahna turned around to follow their motion as they headed outside. When she turned back, the world around her stopped.

Her heart pounded hard.

The blood in her veins raced so much it almost hurt. Time and space didn't matter. She breathed loudly—anxiously. She stared ahead, lost for words, and lost for anything else. It was like the ground had swallowed her whole. She shivered, her lips trembled, the chill down her spine caught her by the neck.

There he was. There was no possible shred of doubt about him being alive anymore.

While he took his last steps towards them, his emerald eyes were fixated on a petrified Ahna. It was impossible to read what was on his mind from their shimmer. When he reached her, he raised his arms slightly, as if to hug a wife after a day of hard work. Then he stopped awkwardly, standing a bit too close, looking lost. His arms fell. It was beyond clear he had no idea how to behave.

"Good day, Iedrias." The tall elf's mechanical greeting was nearly comical, given the circumstances. He had not taken his eyes away from the blue elf in front of him, nor had he moved any muscle.

This shook Ahna out of her stasis.

Was he for real? They had not seen each other in fifty years and he spent the first seconds greeting someone else instead of her?

"You're such an idiot," she said, her voice broken into a mixture of laughter and tears.

Unsure herself of her intentions, she had raised her right hand into a fist. But it broke before it even hit Luthan's chest, as her muscles denied her the required tension for a proper punch. The left hand followed the right, just as confused whether it was meant to hurt or simply touch him again. She went on, as every emotion she had ever felt, as well as those she had not allowed herself to feel, flooded through and out of her. Then, he caught one of her wrists and pulled her into an embrace.

Luthan just wanted to calm the woman he had desperately tried to get back to. He pressed her close to his chest. When he did, he had to shut his eyes, overwhelmed by the scent of her silver curls. Ahna struggled in his arms, crying and laughing. Nobody was able to tell what she felt at that exact moment, she herself the least of them all.

By now, the three bystanders had understood that their presence was no longer desired. Jules reluctantly left *the light thingies* behind as they went back outside.

In her long-lost husband's arms, Ahna began to cool down. The quick heartbeat she could hear through his chest was so much more telling than his eyes had been. This man still felt for her, just as she did for him. Ahna sunk into the embrace. In that moment, she lived through all those they had experienced together. The happy ones, mostly. All the comfort and security he had ever given her.

This was where she belonged.

She was safe.

Slowly, her tears stopped, and the laughs grew into heavy, quick breaths. Her breathing tried to keep her emotion at bay— an emotion that was threatening to take over, now that all others had dimmed down. Sparking in her heart, it slowly crept further, before it filled her body whole, burning her skin and reddening her face. Her hands clenched into fists, and she rid herself of the arms that were soothing her, the arms that were trying to tell her everything would be fine. Absolutely nothing was fine. She glared up into his still so confused, yet strangely indifferent eyes. His almost fearful reaction to her stare indicated that he was perfectly aware of the rage that had consumed his wife.

"How could you?" she asked in a destructive whisper.

Luthan sighed, unable to formulate a comprehensive response to that question. "I thought I would never see you again," he said the first thing that came into his mind. Because Ahna kept glaring at him, he added more inanities. "There are so many things I need to tell you."

"Just tell me one thing," she snarled. "How could you?"

"It's a long story, Ahna."

"I will never understand if you don't start!"

Ahna did everything to mask her anger. The wrath she was feeling right now consumed her to the bone. Kairen had been wrong—she was more than angry. She was furious.

"I was deceived!" he started his side of the story. "The Council *lied* to me. The Dean led me to believe you were to come with me, with all of us. I went through an entire army to make sure you would be the first to know we were ready. Ready to enact the plan. They told me you'd come. The Dean gave me your memlock and assured you'd remember. She lied. They *all* lied."

"I had no idea! I was imprisoned!" Ahna's eyes lit with rage. "That useless marble did nothing! I was imprisoned, Luthan, and you all left me to die," she hissed.

"Meriel, you cannot imagine how…how I have beaten myself about not getting you myself. But I didn't know you'd been captured. And there were so many others to save. And I had no reason to doubt…doubt that you weren't aware. I believed them. But to this day, I am so sorry that I did. When we arrived here…" He had to stop to swallow the rekindling rage. "When I couldn't find you…" He took a deep, angry breath. "When the gateway was closed and there was no way back…" His voice shattered in two. "Only then did they tell me that you were never meant to follow."

Ahna squinted at the words of the visibly broken ljosalfar in front of her. So he did apologize. But at this moment, it didn't mean anything to her. The facts were that she had been imprisoned, and he had left. He might not have known the state she had been in, but he had nevertheless left, perfectly capable of realizing she had been missing before making that damned decision.

"How could you leave me…" Her voice broke in the silence of the castle of glass. Tears began to fill her eyes again. This time, they were of nothing but sadness. Sadness from the betrayal and abandonment she felt. She tried to repress them, but they slowly began to flow. Luthan's eyes dimmed as he noticed her despair.

"I was forced to make a judgement call," he said, justifying his words more to himself than to her. "And I have paid for that mistake ever since. But the survival of an entire generation of magi depended on it, and that's how I learned to deal with it."

"I was tortured, Luthan," Ahna rebuked with vibrant wrath. "Xandor threw Thamias down a pit and executed our mother. I would like to say that I'm glad you dealt with your mistake, but I had to deal with so much more on my own! I mourned your death, Luthan, for fifty *fucking* years!" Ahna's heart ached more than anything else. The feeling of having lost him came back to the surface. She had not only lost him, she had lost everything.

Luthan looked down, not able to look into Ahna's eyes. He did not want his wife to see that his eyes were glazing up. Her words had hit him harder than anything in his life ever had. Not only had he left her behind, he had left her at the mercy of her abhorrent brother. He had not kept her away from the harms of her past like he had promised her mother he would. He shed a silent tear. He would not discuss this failure with her. This was his burden to carry. He had to live with what he had done to the woman he loved more than his own life.

"Our entire survival was at stake," he declared instead, his voice emotionless. It was no excuse, it was just the mantra he had been telling himself for years. "Sharr was coming with his army. I had to get as many as I could to Antaris."

Ahna's response was as empty as his. "Tell me something new."

"The Council justified the plan with the absence of a damned choice. And we really had no choice, Meriel!" Luthan was getting sterner now that the conversation was back to facts. "Your cursed brother was killing us. He was hunting us down to extinction," he ended, almost shouting.

The mention of Xandor shattered Ahna nearly as much as the confirmation that her past fifty years had been based on a big fat lie. She had left the battlefield with a torn soul ready for the Underworld. Half a century, she hid from the face of her torments. Mourning her dead friends. But the magi still lived. The magi had saved themselves. The magi had abandoned Bravoure to the oppression of a tyrant, and Luthan, the man of her life, had cowardly left her to fight the war she never could fight.

"I blamed myself for this whole bloody war! I left the city, I blamed myself for way too long!" She lifted her arms to point at everything around them. "You've been sitting in this forsaken paradise while people were being massacred!" Her voice failed her entirely.

Luthan shook his head ferociously. "We had no choice but to save ourselves," he repeated the phrase that had been carved in him.

Ahna could only retort: "And abandon the people of Bravoure?" Her eyes, filled with burning tears, came to find Luthan's dark green stare.

He did not bulge. "It was a judgement call," he justified once again.

And that made Ahna cringe. She stared at him for a shredding minute, slaying him with her piercing gaze. "The people were right," she rasped. "The magi were cowards."

Ahna had enough of this conversation and the excuses the magi told themselves to rectify their cowardice. She shook her head in disbelief. That was when she noticed a small young boy passing them. He was ljosalfar, with very fair blond hair, and a pointy nose she almost found endearing. Luthan's body straightened upon seeing the boy. Ahna dried her tears with her cloak, as the boy went to hug Luthan's leg. The tall elf looked at Ahna awkwardly before whispering something to the boy. The latter ran away laughing loudly.

Luthan took a deep breath, shut his eyes for a second and looked back at his wife. She would find out sooner or later anyways. "Meriel, that was my son."

Ahna's reality crumbled.

Even after everything, after all the distance she had tried to put between her and him emotionally, his words had cut through her soul. She felt a lump in her throat clog her windpipe. She had difficulty breathing, almost like she was moonstruck again. She felt her gut turn on itself, a retching convulsion that made her lose her balance. She staggered to the entrance and stormed out of the citadel of glass.

AHNA SAT on the stone bench by the entrance that faced the village. It rested behind a pedestal without a statue. She stared at the horizon, and her eyes itched with her dried tears. She felt numb, too numb to think anything. She simply stared. Her entire mind was blank. It felt as though centuries passed, until a familiar someone came to sit next to her.

"What happened in there?" Jules asked the sad elf, already picturing her answer in his mind. Since Ahna would not respond, Jules went on. "I take it that it didn't go so well."

Ahna grimaced. She chuckled awkwardly, almost compulsively. Once she caught her breath again, she turned to the blond shrike.

"Luthan is right," she admitted.

Was this a realization, or an act of surrender so she would feel no more pain? Or was it her sense of logic she always relied on? The logic she reverted to in order to make sense of senseless things.

"They made a judgement call," she said and pressed her eyes against the heels of her hands. She exhaled deeply to repress more tears. "Even if I had been aware, I would never have agreed to this"—she waved around at Skyshrine—"paradise." She paused, letting that *heavenly* word settle down. "My place was in Bravoure. Even when I ran, my place…" She had to halt her thoughts and swallow. "My place has always been Bravoure."

Ahna nervously bit her lip and merged with the silence.

"He made the right call," she eventually said. Was this to be her own new mantra? *He made the right call.* Did she believe that? Did she *truly* believe that?

"I'm not so sure about that, Ahna," Jules admitted, him—not so sure. "It's a damned bitch move to make, if you ask me." He looked to the horizon, distant. He had a strange feeling, something he was not used to feeling. Was it...spite? "Leave Bravoure behind like that, to fifty years of misery you can't even call survival."

Jules wanted to ease Ahna's pain, but he could not help but feel this...anger. Still, he wanted to take his dear friend in his arms, to console her, but he was stopped by Luthan's voice from behind them.

"May I sit with her?" Luthan asked politely.

Jules let out a frustrated sigh. When he saw Ahna's accepting nod, he stood to leave his seat to the ljosalfar, lifting his arms in the air as a sign of capitulation. He was annoyed. A protective impulse wanted to shield Ahna from more pain, from more hurt by this excuse of a tall elf. But he would have to bury that impulse, for now.

Luthan came to sit beside his wife. He remained silent for a long while, inhaling and exhaling slowly while she stared in the distance. She did not move. She did not want to turn her face to him. And he had no idea what to say. He just wanted to be close to her, close to the woman he had lost. Close to the woman he had caused so much pain.

"What's his name?" she asked, emerging out of the silence.

Luthan simply smiled, yet he felt so ashamed. Could he even bear to tell her his son's name? The son he had with...another woman. He had left his wife behind and had a new life here, with another woman, and a son. One thing he and Ahna could never have. But he would not let Ahna see his distress, so he gave her an emotionless answer: "Tiberius."

Blank. Ahna's mind was just blank. "He's ljosalfar," she said, as if that mattered right now! "Who is his mother?" she asked the question, but she really could not care right now.

Luthan took a deep breath. He did not want to tell her, but

she was asking, so he had to. "Her name is Ellyra. She was from the School of Elgon." He looked to his feet, down in shame, and let the silence sink in.

Ahna's heart constricted. It was like she wanted to cry but had no tears left to shed. So she returned to her previous catatonic state.

"Do you…love her?" she asked. *Now*, this question mattered to her.

The tall elf simply exhaled. He searched for Ahna's eyes, not ever finding them. She would not look at him, and that was his fault. "I never married her," he answered, then another one of these long silences settled in.

Ahna scoffed—that was no answer. But fine, she would let this one go.

"Fifty years, Luthan," Ahna said with distance laced in her tone. "Why did you not come back?" She took a deep breath and raised her voice. "You had fifty years to come back!" The anger and frustration were rising again.

That, he could react to, just fine. Luthan hushed her with his fierce emerald eyes. "Don't you think I tried, Meriel? If you let me explain, we wouldn't be shouting at each other."

Idiot. "How did you expect me to react?" she challenged, feeling almost insulted. She could almost stab him with her glare.

But the look in her eyes brought Luthan back to a long time ago, when they had just met. Not the right place nor time, but a slight smile drew on his face. He could not stop it. "By Arcanis…" he sighed. "You're as stubborn as when I met you!" He instantly regretted saying that last part.

Luthan's last words, the memory of the first time they met, why was he even bringing that up? It did not fuel the anger that had begun boiling again. It just…confused her. Actually, perhaps fortunately for him, it brought her mind back to this blank state of blankness.

"We've been stuck here," Luthan continued, acting as though

he had not said that last bit. "We've tried everything to get back, but we've been stuck here!" The shreds of his voice dissipated in the absent wind, and Ahna simply remained silent. A sudden realization caught his thoughts. Ahna was here. But it was not her presence that was odd. It was the fact that she had traveled here, through the stars. A journey Luthan had not achieved to take in fifty years. So one pressing question remained to ask: "How did you even get here?"

Finally, something else Ahna could focus on. Something concrete, tangible, something that required logic instead of dealing with emotions. "An augmented rift," she blurted out, practically in one syllable. "With the help of Farooq. And a huge gamble." She chuckled lightly on that last part, because it felt like she was referring to a crazy idea. Well, actually, she was. All of this was crazy. She was on Luna! Anywhere else would have been less crazy than on the moon.

Ahna's laugh made Luthan relax his posture. He finally dared to look at her himself, the woman who had taken his heart a lifetime ago. He examined her. He could see her clearly, past the veil of resentment that shaded her face, in the bright light of Sol. He contemplated how her loose curls caressed her neck. He looked closer to the little bumps on her blue skin that betrayed her distress. At this moment, he wanted nothing more than to hold her. An old, familiar feeling spurred him to. However, before he could act on it, her voice pulled him out of his thoughts.

"So, tell me…" Her tone was lighter. "What have you tried?"

Luthan cleared his throat. He had so much to tell. He did not even know where to start. "That's a long story." That was the best he could muster.

"I have centuries."

He smiled. He recognized that determined look. Oh, how desperately he wanted to hold her. "We've tried augmented rifts, but there are so many of us. There was no way to acquire such power, and with Luna's pull—impossible."

Ahna shook her head. One thing didn't seem to make sense. "There are so many of you. How can an augmented rift *not* work?"

Luthan smiled. The didactic smile of a teacher. "You know how the Arcane Law of Planar Energy Conservation works, right?" Ahna gave him an evident nod. Of course, she knew. It was foolish of him to ask. "For a while, I did try to open a rift, with all I had. Every single day. I exhausted myself trying to get back to—"

He was quickly interrupted by approaching footsteps.

"I forced him to give up!" Iedrias, who had joined them, declared with a serious tone. "Luthan was losing his mind."

The tall elf looked to his feet again. That part of his life here he did not wish to remember. After desperately trying and trying to get back to Terra, to get back to Meriel, for years and years, he had begun to lose himself. Even worse, he had almost wished to take his own life. As such was the reality. He had been to insanity and back. But there was no way he would let Meriel know. That was something his pride could not take. And he was damned well aware of that.

"What about the Planar Mask?" Ahna wondered, unaware of what was going on in Luthan's mind. "The one here, on Luna? Oh wait…" She halted her initial train of thought. "Is the other end destroyed? Is that why you weren't able to use it again?"

Iedrias shook his head. "No, that's not the problem."

Luthan raised his. "The Planar Mask in Antaris is still intact."

Ahna rounded her eyes. Then how had they not been able to get back? She looked to the two archmagi in search of an answer.

Noticing her confusion, Iedrias proceeded to explain. "Well, the Planar Mask on Terra wasn't *exactly* in Antaris," he disclosed. "We kept it miles beneath the earth." Since Ahna still looked perplexed, Iedrias resumed his argumentation. "If Sharr destroyed Antaris, then he buried the tunnels, and he never got to the Planar Mask."

"Plus," Luthan raised. "There's no way a mortal can destroy an Item of Power."

Ahna was still not convinced. She still had not received the answer she had been asking for. "So, what was the problem?" she asked again, her tone growing impatient.

Iedrias's eyes darkened. He had this concerned look, as though something troubled him greatly. "I guess it's something with how Luna moves. When we came here, we were engulfed in darkness. It was…"

"It was horror," Luthan completed his sentence, also with dread in his eyes. "I don't think the Ancients meant it to be this way. We were able to make it to the light, but a few of us were…taken."

Iedrias continued. "Luna's course through the stars has changed in the last centuries. The Planar Mask on this end is… not in a pleasant place."

"Where is it?" Ahna definitely wanted to know more.

"It's on the far side of the moon," Luthan answered, and Iedrias confirmed the statement with an ample nod. "There are creatures there…very dark creatures." The tall elf shuddered at the mention of these…monsters that still seemed to give him nightmares.

Ahna could not be bothered by dark creatures. "Did you attempt to retrieve it?" she inquired. "Did you try to take it back here?"

The two archmagi nodded simultaneously.

"We had dozens of explorers, every day, who strived to get to the Far Side," Iedrias explained with a dark tone. Something else was in his voice, something he desperately tried to mask with a smile. Ahna was not sure what it was, but it resembled grief. "Once you get to the darkness, everything becomes unreal. Nothing makes sense anymore."

This all sounded like thinking of retrieving the Item from the Far Side was a desperate mission. Iedrias and Luthan looked as though they had already given it their everything. They seemed to have lost so much to the idea of ever getting back to Terra that way.

But enough lamentations! Ahna rose to her feet. Her saddened eyes had changed to the determined shade of violet. She spun on her heels and faced the two archmagi as she brought her hands to her hips. She was going to get back to Terra. She did not yet know how, but this was her resolve, and she was determined to get the job done.

"Well, how do we get to the far side of the moon?" she asked.

They both compulsively laughed, as though Ahna had made a joke.

"You want to get the Planar Mask and fight your way through an army of monsters?" Luthan checked, just to make sure he had heard Ahna correctly.

"Just answer the question," she retorted as she shook her head. She had no time for doubt or hesitation.

"You'd first have to get to the *Eidolon Forest*," Iedrias declared before Luthan could retort.

Ahna remembered where she had landed on Luna with Jules and Farooq. The curious flora she had seen. "The forest with the strange purple trees?" she wondered, out loud. As the two nodded together again, she raised another question. "And then what?"

Luthan's eyes met hers. He seemed unwilling to answer, because he knew what it would mean for his wife. She would go there, no matter what he would say. And he might lose her again. Still, he would not show her his anguish. "Then you travel for days until you reach the darkness," he gave her the answer she had asked for.

Iedrias clapped his hands together. It was time to move to another subject. Ahna looked miserable right now, and Jules and Farooq by Skyshrine's entrance looked like they really needed food and sleep. "My friends, dinner is about," he announced. "Let's let this idea slide for a bit, shall we?"

Dinner. Ahna's stomach growled intensively at the mention of the holy word. Fortunately, no one had heard, but it hit her how tired and hungry she was. It was practically the middle of the night for the three Terrans. Jules and Farooq had waited patiently. Or maybe impatiently. They were repeatedly yawning and stretching their arms to kill time. Iedrias motioned for them to join them by the bench.

"You are all welcome in my home," the Taz wizard said with a warm smile. "Just follow me, I'll lead the way." He then turned to Luthan, who looked just as miserable as Ahna. "Will you join us?" he asked, expecting a no.

But the high elf paused for a moment to think, then he stood straight. "I will. But give me an hour."

Surprised, Iedrias still gave him a smile. "Good." He turned to the travelers. "Meriel, you and your friends can take a rest while I prepare something nice!"

Iedrias led them down the staircase while Luthan stayed behind. For a brief minute, Ahna hesitated to look back to the tall elf. Her mind was now more peaceful, less thoughts rushed by, but she still felt like she had a lot to process. Now was not the time, though, she needed food and sleep. Never make a decision on an empty stomach! She wondered for a bit who had told her that. Maybe it had been Iedrias, or someone else from her past. Maybe it had been her mother... Ahna took a peek over her shoulder and observed her husband as he faded away, back into the castle of glass.

8

CASTLE OF GLASS

*L*uthan examined her and observed the movements of her chest as she breathed in and out. Ahna was fast asleep, and she simply looked so beautiful. He sat on a stool in the home of Archmage Dallor, in the guest room assigned to his long-lost wife. Her two other companions rested in the meditation room upstairs, both sprawled out on pillows on the floor. They had missed dinner, too exhausted from their interstellar travel.

The blue elf suddenly turned to her side, her back toward Luthan. He was startled for a second, thinking he had awoken her. But her eyelids remained shut. She seemed deep in a dream. Luthan longed to know what she could possibly be dreaming about. He leaned closer to her, contemplating the dawn blue of her skin lit by the small egg-shaped lantern beside the bed. He wanted to stop himself from staring, but he just could not. She was too beautiful. And she was here. His wife was here.

Luthan thought back to their reunion, to the moment he had first laid eyes on her after half a century. How, for a short moment, he had only been obsessed with the scent of her silver curls. Dokkalfar maybe had the gift of an incredible ear, but ljosalfar were fair competitors when it came to the nose. And after that, blank—Only Ahna's anger remained in his memory. Ahna's pain. How could he face her after what he had done? He could not bring himself to reflect on how the argument had gone. *Poorly*, was the answer. The things he had said…stupid things. *A judgement call.* He had left Ahna behind, to be tortured, to suffer the loss of everything she had held dear. And Luthan, that idiot, could not bring himself to tell her how many years he had spent destroying his very soul to get back to her. Iedrias had come to his rescue, from the deepest pit of despair.

Nowadays, his son, Tiberius, was all that kept him going. And his partner, Ellyra, who had been there for him. She had lost her husband to the fires of war. He and Luthan had grown close. After Luthan's downfall into an abyss of self-blame, she had been there with Iedrias. She should be all there was on his mind. Yet here was Ahna, and here was he, lost in her sight, dimly lit by the magical lantern. The old flame that had remained dormant at the bottom of his heart burned again, brighter than he had ever imagined was possible.

Ahna turned. "Luthan?" she whispered.

Startled by her sudden voice, the high elf jumped to his feet. He looked at Ahna with his mouth slightly open. "I'm sorry," he apologized. He felt awkward, knowing how she might feel realizing Luthan had been in this room all along, watching her sleep. "I didn't mean to intrude. I will leave."

Ahna had to recollect her thoughts for a minute. How long had he been here? She had not heard him at all while she should have. Her growling stomach interrupted her wonder.

"Wait!" she called as he was about to leave. "Did we miss dinner?"

Luthan's lips folded in a dear smile. "We have some leftovers for you travelers." He was about to step out of the room when her voice chanted between his pointy ears.

"Luthan, there's something I need to say." She sat straight, and he turned to her.

She noticed the linen sheet was about to fall off her chest. Her shirt was slightly open. She blushed, pressing the sheet against her chest. With a hesitant look, she searched for his eyes. She needed to say it, to repeat her new mantra again. She wanted to stop being angry, and this was her temporary solution.

"It was the right call to make," she told him. "The magi would have died there." She paused as though to ponder on one last thing to say. "I would have never followed, and you know that."

Luthan's gaze explored her. No, it was not the right call to make. No, he should have never agreed. No, he should have never left her there to fight alone, to be tortured, to lose everything. He should have never left her. His heart beat faster in his chest. The more he looked at her, the more pain he felt. But he would not let her see.

She must have noticed something because she softly bit her lower lip in hesitation to say anything more.

"I will leave you to rest," he said with a careful tone.

He turned around. When he passed the threshold, he cast another glance over his shoulder and closed the door behind him. There were tears in his eyes he could not hold in.

AHNA SLEPT for a long time before waking again. The sun shone still brightly in the sky above them. She heard a few voices coming from outside the guest room, probably from the living room. Iedrias Dallor lived in a modest, windowless house made of white moon rock. It reminded her of the little stone house she had lived in back in the dwelling of Miggdra, which seemed so long ago. The only difference was the complex construction concerning the lighting. Similar to the Taraxacum in the castle of glass, a large egg-lantern connected to the ceiling lit each room.

Iedrias explained they were linked to the castle's power source, the one that drew energy from Sol itself.

Ahna rejoined Jules and Farooq, who sat at the large wooden table in the center of the house. She felt lethargic and still numb, which was a better alternative than angry and spiteful. Her two companions were munching on large loaves of bread served with butter and jam. They had just finished Iedrias's leftover from the dinner yesterday: momrogis! Although, these were slightly different, made of a vegetable discovered on Luna.

"We call it *gombo* ," Iedrias explained. "It's very bitter, and you need to cook it for a very long time if you want to eat it!"

Farooq remained silent and ate all he could. Jules finished his cup of silver-leaf tea. As it turned out, the grey fields were colored by sweet minty grass! Ahna immediately gulped a piece of bread and poured herself some of that tea. She exhaled deeply as a sign of relief.

"It is excellent to meet you all," Iedrias said with a smile. He was happy his guests enjoyed his food so much. "Tell me, Farooq. How long have you been practicing?"

Ahna answered for the young man. "He just found out about his power."

Farooq nodded to confirm. "I have no idea what I'm supposed to do."

He passed a nervous hand in his wavy black hair. Iedrias noticed his discomfort and offered him another cup of tea.

"Archmage Arkamai was the best teacher I knew," he said with a dear smile.

Ahna blushed immediately. She complimented Iedrias for his own skills. At the mention of teachings, Jules raised a hand.

"So, which school are you?" the blond shrike asked Iedrias.

The wizard smiled. "I am a human-elf from Tazman—we are proud mysticists!" As Jules wanted to know more, Iedrias continued. "I understand the mind and the soul. The weather, the trees, the air. I can speak to animals!"

Jules chuckled. "Do they speak back?"

"Sometimes."

They continued their conversation about Mysticism, but Ahna's mind wandered off topic. "How did you build all this?" she interrupted Jules, who was making up small talk one would have with a hedgehog.

Iedrias looked at her. "It was already there. This is one of the cities the Ancients left behind. You know, the one from the texts. Skyshrine, the citadel of glass. We just never knew it would be here, on Luna."

"How did you get everything to work? The lighting, the Taraxacum, the waters, even the protective dome?"

"Everything was already in place when we arrived," Iedrias revealed. "The city is powered by the light of Sol and the annealed moonstones of the castle. The entire system was functioning as it was many centuries ago." The Tazman-elf paused. He frowned for a second in timid curiosity. "Meriel, could you tell me more about the Resistance?" he asked, hesitant.

Ahna replied with a warm smile. She looked at Jules, his grey eyes revealed pride. "The Resistance. An army of righteous souls who gave their everything in the name of freedom, and they won."

Jules nodded in response. Iedrias wished to learn more about the movement that had shaken the false king until death, so Jules began to tell the story of the brave rebels who had fought for fifty years. He told him of the history of the first commander, who had picked up the Royal Claymore. The Uprising, the one that, despite all efforts, had failed. And lastly, the ten-year building of a new army that had fought to the death. Of course, he mentioned Ahna's arrival and how it had affected his own view on magic and the arcane. And even more so, he praised her accomplishments to restore the Magi Academy of Bravoure. During his entire story, Iedrias looked at him with a passionate flame in his eyes. He followed Jules's words of every battle to the syllable. He felt he could have been there. He should have been there.

"So, Iedrias," Jules said, away from the subject. "You must be very old, like Ahna, since you are elven!"

Iedrias laughed, and with his loud and warm voice said, "I have elven blood. My mother's mother was *vidthralfar*, the rest of my family is human."

"I've fought side by side with vidthralfar! They had an entire platoon of rangers, the wood elves of the Antlers."

Iedrias listened attentively to the story of the rebel archers and rangers that had fought the war. He felt a slight ache in his heart, the pain of having missed the fight. He was taken by a sense of regret.

"Iedrias." Ahna caught his distracted attention. "Who is the Dean nowadays?" she asked.

The Taz wizard chuckled. "You're looking right at him!"

Ahna cheered in happy surprise. She congratulated him, and he continued. "After her death, they picked me, their Grandmaster Mysticist!" He then laid his hand on Ahna's. "Meriel, when I found out you were not aware of this, I was utterly furious."

Ahna pulled her hand back. She had figured Iedrias had not been aware of the plan to leave her behind, but that did not make her feel any better. The mention of this whole secret plot of escape brought that retching feeling to her stomach again.

"It was absolute secrecy," Iedrias continued. "No one spoke of it outside the Faculty. We used the memlocks to forget. I resented the Dean for it."

When Jules noticed Ahna's disconcertment, he raised another question, changing the subject. "How many people can live here, actually?"

Iedrias turned his head to him. "Hundreds. Many houses in the village are still empty. We only occupy the ones closest to Skyshrine."

"Do they all have this Tar…axara…cacum thing?" Jules stuttered a question.

Iedrias and Ahna laughed together. "All houses are connected to the *Taraxacum* in the citadel," the Taz wizard replied. He paused for a brief minute before turning his head to Ahna. "How did you know we were on Luna, Archmage Arkamai?"

Ahna exhaled deeply. "It was the only explanation that made sense." She looked to Jules, remembering that it was he who had come up with this whole idea of interstellar travel.

Farooq, who had remained silent through the entire conversation, still lingered in his mind on the many stories of the Resistance. He looked at Jules, who appeared to be just slightly older than him. He wondered how this valorous man had ended up following such a dangerous journey at such a very young age. In that minute, Farooq saw himself as a coward. While he had been living the recluse life of a farmer, Jules had fought the war of the century.

Iedrias rose to his feet. He was meant to give a lesson to young apprentices today, yet he was not sure anymore what to do. He was going to teach younglings the basics of the arcane, but that did not really matter anymore, did it? The arrival of the three Terrans had caused tremors among the inhabitants of Skyshrine, and he needed to tend to what was expected of him. But the strongest tremor was perhaps the one in his own heart. For the first time in decades, he felt something long lost return. The wish to leave this place. Ahna must have noticed, because she looked to him with the purple eyes of someone who can read one's soul.

"I am needed in Skyshrine," Iedrias said, averting her gaze, and he turned to Farooq. "As you can imagine, I have a ton of matters to solve, now that you're here."

He invited Farooq to join him in the citadel of glass, to get a perspective that could potentially change the young man's life. Farooq accepted, and the two headed out into the village.

. . .

HOURS LATER, Ahna still sipped on a cold cup of tea. Her gaze landed on Jules, who appeared to be in a deep trance of racing thoughts.

"Is something on your mind?" she asked him, concerned.

Jules leaned back and dropped his shoulders. He had a frown Ahna had rarely seen. He was unsure what to say, so he said the first thing on his mind. "Speaking of the Resistance like that," he began, expressing himself in such a careful tone. "It makes it sound so glorious."

Ahna hesitated to respond, so she let him talk instead.

"We freed a kingdom, but we lost so much doing so." Jules let his words sink into the silence. "I just can't help wondering what would have happened...had the magi stayed."

Ahna's heart ruptured. She felt his hesitation, the slight resentment that quailed in his heart. She had been angry enough, but Jules's words kindled a fire again.

His eyes turned dark. "I'm not staying here, Ahna," he declared. He was not staying in a place that reeked of cowardice.

"I know," she said as she nodded. Then she began to think. How would they get back to Terra? What would be their next step? Iedrias and Luthan had talked about the Eidolon Forest, and the Planar Mask being on the far side of the moon. But they had tried to retrieve it themselves and had failed. Yet this did not dissuade her. On the contrary, she started thinking about what she could do differently...

"You're making a plan in your head—what is it?" Jules asked the elf not a minute later.

Ahna pursed her lips together before speaking. "I don't know how to get back to Terra," she confessed. "But I am thinking about it!"

Jules leaned back in his chair. "Can't we try the same way we came here?"

The elf shook her head. "No," she sadly replied. "My magic seems to work differently here. The law of conservation of energy..." she took a deep breath to explain. "It depends on several factors, one being the pull of Terra. Something on Luna makes it impossible to open rifts."

"So, we can't get back with a rift," Jules inferred.

Ahna confirmed his statement. She looked at the shrike with sorry eyes. "I'm sorry I brought you here, both of you."

Jules would not take her apology. "Any adventure has its risks!" He smiled to appease her. "So, let's think! What was that talk yesterday of the Planar Mask and the darkness?"

"The other end of the Planar Mask, the only way back, is on the far side of Luna." She made a spooky sound to indicate something mysterious. "They say there are...strange and deadly creatures there."

"Let me guess," the blond shrike began. "You're thinking of going there!"

Ahna looked through the window to the outside. The light of the sun rained on the opalescent pavement. A sight of such beauty... The shimmer of the Dome, the sparkles that lit Skyshrine like a falling star, everything made it a place only dreams could fathom. But this place was haunted. At that moment, Ahna felt the same as Jules. This place reeked. It was too perfect. Too pretty.

"I'm not staying here, no," she distantly murmured.

"Let's find the Planar Mask then," Jules said with a smirk of determination. "How do we get to the far side of Luna?"

Ahna slightly chuckled, but then she seriously began to examine the possibility. "Well, most made it out of there, and they weren't trapped for days, so it shouldn't be that far. It's going to be dangerous."

"My entire life was danger."

"And we have something they didn't have," Ahna added. "We have an Item of Power."

Jules slightly smiled. "The Cursed Bow? I thought you hadn't brought it."

Ahna mirrored his smile. "Looks can be deceiving," she winked.

Jules wanted to say something else, about the time Ahna had retrieved the item from the battlefield of Orgna, but he figured this was not the topic at hand. They stayed silent for another minute while Ahna was concocting a plan.

"If we bring the Planar Mask to Skyshrine," she stated. "We can give people a choice to come back to Terra. Most have built a life here…" Her thoughts went to Luthan, to him, his son, and the new woman in his life. Her tone saddened, and she struggled to speak. "So, I'm not sure any will want to get back."

Jules responded with a comforting gaze. "As you say, we can give them the option."

Ahna rose to her feet. She needed to think this through, but deep down, she had already made her decision. And so had Jules. They were leaving. They were going to try and find the Planar Mask. She had said it herself, the Far Side was not far. There was just this *Eidolon Forest* they had to cross, the one her old friend Iedrias had mentioned.

Ahna needed to know more about this forest. She needed to acquire more information. "I'm going to the citadel," she told Jules. "You can come with me if you'd like."

Jules pursed his lips to fake hesitation, but in reality, he still needed to deal with that dark feeling he still felt, alone. This place did not make him feel easy.

"I'm going back to sleep!" he simply announced.

The elf acknowledged and went to gather her belongings. It was quite warm outside, so she did not need her cloak. She put on her traveler's tunic and tied her hair in the knot she always did. She hesitated for a second to take her bow and dagger. After a short moment of reflection, she seized her satchel and strapped her quiver to her back.

"Always prepared?" Jules teased.

Ahna answered with a smirk. She spun on her heels and headed toward the door. As she passed through the threshold, Jules was clearing the table and was about to isolate himself in the meditation room, where he could work on setting his angry feelings aside.

As she walked through the paved street, Ahna took a few moments to examine the potted flowers that reminded her of the fire lilies on Terra. Except that these ones had red and blue petals and a stem that had the same color as the barkless trees on Luna. A few people ambled the streets of the village, some wore apprentice robes, other more decorated tunics. They cast peculiar glances at her with curious eyes, or perhaps cautious glares. She was one of the few elves here and the only dokkalfar. They avoided her. They circled around her not to come too close. Ahna noticed. She recognized these stares. Those of the fear of her kin. It made her feel uncomfortable and perhaps a little sad. Fifty years ago, the magi had accepted her for who she was. Now, they looked at her like they would look at a total stranger.

Iedrias lived very close to Skyshrine, the citadel of glass. Not a while later, Ahna had already made her way on top of the staircase, and she passed the large open gates. She paused for a moment to contemplate the beautiful structure of light—the Taraxacum, with its many garlands that ended in arcane-lit tips. Each shimmered with a bluish light that imprisoned Ahna's gaze with their elegance.

"Meriel?" a voice brought the elf back to the moment.

Ahna glanced over her shoulder and faced a slim woman.

"You must be Meriel!" the woman said with a joyous tone.

Ahna examined her interlocutor, a tall woman with apparent distant Taz origins and big brown eyes, and a mane with a myriad of coils. She had a light brown skin covered delicately by her silky lilac robe, the one that adepts of Mysticism wore.

"I am Clarice," she introduced herself.

A vision flashed behind Ahna's eyes. *If I ever have a daughter, I will call her Clarice, in the memory of my mother.* Iedrias's words after a glass of goldrain rum on a summer night in Bravoure City, right before everything had...collapsed. The elf recognized his gaze in the eyes of the tall woman.

"You are Iedrias's daughter," Ahna said.

"Yes, my father has told me so much about you. Speaking of the Tazman devil..."

Archmage Dallor walked up to them from the left corridor. He had just finished his lecture, abridged, considering the circumstances. He kissed his daughter on the forehead and greeted Ahna.

"I see you've met Clarice," he said. "She's my favorite apprentice!"

Clarice laughed. "I am more than an apprentice by now."

There was a slight mystery in the air. Iedrias had welcomed the three travelers into his home, where he lived *alone*. What about Clarice's mother? Ahna wanted to ask, but she was interrupted by Farooq, who appeared from the same corridor. He came to her with a smile until his ears.

"Ahna, this place is amazing! I've learned so much, and met so many people, people like me." He was so joyous.

Iedrias laughed with his daughter. "Clarice, please show Farooq around the citadel. I need to show Meriel something."

The young sorceress acknowledged and led Farooq to the furthest set of stairs, the one that stretched and slithered to the back of Skyshrine. Iedrias turned to Ahna. His eyes had darkened, and he seemed to distance himself.

"I know you plan on finding the Planar Mask," he declared. "And I know I won't be able to dissuade you."

He motioned with a swift flick of his wrist for Ahna to follow him up the coiled staircase to their left. They reached a small, circular platform above them, that was built against the tall bookshelf wall of the main hall. The platform was enclosed by a wooden railing and leaned over the rest of the grand room. There was a desk with parchments and books that lay piled. By the fence, there was a lectern with an open tome, as though someone could read out words for a gathering in the main hall. This was the Dean's office.

"This is where I spend my days," Iedrias said.

"It's a very nice office," Ahna complimented.

"You will be going to the Eidolon Forest, and there is someone who wishes to come with you," the Taz wizard declared.

Ahna rounded her eyes, so Iedrias continued. "Clarice has the heart of her mother. Skyshrine is too small for her adventurous soul. She wants to discover the world, but Luna is no place like… like home."

Home. He had said this with deep regret in his voice, leaving no room for doubt that he dearly missed it.

"Are there more who wish to get back?" the elf asked.

Iedrias's eyes shone with a candid light. "Some. Some like me who want to go home," he admitted his truth, the truth that he wanted nothing more than to return to Terra. "However, it's a hopeless mission no one has dared to try in years."

Ahna cleared her throat. "We are willing to give it a try," she declared with resolve.

"I know, and so is Clarice." Iedrias went to his desk to fetch a book, a black leather journal with many doodles and scribbles. "This was my wife's. She took many magi to venture into the Eidolon. One day, she did not make it back." He swallowed, perhaps to the hide tears that had climbed to his eyes. "You can take it for your quest."

Ahna felt sorrow delve into her heart. Iedrias's grief for having lost his wife to the idea of getting home. He handed Ahna the book with a sad look in his eyes. The elf quickly scrolled through it. She handled it with the utmost respect.

"What is the Eidolon, exactly?" she asked.

The Taz wizard inhaled deeply. "It draws a ring around Luna, one that borders the far side of the moon. It lies in the penumbra of Sol. You will have to traverse it to get to the darkness."

Ahna noticed a drawing of a map Iedrias's wife had made as accurate as she could. It started at the edge closest to the city, possibly the one Ahna and the two travelers had come from. Behind this page, there were a multitude of sketches of the different creatures of the Eidolon. Some small, some terrifying. There were botanical illustrations of plants, with their properties listed. Many were edible, and some even mentioned as tasty— that was very important!

"The bow that you carry," Iedrias began out of the silence, looking at Ahna's bow hooked on her quiver. "You can hide it from most, but not from a mysticist like me!"

Ahna reached for her crude bow and held it flat in front of her.

She closed her eyes and exhaled deeply. "*Siina...*" she murmured. Cracks of light engulfed the wood, which morphed into familiar adornments. Ornaments of an Item of Power, the Cursed Bow the elf had kept safe, close to her, all this time. "I'm no illusionist—this was no elaborate disguise."

"How did this Item of legends come into your possession, Archmage Arkamai?" Iedrias asked.

Ahna smiled wistfully. "The Resistance had it, but I, myself, am still not sure how."

Iedrias examined the bow. "Perhaps you have a chance, now, a chance to do better than us," he distantly said. "You have an Item of Power, after all. You do know it's not its true form, right?"

"What?" Ahna gasped. She was genuinely surprised. And no, she certainly did not know.

"Let me show you!" Iedrias enthusiastically exclaimed, heading to the closest bookshelf.

Among the many tomes they had brought with them from the Antaris Faculty was one thin, peculiar brownish volume Iedrias pulled in his hands. He read the title out loud: *On the Schillers of the Arc.*

"This is very old," Iedrias said. "The monks who studied the Items of Power wrote it."

"I have never seen this book," Ahna confessed.

"It's not surprising," Iedrias commented. "Most believed the Arc of Light to be lost. The appellation of *Cursed Bow* only appeared after the monks concealed the Arc into a...bow."

Ahna slid Iedrias's wife journal into her satchel, and she began to read the new book the Taz wizard handed her. It described the powers of the Arc of Light. There was no mention of the immense pain one felt when wielding the Cursed Bow, the pain that had given it its name. The book spoke of a way to restore this Item of Power to its pure form. Little by little, Ahna understood the powers of the bow and why it reacted with such... ancient energy when she held it.

"*Where there is darkness, only light can vanquish.* Do you remember these words?" Iedrias asked Ahna with a melancholic smile, remembering the words of prophecy distant in his memory.

Ahna gave him a nod and a smile. "The prophecy... The one that doomed my brother to die."

"Perhaps it had a different meaning, for us here, castaway." Because Ahna did not respond, Iedrias straightened his posture. "I need to solve another matter," he declared. "Take this book too, and see what you can do with it. You're an archmage, it will be child's play."

He was about to head back to the coiled stairs when he turned to Ahna. His eyes expressed more devotion and determination than ever before. There were almost tears hiding behind the moss of his irises. Ahna distinguished the glimpse of grief again.

"Meriel, my wife's greatest wish was to find her way home," he said. "Please make her wish come true."

9

THE ARC OF LIGHT

*I*t should have been night by now, though the sun still shone brightly. Farooq had learned that days here were at least twenty-five times longer than on Terra. The Dome is what kept the inhabitant sheltered and protected from too much sunlight. After his short time exploring the Skyshrine citadel, Farooq went back to Archmage Dallor's house and found a passed-out Jules on the sofa. The blond shrike awoke a few moments later.

When Ahna rejoined the two travelers, she showed them the journal about the Eidolon Forest. She had all information she needed to know precisely where they would start and in which direction they would then go. She handed the journal to Farooq, who began to scroll through it with light eyes. Jules had already readied his scabbard.

"Hang on, shrike," Ahna said with a chuckle, amused by Jules's eagerness to leave. "We should get some more rest."

Jules sighed and returned to the sofa. More rest it was! Farooq, who was less excited to leave, felt the grip of fear around his throat. He had already gone farther than at any place in his life. Should the young man go even further? However, Jules's determination sparked the light of courage in his heart. He would not let his fears dissuade him. Farooq was convinced this had been his true calling all along. He needed to discover himself and who he truly was, and this adventure had all the chances to lead him to answers.

Clarice joined the band of three with her father, and they all sat for dinner. She revealed her determination to join them on this mission, the quest to find the Planar Mask. There was no way she would let her father restrain her. Farooq recognized Clarice's resolve. He would not have allowed his grandfather to tell him what to do.

For a short while, he contemplated the beautiful young woman who spoke at the table. Her features showed a long and distant elven origin, especially her high cheekbones. She waved her lively arms in the air as she told stories of her mother and tales of Skyshrine.

"You travelers came from the south," she began. "Mother always went east, back to where the magi had first come from. We're at the edge of Eidolon, so it will not be a long walk before we reach the forest."

The young sorceress explained all the efforts her father made to keep the magi always hungry for more knowledge. Iedrias came with stories of their study of Luna herself. He went to fetch a few cups to offer his guests, then went to sit next to his daughter.

"The moon changes with time," he explained as he poured a blue liquid in each glass. "And as the Far Side moves, so does the Eidolon Forest. We suspect that Skyshrine was at the center of the light when the Ancients still lived. And we also know that, in a few thousand years from now, Skyshrine will also disappear into the dark."

So, this entire place ran on a ticking countdown, but a few thousand years were like eternity for mortals, even for elves.

Farooq and Jules inspected their glass with curious eyes, taking in the information but not processing it.

Clarice laughed at the two travelers' wonder. "This is moonberry juice. Moonberries are blue—we will see them in Eidolon!"

Farooq still held the journal in his hand. He turned to a page that made him snap his eyes wide open. He showed the others.

"What is this?" he asked with slight fear in his voice.

It was the drawing of some kind of beast that had caught his nervous attention. It looked like a dog—no, a wolf, but it had eight eyes and claws the size of its maw. It had horns. Were they horns? They looked more like two pairs of extra limbs that surged from its head.

"Your mother could most certainly draw, Clarice," Jules observed.

"Drawing is a magi thing," the young sorceress retorted with pride. "Mother called it a *lycaonite*."

"I hope we don't meet one of these," Farooq said.

Clarice's eyes rested on Jules and Farooq, and her gaze lingered there for a minute. She still had many questions about where they had come from, and she hesitated on how to formulate them.

"So, what are mountains like on Terra?" The question finally escaped her lips. She continued, as the two looked at her with uncertain expressions. "Father always spoke of the mountains. What are they like? What are forests like?"

Jules cleared his throat slightly. "He must have meant Gurdal, and the forests that surround it. Gurdal is...simply majestic."

"Is that a mountain?" she asked, innocently.

"No!" Jules chuckled. "It's a chain of mountains. Mountains surrounded by forests of everlasting green. The highest peaks even touch the sky."

Clarice's eyes were simply sparkling in wonder. Jules found it awkward but endearing. Her gaze lingered on the blond shrike. He blushed as she still would not look away.

Ahna had grown more and more distant from the conversation. She looked to her satchel and caught a glimpse of the small brown book Iedrias had given her. Something she could focus on instead of everything else. All that had been in her mind so far: how to activate the Cursed Bow, to recover its true form. She grabbed the brown book and searched through it.

"What is this one?" Farooq asked Ahna when he saw the book in turn.

Iedrias smiled as he spotted a familiar look in Ahna's eyes. The look of yearning for the unknown, the appetite for riddles and mysteries.

Ahna rose to her feet. "It's something I need to do." She went for her bow by the entrance and stopped at the threshold to turn to Iedrias. "Is there a quiet place around here?" she asked.

"There's a lake down the road," the Taz wizard answered. "Some people like to go for walks there, but you'll remain undisturbed for sure."

Ahna nodded and indicated she was to return soon, before stepping into the streets of the village. Further away from the citadel, there was a path leading to a large pond she had not yet seen. The small lake was almost at the edge of the Dome. There was a trail slithering by the pond. There were even Terra trees that perhaps the Ancients themselves had scattered around the water, some oaks, mostly. The silver grass grew wild in this modest shimmering park.

Ahna reached the path and strolled around for a few moments. She contemplated the pond, the clear water that sparkled in the sun. She even thought she saw some kind of fish swirling around. She heard the distant buzz of bees, *moon-bees*. Well, it sounded like bees. The elf breathed in deeply, to dive in the scent of the lily-like flowers that populated the park.

As she made her way up a small hill, the shadow of a little boy caught her attention. He was chasing some kind of butterfly-like insect, but it was no butterfly, it only had two bright yellow wings. She noticed the boy's mother, a ljosalfar woman, much taller than Ahna, with long and wavy copper hair. The woman wore an emerald gown that touched the ground. She radiated with a particular light of kindness that could almost have brought warmth to Ahna's heart. However, as much as she wanted to study this innocent moment of a boy chasing a butterfly, Ahna knew very well who this woman was. Because behind them, the boy's father sauntered toward his son. The tall elf with his long hair, almost white, that flowed behind his steps.

Ahna instantly avoided their path. She wished to remain unseen. She had no time for this, no. The lethargy had quickly turned to angst. She continued her march in the opposite direction, but the chill down her spine manifested itself. The tall elf had his gaze on her, she knew that for sure.

He simply called her name. "Meriel."

She froze, and Luthan ambled toward her.

"I don't want to come in the way of your evening stroll," Ahna excused herself. She really had no time for this. She was about to walk away, but he caught her arm.

"I don't want us to be like this," he said.

Ahna raised her eyebrows in consternation. How would he expect them to be? She wanted to pull her arm away, but his grip intensified. Ellyra and the boy had almost reached them.

"Please let me go," Ahna implored.

And so, Luthan heeded her order. Ahna met Ellyra's eyes, and the graceful ljosalfar simply greeted her with a peaceful, tolerant smile. Ahna had never met Ellyra in her time at the Academy nor in the Faculty of Antaris, so she assumed the ljosalfar had never left the School of Elgon, close to the border with Fallvale, the land of the elves. Ahna had expected to feel pain or jealousy when she looked upon Ellyra, but, surprisingly, it was none of the sort. It was something like...gratitude? Ahna did not understand why she felt that way. Thankful. Thankful that Ellyra had given her husband something Ahna never could have. The boy, Tiberius, remained silent, examining Ahna's blue skin. His pointy ears flickered when she looked at him. He obviously had never seen a dark elf before.

"Why are you blue?" the boy asked.

Ahna raised a brow, not knowing how to react. Her purple eyes sparkled but revealed no emotion at the same time. She leaned over to come to his size. "It's because we get no Sol in the Dwellunder," she answered.

The boy gasped. He had never heard of the Dwellunder, but he was too caught in the twinkles of Ahna's eyes.

"Why are your eyes so pretty?" the boy asked again.

Ahna let out an awkward chuckle. She definitely had no time for this. She looked at Luthan in search of something to say, something that would not make the situation any worse than it was. The tall elf simply observed her short interaction with his son. She pursed her lips and quickly waved goodbye, dashing away, never answering the boy's question.

AHNA HEADED toward the pond and came to sit on the bench right by the water. She crossed her legs, balancing the Cursed Bow on her knees, with the old book opened at her side. She turned each page, scanning for some clue on how to *activate* it. The language was practically ancient. Old Tongue, the language of the monks from centuries ago. She could piece the words together, though it took her a very long time. *Something about Photomancy*... The more she read, the more she understood. She seized the book between her hands and scried further. *So, I need to hold it like this.* She gripped the riser, carefully, with her left hand. As long as she did not use it with the will to kill, she would not feel any pain. Because that was why the Cursed Bow had earned this name. The pain, the torment the wielder needed to master. Ahna only knew of one person before her who had tamed this Item.

After the Rebellion, many soldiers had returned to the valley where the Battle of Orgna had taken place, in search of survivors, or to wander the ruins of the mines that had sheltered them. Some had been on a solemn mission to retrieve the lost Royal Claymore but faced the poignant realization that the symbolic weapon would be lost forever. To this day, it was never found. Ahna had followed them, in search of something she had also lost. She had found it close to where she had faced Xandor for the last time, buried beneath rocks, still intact. Still radiating Power. The power she felt now.

Oh, I need to aim it at—no, this can't be right. She squinted to focus. *At myself?* She attempted to grasp more words. *And I need to cast something...*

Ahna seized the riser in her left hand again. She shifted the bow to lay on the opposite side, to aim at herself.

"I think I know what to do," she said out loud.

She then focused all her energy to the bow. She felt the arcane flow move through her veins to her fingertips. Her eyes lit with a white glow, and the bow began to shine. The encrusted writings shimmered, almost too brightly. Ahna exhaled deeply, concentrating on the light with all she had. The engravings on the bow began to detach themselves from the wood. They followed its limbs in the direction of Ahna's clasped hand. Once they reached it, they climbed on her fingers and crawled all the way to her shoulder, lodging themselves on her skin.

It did not hurt. She sensed that it never would. How, she did not know, she just felt it.

The markings appeared on the entire length of the elf's arm, adorning her blue skin with lighter glyphs of powerful magic. They came to place themselves in coiling patterns from her wrist to her shoulder. The rest of the bow disappeared into thin air. She took a moment to contemplate the beauty of the paintings on her skin. It looked like her arm had become the Cursed Bow itself.

Ahna rose to her feet. She still examined the glyphs for a few minutes, whirling her hand repeatedly before her, then she focused her magic again. The markings lit as she extended her arm in front of her. A blinding beam suddenly burst from her hand to the sky and floor in an arc of light. A curved ray that radiated in the shape of a bow. This sight emitted the distorted sound of a thousand tiny lightning strikes. Ahna turned to the pond and brought her right hand to the flashing light. She seemingly pulled on an invisible bowstring. From her fingertips to the light stretched another bright beam, like a missile arrow that she could shoot at will. The elf simply laughed with amazement. She felt her power increase the longer she held the arc this way, it almost got to her head. She had to let her focus go. The light dimmed, and the glyphs on her skin returned to faint white paintings that spiraled around her arm.

The elf still smiled from the awe she felt, and especially from the surge of power that flooded her veins. This power enraptured her, almost like a divine fervor.

Ahna was too immersed in this moment to hear Luthan's steps behind her.

"I will be going with you," he firmly declared, as though he left her no choice. He had not noticed Ahna's gleaming demeanor.

His voice startled her, but not as much as it would have under other circumstances. She turned to him. Her purple eyes sparkled like new-formed gems. Luthan stood there, behind her, so close she could hear his shallow breath.

Luthan was instantly reminded how beautiful she was, there in the shimmer of the sunlight over the pond. It took him by surprise. An instinct inside him awoke. He wanted to hold her, to take her in the comfort of his arms. He wished to come closer, but everything else ordered him not to give in to his weakness.

He had made a choice tonight, one that not even Ellyra could contest. The decision to go with Ahna and her friends and find the Planar Mask. He was resolute, determined to help them find their way back. Determined to find his way back, Iedrias had come to him with the blue elf's plan to venture through the Eidolon Forest, despite all warnings. There and then, Luthan had decided to join her on her perilous quest.

"I spent decades trying to get back," he explained. "I almost went insane."

Ahna had heard this before. She would have shut him up, but right now, the euphoric energy flowing inside brought peace to her mind. "Why would you start again now?" she asked.

"Because you'll need help."

"I have Jules and Farooq, and Clarice," Ahna calmly retorted. "You have a son."

Luthan's shoulders dropped. "I have a son who deserves more than a dome for the rest of his life." He exhaled deeply, his eyes had turned to a pale green, almost as though he was begging Ahna to let him join this mission.

Ahna shook her head. She was not dismissing him, she was just surprised he had not noticed everything that was happening in her mind at this moment. All this stupor and splendor rushing through her veins. She turned around to rest her eyes over the pond and smiled distantly, absorbing the landscape's beauty. The uncaught silver curls along her neck moved to her rhythm.

Luthan took a step closer to her. He could no longer control himself. Her smile, the smile he had not seen in decades, it was simple yet so beautiful. He lost himself in her vision.

Ahna turned to him. Her smile faded slowly and left room for another kind of expression. She came closer to him. She searched his eyes, his beautiful emerald eyes. She saw his pupils dilate as her tempting gaze delved in his. The euphoria took over, and she did not think anymore.

His curious hands slid into the curve of her back, and he pulled her in, towering above her. Her face came close to his chest, too close. He caught her scent and pressed her closer to him. She let out a small squeal from his embrace. The little sound pulled Luthan back to reality. What was he thinking? He could not do this, not with Ellyra and Tiberius still in the area. With the utmost regret, he abruptly let her go.

Ahna took a step back and recollected her thoughts and belongings. She blushed and pressed her lips together. That euphoria she had felt—inexplicable. Caught in this moment with her long lost husband, she had just wished for him to take her lips. She had ached for it. What had she been thinking? She went for *On the Schillers of the Arc*, which she clumsily waved around then clenched against her flank. She left without saying a thing.

Luthan remained here, silent, watching the woman he had once called his wife stroll away, away from him and out of his reach.

AHNA HASTENED BACK to Iedrias's house. Her heart pounded in her chest. Luthan's burning touch lingered on her skin, and his enamored eyes still rested on her. She had to dismiss thoughts that began to grip her mind, lustful thoughts of his lips on hers. Memories of his fingers interlocked with hers as he—*no!* Gods, no. She had to roar the fantasies away. This anger, numbness, resentment...joy? Since when could all these emotions collide into such a burst of intense lust?

When she made it back to the moonrock house, Jules and Farooq had already gone to sleep. Iedrias sat beside his daughter on the red sofa. He seemed very concerned, and Clarice consoled him.

"If this is our chance to get back, I am willing to take it," his daughter declared, resolute.

She kissed her father goodbye and headed toward the entrance. She waved at Ahna and disappeared into the village. Iedrias let out a long, grieving sigh after she was gone.

"My wife died there," Iedrias conceded gravely. His voice seemed to implore rather than explain. Implore Ahna to succeed.

"The deeper in the forest you go, the darker it gets, and the darker it gets, the more…strange things start happening."

Ahna came to sit beside him. "How strange?" she wondered.

Iedrias inhaled deeply. "*Reality folds on itself*, that's what my wife used to say." He cast a warning glare at Ahna. "Don't let the Far Side fool you, Archmage Arkamai."

The elf gave him a firm nod of acknowledgement. "Clarice is a mysticist," he informed. "She can keep your mind in check."

"I will do everything to keep her safe," Ahna promised her old friend.

"Keep yourselves safe too."

Iedrias stood. He went to his kitchenette and poured Ahna a cup of moonberry juice. She thanked him and took a careful sip, and winced instantly.

"This is very sweet," she noted.

"I thought dokkalfar had a sweet tooth!" Iedrias laughed, and so did Ahna.

After a minute of tender silence, he stood and looked to the elf.

"I can't wait to see what you've done with the Academy," he said, hesitant, then his voice took a darker tone. "I am so deeply sorry you had to do this alone." He almost had tears of regret in his eyes. "I am so deeply sorry…we left you."

Ahna had not been angry at Iedrias. Ahna actually did not have any energy left to be angry. She dismissed him, shaking her head slowly. "The Phoenixes stand again," she said, taking the opportunity to change the subject. "I can't wait for you to see them."

Iedrias wistfully smiled. He sat still for a minute, then bid Ahna goodnight.

She gazed dearly upon him, hoping his sleep would not be too troubled by his worry for his daughter. She remained here for a moment, sipping on her cup of juice, enjoying the still of the night. Well, Sol shone high in the lunar sky, it would take a few days at least before the real night would return. But the window-less moonrock house was in the darkness, at least.

The sudden vision of Luthan rushed behind her eyes. His son, Tiberius, full of life, who looked just like his father. In this moment alone, the ache had returned to Ahna's heart. *They left me behind.* Words raced through her mind. Mohindra's voice, *You were Sharr.* Luthan's voice, *The Council lied to me. She lied. They all lied.* Her own, *I would have never followed. The magi were cowards.* She hated it. Jules hated it too, as much as he tried to hide it or cope with it. But the magi had indeed saved themselves. They had saved themselves from the horror that her twisted brother was. And they had left her behind because of who she was. The guilt of her past pierced through her like a holy sword of retribution, but it was quickly replaced by raw anger. Though that anger would never lash out. Those who had made that decision, the Council of Magi that preached balance and tolerance and all that nonsense, they were all dead anyway. Ahna could not scream or shout at them, or blast them out of existence like that darkness inside her wished for. She was decades too late for that.

Ahna closed her eyes to repress tears. All these clashing emotions—she could not bring herself to cry now. She had cried enough. The magi still lived. Her husband still lived. He was there, just in reach, and they had almost shared a kiss. Oh, how she ached for him right now. She needed his embrace, the security of his arms, the way he had always made her feel safe.

By her side, the Eidolon Forest journal rested on a small stone table. Ahna observed it expectantly. The apprehension of what tomorrow would bring was all she felt in her heart as she gazed upon the leather booklet. What creatures would they encounter? What did Iedrias exactly mean with his stern warning of the Far Side?

Ahna looked to the faint glyphs on her left arm. The newly acquired power she felt, though did not quite understand. *On the Schillers of the Arc* spoke of an additional state of the Item of

Power, something only the strongest of magi could unleash. The elf had not quite understood the words. She needed to do more research. She opened the book again, the one she still held in her hand. Some words confused her, words that translated as *ascension* or *chimaera*. Out of context, these two words made little to no sense at all.

Moreover, there was the mention of the arc's...*soul conduit*, or at least she thought the word meant soul—something about the coalescence of the soul. Something that reminded her of the naming of a Dragonborn, which she had done *twice* in her life. The one ritual where the divine *soulling* of a dragon-god merges with the soul of the *chosen one*. Her thoughts raced to her brother, Thamias, the golden dragon who was still healing from the wounds of war and wounds from days unforgotten in the Dwellunder. She missed him. She missed him so dearly. This hole in her heart gave way to someone else's image. The second Dragonborn. Cedric Rover...the fallen hero. Fallen to a fate, a curse, something she could not explain. Yet another thing she blamed herself for. The memory of his face was so clear, she could almost touch him. She wanted to. But that feeling, that longing for him, she had to wipe it off her mind. She had to bury it, because it only brought her sorrow, and she was already feeling so helpless.

Ahna clenched a fist and focused this new energy she felt. If she had to be honest with herself, this power both intrigued and scared her. Now that she knew how to activate it, she had the ability to return it to its hidden state. Ahna closed her eyes and let the ethereal glyphs swirl along her arm again. They gathered in the palm of her hand and spread out to form the shape of an adorned bow.

10

JOURNEY

*A*hna readied her satchel that contained a brown book and enough stuffed bread to last for a couple of days. She strapped her quiver to her torso and hooked her bow. She attached her dagger's scabbard to her right boot and dived into her white linen shirt. To top it all, she put on a black tunic that matched her breeches. It was cut at her shoulders and in an oval cleavage, though a little too tight around her chest. This tunic was from Clarice's mother. The young sorceress had tailored it slightly to fit Ahna's figure. Her mother had worn it for her travels to the Eidolon Forest, mostly to protect her body from thorns or dangerous vines. The reinforced leather would serve as better protection than simple clothing.

Ahna examined the blue skin of her arm for a minute, the spots where the arcane glyphs had shimmered just the night prior, from her wrist to her shoulder, then she let the sleeve of her linens swallow her arm.

"It suits you!" Clarice exclaimed when she noticed Ahna step outside the house. "You can leave your cloaks here, it's too hot on Luna."

She waited for the elf with the rest in the street, and they were ready to leave. Jules had already strapped his shortsword to his back, and he still wore the black leathers of the shrikes. Farooq used one of Iedrias's brown vests, and Clarice had her favorite lilac sorceress robe. The long tunic almost looked like a ceremonial gown. It reached her knees and touched her beige leather boots. She firmly held a quarterstaff made of the barkless tree wood in one of her hands. It glowed with a silver hue and ended in a claw enveloping an annealed moonstone. In the other, she carried her mother's journal. Iedrias stood by her side.

"Take these loaves in your satchels," the Taz wizard said as he handed the band more rolls of bread. "And before I forget"—he walked to Ahna—"take this."

Iedrias handed the elf a small rhodium ring. When she touched it, she felt the vibrations of its magic. She immediately recognized it.

"A vox-ring," Ahna observed.

She looked to Clarice and noticed the same ring around her finger.

Iedrias handed one to Farooq. "Use it to communicate, in case you lose each other," he instructed. As the young man looked to him with rounded eyes, Iedrias proceeded to explain. "You activate it at will, then you speak to it in thoughts. The rest will hear your words in their minds."

"It will only work within a certain radius," Ahna warned. "So let's not stray too far away from each other."

Iedrias showed his own ring. "I will have one for as long as you're in range. Then it's all up to you."

Ahna's gaze ventured around. Her three traveling companions looked expectantly at her, as though she had to make the call for the band of four to leave. Or better said: the group of five. Luthan appeared from further down the street. He marched with the notorious garments of magi warriors, a blue robe hardened by a thin sheet of steel. This one drooped from his shoulders to his knees and was open by his breeches, past the thick leather belt equipped with a satchel that girded his waist. This allowed him to move freely and quickly, with the dexterity of a fighter. He had not worn this steel blue suit since the war, since his joining of the Guild of Battlemagi. In his right hand, he carried a quarterstaff similar to Clarice's, but his was adorned with red veins and finished in a dark prismatic diamond. His eyes were grey and did not shimmer. Ahna recognized that look of concern on Luthan's face. Something was not right with him, but he did his best to hide it. Was it because of Ellyra? Had she been against him leaving to find the Planar Mask? Ahna really had no idea, but her husband definitely looked troubled. He joined the group, and Iedrias handed him a ring in turn.

"The air is thin outside the Dome," Iedrias informed them. "Once you're in the forest, it will be easier to breathe."

Luthan slipped his finger through the vox-ring and immediately experimented with it. He clenched a fist and closed his eyes. *"One, two, three..."*

Ahna, Farooq, and Clarice heard the echoes of the high elf's voice in their mind. They nodded to indicate the ring worked just fine.

"Why don't I get one?" Jules asked with a small pout.

Ahna chuckled. "It only works if you're a mage."

Jules expressed his disappointment with a humorous sigh, then he turned around and waited for Ahna to make a move. She spun on her heels and headed down the path out of the Dome of Skyshrine.

THE BAND of five were set on the path to leave the Dome and headed east toward the Eidolon Forest. They march together, Luthan and Clarice leading, Farooq in the middle, and Jules and Ahna at the tail. They followed an ancient road traced in the silver grass fields that stretched all the way to the eastern edge of the forest. Ahna was deep in thoughts when Jules's whispers brought her back to reality.

"I see you've switched your crude bow for the Cursed one," he noted. He had probably noticed much earlier.

Ahna gave him a single nod. "I concealed it for safekeeping. Now, I might need to use it…"

"Let's hope it doesn't get to that!" Jules said with a cautious smile and a hand shaking his hair. He looked to the front, to Luthan who walked ahead. "Have you spoken to him since…your last encounter?" the blond shrike asked in a whisper, pointing at the tall elf with his chin.

Ahna sighed. "Not really, no."

"He hasn't said a word to me at all," Jules said and paused to think for a moment. He did not want to pry, but his curiosity took over. "How long were you married before…?"

"Over fifteen Sols," the elf said with no emotions.

Jules gasped in surprise. "That's a long time!"

"Not really. Time, for elves, is different. And so is love."

Jules grew more curious. "How so?" he asked.

"When you love someone, they don't just become part of you. They become you, and you become them." Her words were intriguing, but her voice was as solid as ice. Ahna had built a wall and was hiding behind it, and Jules had definitely noticed. But he also had noticed the way she looked at Luthan, the shimmer in her eyes as he walked in front of them.

An elf's life, for most humans, may have seemed like an eternity. When one lived for more lifetimes than a hand could count, emotions, the motions of the heart, took on a whole different meaning. For ljosalfar, emotions were the fires one must keep under control. Anger must be kept at bay. Joy must remain still. And love was a contract for life, a partnership to face the world together. For dokkalfar, emotions were weapons. Dark elves worshipped the flames of love, pleasure, and passion. Men and women consumed their emotions, regardless of sex or gender.

Life was to be lived to the fullest of their beating hearts. Vidthral-far, on the other hand, praised the balance of their two counterparts.

But for Ahna and Luthan, this story had been very different. The dokkalfar apprentice at the time had let her heart be swayed in different ways than the usual inferno. Her emotions had not raged with the dramatic fury dark elves favored. They had rather smoldered with the embers of an eternal, soothing flame. Luthan had brought only peace to her tumultuous heart. He had brought her the security she had desperately needed. He had taken away her fears, her anger, the trauma of her past in the Dwellunder. He had kept her safe. Luthan, on the other hand, had been the ljos-alfar pariah who had fallen hard for the bane of his kin. And had been cast out of Fallvale for it. But Luthan had never cared. Banned or not, Ahna had been everything he had wanted to live for.

"How do you feel now about all this?" Jules asked suddenly.

Ahna shrugged Jules's question away. Luthan's fire vanished from her mind, and she had other things to think about. Tangible things.

The band slithered down the path, between the silver hills, until, in the distance, they could see the purplish shadow of odd-looking trees. It was about time. An intense feeling of vertigo from the light too bright had already begun to take Ahna over. She had to do her best to keep on walking straight. She squinted so as little light from the sun as possible could reach her eyes. Once the band stepped between the trees, relief instantly flooded Ahna's lungs.

"I'm dokkalfar," she said as she winced. She pointed at the sun. "This is no Sol for me."

The elf pulled her canteen out of her satchel and took a large sip of water. The others mimicked her movements when they realized that they too were immensely thirsty. After this short break, Clarice used her vox-ring to make contact with her father, to tell him they had reached the Eidolon Forest. Iedrias was still in range.

Farooq and Jules were already on the path among the barkless trees. Ahna took another sip of water before following them. There were drops of sweat swirling down her neck. She immediately wiped them off and adjusted her silver knot as she walked. Clarice came to stroll beside her, she was holding her mother's journal.

"If we follow this path," she began. "We'll reach a waterfall. According to my mother, there is a collection of ponds if we keep moving east, like hot springs..."

Jules immediately turned on his heels when he heard the mention of hot springs. "Yes!" he exclaimed with his fists against his chest and a big smile.

Ahna suddenly heard a far screech, the echo of the same animalistic roar they had heard upon their arrival on Luna.

"Did you hear that?" she asked, cautious.

But Clarice and the others shook their heads. Luthan paused for a few seconds. He gazed deep into the woods that darkened by the distance. He seemed to scan the horizon for something that could answer Ahna's question.

"Do you see anything, Luthan?" Ahna asked.

His lips curved down, and he shrugged. "We'd need a wood elf to see through these trees," he mumbled.

Clarice raised an innocent hand. "I'm part vidthralfar," she exclaimed with enthusiasm, but the tall elf did not respond.

The band of five continued on the path. It was a trail made of stones that had aged over the last centuries. Clarice had mentioned this path to have been laid by the Ancients themselves, from Skyshrine to a distant vault. Since their arrival on Luna, the magi had dug new meanders and trails all across the forest during their countless explorations of the Eidolon's wonders.

Ahna began noticing the diverse flora scattered all around

them. The barkless trees and their opalescent leaves were one thing. However, she spotted strange flowers with petals that looked like oscillating tentacles. The most striking thing was that these yellow petals seemed to freeze in her direction as soon as she looked at them. They also glowed a soft golden light, the kind of light Ahna would see in the sunset above the city of Bravoure. When she veered her gaze away, she thought she saw the petals move freely in the corner of her eye. She looked again. The flowers were petrified. She swore it felt like her gaze somehow captured these strange plants just by landing on them.

Ahna was so caught by the flowers that she had not seen how the forest had begun to evolve. The barkless trees grew taller, more robust, like a purplish version of Bravoure's oaks. The leaves that looked like they were made of ice extended as spear-heads into the air. Some, too heavy for the branch, seemed to sink down and point to the ground. One was just in Ahna's reach. She brought a finger to it, gently touching its surface. To her honest surprise, the leaf was soft as a sheet of paper, though it looked solid as glass.

Farooq and Jules were in complete amazement for something else. They both stood by the foot of one of the taller trees. There, in the crook of its roots, lay a giant, white mushroom cap of a convex shape, the size of Jules's foot. The stalk was thick and of the same color as the roots around it. What had immediately caught their attention was the following: Jules tapped the cap once, and it lit up!

"Look at this, Ahnny!" He tapped the cap again, it lit up even brighter. "What do you think will happen if I tap it again?"

"Do it," Farooq pushed with a curious smile.

Jules tapped it again. The cap seemed to let out a long sigh. They even heard a faint whisper come from underneath the mushroom. It shrunk and shrunk until it became a smaller ovate bulb. The two experimenters giggled together, almost like two children.

"I've never seen anything like it!" Farooq exclaimed with a sweet laugh.

"You tap it," Jules pressured the young man.

And so, Farooq heeded the order and tapped the mushroom cap one more time. Then, within the fraction of a second, the mushroom sunk deep into the ground. The two laughed and expressed their awe with a loud, enthusiastic, "Wow!"

Ahna simply shook her head and smiled at the two curious souls. They seemed to really get along in this strange forest.

"It takes little to amuse these two," Luthan said with a serious voice, behind her.

Condescending, much? Ahna veered to him, triggered by his tone. "Don't wear that magi arrogance on your face, Luthan, it doesn't suit you."

She then saw his eyes, the gems that sparkled with the humorous light of a playful mind. He raised his gaze to her and smiled. "Magi or ljosalfar arrogance?" he teased with a chuckle.

"Maybe a bit of both," Ahna returned his smile, but hers was shallow.

She distracted herself by looking back to Farooq and Jules who had found another mushroom to play with. She told them to return to the stone path and keep on moving. Clarice searched her mother's journal again, checking if they still walked the right trail. Yes, they did! And the young sorceress began to lead the pace of the group of five.

THE TRAIL SPLIT IN TWO. One kept on leading east, the other seemed to lose itself among the trees, trees that had now grown so thick and high they could no longer see the sky. Even the stones on the ground had faded with time. Temperatures had dropped significantly. Ahna and her companions felt they could finally breathe properly in this deep forest. But the path they walked seemed odd, out of place.

"Something's not right," Clarice said with a hint of worry in her voice. She tried calling to her father with the ring—no response. "This trail doesn't look like it belongs."

Jules came to stand near her. "No, it doesn't, and it looks fresh."

Clarice looked to the blond shrike with surprise. "How can you tell?"

"The color of the ground," Jules observed. "It's darker. Even if the stone path has disappeared, this is still darker than the dried mud we've been walking on."

Ahna most certainly did not feel reassured by Jules's words. Another distant sound caught her pointy ears, which fluttered intensively. Luthan did not miss this detail.

"Your ears betray your distress, *kyære*," he murmured beside her.

That word he had just called her, *kyære*—a tender word. One she had not heard in a long, long time. Her initial thought: how dare he call her that? How dare he, after all...this? Still, her heart had leapt in her chest upon hearing it, and now felt soothed by its echoes. He had probably not noticed at all, the word he had impulsively said. Or maybe he had and he just did not let it show.

The elf cleared her throat to clear her mind and move on. "I'm not sure we should stay here," she uttered.

The sound rang again across the forest. This time, the others heard it. They immediately looked back and forth to each other. Jules took a deep breath, unsheathed his sword, and brandished it close to him. Clarice, who stood by him, clenched her staff. Another distant howl. Farooq gasped in instant fear.

"What is that sound?" he urged as he held his baton and mimicked the blond shrike.

Ahna hushed him. She focused her hearing and analyzed where the sound came from. Yet another distant howl.

"I can't figure out which direction," the elf alarmingly rustled to her companions. She heard another howl. This time, the sound was too complex, as though there were different pitches in its melody. And then it hit her. "I think there's more than one!"

Before Ahna could say something else, the band heard the gallops of a giant creature across the forest. It sounded like beats of a loud drum that repeated over and over and amplified with time. It came from their right.

Luthan caught a glimpse of its eyes. The creature, a monstrous beast of black and blue, emerged from between the thick trees and leapt toward them. Luckily, Luthan was just in time. He raised his quarterstaff in the air, and the diamond lit red. And so did his eyes. A massive burst of flames spread from the length of the staff to each side, forming a blazing barrier that stopped the creature from reaching them. The beast yelped and turned back, cowering away from the group.

"What in the Hell was that?" Jules asked in a panicked shout.

Farooq briefly only had eyes for the flames. "That was amazing!" he exclaimed in awe as he looked to Luthan.

Luthan hushed them both. This was far from over. The creature in the distance spun on its claws and dashed toward them again with full speed.

Clarice saw the creature's full body in the light. A lycaonite, like the ones her mother had drawn in her journal. Its eight eyes burned with fury as it raced toward the group. Luthan seized his staff with his two hands and pointed the crystal at the enlarged wolf. His eyes turned red again, but before he could launch a column of flames, he caught the sight of a second lycaonite to their left.

Clarice veered to the other beast, thinking as fast as she could. But she was no elementalist with spells of offense. Fear began taking over as the wolf approached. Before it reached her, Ahna stepped in to protect her.

"*Katl a frumur,*" the elf whispered in front of Clarice.

Flashes of silver flickers sprung from Ahna's shoulder and bounced around her arm. The bolts slithered to her fingers and spiked straight into the air. They merged and clashed against the enraged creature in a loud, hammering roar. As Ahna conjured another bolt around her wrist again, she aimed at the first lycaonite and unleashed her thunder straight into its heart. The two beasts, albeit stunned by Ahna's magic, quickly rose to their feet and pawed away in a loud stampede.

"Do you think it's over?" Jules asked, still holding his sword tight.

Ahna's bolts of lightning still danced around her arm. She turned to the shrike. "We should move quickly!"

With a flick of her shoulder, the lightning faded away. She wanted to head back onto the main path when she heard another loud roar. The band gazed into the darkened forest from each side. Back to back, they formed a circle to better scan their surroundings.

"Jules," Luthan called quickly. "Show me your sword."

The shrike mechanically pointed his shortsword in the air so Luthan could see it. Luthan's eyes lit again, and a wild, flaming hot flare appeared around Jules's blade. Jules looked at it in amazement.

"This will help," Luthan assured.

"How do I use it?" the blond shrike asked.

"Like you use your sword."

"Ahna, why did you never do that?" Jules whispered as a badly timed joke.

Farooq and Clarice had no time for Jules's humour, they were dead afraid.

Ahna cast a confused glance toward the shrike. "I'm no pyromancer like Archmage Hyehn."

They heard sounds again, all around them. Pounding sounds against the forest floor. Clarice squinted to see better through the thick foliage. Then her eyes snapped wide open. Another lycaonite charged them, with fierce claws first. It sprung from the ground and crashed violently in front of Ahna. The shockwave from its landing sent the elf flying. She landed on her back, almost snapping the Cursed Bow in two! And losing a few arrows. The beast came to stand right above her. It stared her down with its eight black eyes as she attempted to crawl away. It growled deeply, drooled over her. Before it could lock its jaw around her, Jules struck it with his flaming sword into the maw.

The beast howled in pain. Jules took another swing at the enlarged wolf. The fires of his blade burnt one of its eyes. Ahna quickly rolled to the side and stood back up. As the beast moved to take a fierce bite at Jules, the shrike dashed forward. He slid with his feet on the muddy ground and cut through the lycaonite's flank. He then anchored his balance into the lunar soil, spun on his axis, and plunged his sword into its hip. The beast roared loudly. The flames of the blade burnt through its flesh, Jules could almost smell it. He pulled his shortsword out of the wolf's skin and cut through it again. The blood splattered all over his torso and face. The beast lost its balance, fell to the cold ground, and let out a dying howl. Jules came to stand close to its quivering body and sank his sword deep between its ribs.

"One less," he said as he bit his lip and wiped the blood off his face.

The shrike contemplated the lycaonite's corpse for a moment, especially its long coiling horns to the side of its massive head. He noticed that it was definitely not a wolf, perhaps something closer to a giant carnivorous ram. Its eight eyes closed one by one.

Ahna held her guard. She could still hear faint movements between the trees, but it was too dark to see. The band began to haste in the opposite direction. They had almost reached the previous intersection when another one of these beasts jumped out of the trees. This time, the lycaonite did not hesitate to charge into the group. Jules and Clarice were cast to the side. Farooq landed on his stomach with his leg in the air, and they could not see where Luthan was. From behind them, a third enlarged wolf attacked them. Ahna noticed Clarice's quarterstaff on the ground. She dodged the tail of the lycaonite beside them and slinked on the mud to seize the staff. Once she rolled back up, she held it like a spear and focused her energy. She had not wielded a magical staff in a long time.

A burst of lightning flashed out of the annealed moonstone and struck the third lycaonite in the jaw. Ahna cast the quarter-staff in Clarice's direction. The young sorceress caught it just in time to launch Ahna's charged bolt toward the beast that faced her and Jules. There was one charge left. Despite the powerful force of their lightning strikes, the lycaonites seemed unmoved. A fourth one appeared out of the shadows and galloped toward Farooq, but Luthan was quick enough to launch another column of fire. He slipped between the beast and the young man and propelled his flames with all the strength he had. His staff began to burn beneath his fingers. The flames turned blue. Ahna slid beside him and stretched the Cursed Bow's string. The pain she had not felt in two years returned, but it had significantly less-ened. She felt one with it, like it was meant to be this way. She released the arrow, launching a blast brighter than Sol at the lycaonite. The two waves merged together and spiraled in a tornado that set this whole part of the forest ablaze. The lycaonite burned to cinders. They thought they could catch their breaths, but when the two elves turned around, they saw another lycaonite charge onto their paths.

"Run!" Luthan shouted.

Ahna rushed to help Farooq stand, and the two headed for the path. They ran as hard as they could. Luthan gathered the fires around the forest and summoned a wall of flames between them and the lycaonites. Jules and Clarice were soon running after them. They were almost back onto the regular trail when a final enlarged wolf split the group in two. At this moment, Jules's sword lost its fire, so the shrike seized Clarice's wrist and began to run in an arbitrary direction. In a final attempt to distract the beast, Ahna threw her dagger straight at one of its eyes on the back of its head. The lycaonite, stunned and dazed, pawed around in confusion. Jules and Clarice had a head start among the woods. Farooq and Luthan were already out of Ahna's sight, so the elf ran east. She slid among the trees and foliage, one branch cut through her right sleeve into her arm, and one thorn almost scratched her face. Ahna ran until she rejoined the path where she saw Farooq and Luthan up ahead. Behind her, among the cloud of the inflamed forest, she heard the howls of a dozen more lycaonites.

THE EIDOLON

*J*ules ran with all the endurance he had left. Clarice, the young sorceress, galloped beside him, holding her staff firmly. They made it out of the thick woods into a clearing. They no longer heard the enraged beasts behind their steps.

"Hold on," Clarice called. She had to gasp for air. "I think we..." She was out of breath. "I think we lost them."

Jules stopped and panted. Each breath that filled his lungs made the side of his breast hurt more and more.

"We lost the rest too," the blond shrike exhaled.

Clarice took a moment to catch her breath, then she brought her hand close to her face. She clenched a fist, and the vox-ring around her index finger lit. "*Archmage Hyehn, can you hear me?*" she asked in her mind. No response. "*Meriel?*"

She waited a minute with her hand in the air. She was about to give up when the ring vibrated, and she heard a faint voice.

"*I'm here.*" Luthan's words echoed.

Clarice nodded, and Jules immediately rushed to the ring. He had to know if Ahna was all right. "Ahna, are you there?" he asked, urgently.

Clarice had to summon his question in her mind to transmit it through.

"They're with me," she heard Luthan say again and redirected the information to Jules, who sighed in relief. *"We don't know where we are, but we're back on the path, and we have a much better sight here."*

Clarice checked her satchel—her mother's journal was still in there! She spoke to the ring again with her thoughts. *"Whatever you do, just keep on heading east. Let's try and meet at the hot springs. Always keep in check with us if you don't fade out of range."*

Luthan acknowledged, and she lowered her hand. She grabbed the journal and opened it to one of Eidolon's maps. She analyzed it first, and turned to Jules to show him.

"I think we went north," Clarice said with a worried timbre. "If we continue here"—she pointed at the part of the forest ahead of them, with a light slope—"we should reach the waterfall my mother wrote about."

Jules took another deep breath, letting it out slowly. "Let's just remember not to go into the darker woods!" He continued his march, leading Clarice toward the hill.

THE TWO WALKED for what seemed to be an eternity. The small hill had quickly run back down and muted into another thick bouquet of barkless trees with odd leaves. They still followed the trail according to the journal Clarice carried and regularly consulted. Jules began to grow thirsty and hungry. He pulled the stuffed loaf out of his satchel and gulped it almost instantly. He then opened his canteen and swallowed the water whole.

"I just ran out of water!" the blond shrike announced.

Clarice chuckled. "You should have saved it. If we keep walking at this pace, we will reach water soon."

"How soon is soon?"

"Patience, Jules, is what we teach at Skyshrine."

Jules scoffed jocularly, amused by Clarice's words. He still walked in front of her. The path was narrow, and they felt as though they had to keep their steps on the dried mud. Otherwise, something terrible would happen.

"Did you know Ahna was not her real name?" Clarice asked out of the silence.

"Yes, but does it really matter what her real name is?" the shrike retorted.

Clarice emitted a soft hum to think. "It's like she hides that part of her."

"What do you mean?"

"That…part of her past?" Clarice was careful with her words.

Jules simply shrugged and moved on. He knew but a shred of Ahna had been through in her life. He did not want to linger on it. He did not feel like it was his place. She was here now, and she was his friend. And he would not let anything happen to her.

There was another hill up ahead again. Jules paused for a minute, just to calm his breathing, then he marched uphill. Clarice sighed. She switched hands regularly to not wear out her arm from carrying the quarterstaff. Jules had offered to help, but she had firmly refused.

"How did you two meet?" Clarice asked again.

She was insistent with her questions, almost as curious as Jules's usual self, he thought. He smiled a smile she did not see. "We fought a war together," he said. *One which none of you fought*, the thought came but did not manifest itself out of Jules's lips.

"You saved Bravoure together?"

"And with many more!" Jules exclaimed. "There was the commander, from Tazman, like your father. There was our dear leader, who gave his life for the rebellion. There were swordsmen and women always eager to fight. They fought bravely for the cause, the ideals of hope and freedom, that's why we won. And there was my captain, of course, Cedric Rover, he was…all of this at once!"

Jules spoke so dearly of his brothers and sisters in arms, it spurred Clarice to learn more about the legend that the Resistance seemed to be. She wanted to know more. Though something in the shrike's reverent voice caught Clarice's attention. The way he had spoken of his captain.

"Where is your captain now?" the young sorceress asked.

Jules paused. His posture froze, and his smile faded. "To be honest, I'm not so sure." His voice had changed. Everything about his joyous allure had changed. Remembering Cedric, like that, made him feel...uncomfortable. Uncomfortable to linger further on his memory.

Clarice had brushed a touchy subject here, and she had better not venture further. She did wonder, though, why the mention of this man's captain brought so much pain to his usual joyous heart. Clarice could feel his distress. As an adept mysticist, she had all the powers that allowed her to.

"So, Clarie, what do you do?" Jules asked as he recovered his march.

Clarice chuckled loudly. "Clarie?"

"Yes, get used to it."

She could not stop laughing at the shrike. "Do you call everyone names?"

"Well, yes!" he realized himself. "Ahnny, Rooqie, that's who they are in my mind! So, what do you do?"

Clarice shook her head to stop laughing. Jules seemed to fancy humor used as a distraction. "I read the mind," she said. A spooky sound came out of Jules's mouth, and she continued. "I'm in touch with nature, and I can feel what it feels. I can also alter or bend magic to my will. That is why, for example, I could control Meriel's lightning with my staff."

"Like a shaman?"

So, Jules knew about shamans... Interesting! Clarice nodded slightly. "A shaman is more in touch with the divine. I am on the arcane side."

The two soon reached the top of the hill. Now, they had a view above the trees, even the ones with higher branches.

It was simply marvelous.

The light had changed—it was the warm and ethereal hue of a commencing sunset. Jules's jaw dropped as his eyes landed on the scenery. Far ahead, they could see the contours of low mounts that surged above the trees. In their curve, they saw a large lake and scattered ponds, and the sparkling waters of a waterfall. Beyond this beautiful sight, the forest grew larger and thicker, they could not see past it. It seemed to turn dark, and they did not dare to look longer.

"It looks like we'll have at least a day of travel before we reach the waterfall," Clarice observed.

"This sight is just marvelous!"

Jules's grey eyes were lost in this fantastic view. He had never seen such colors on Terra, a hundred shades of purple, green, and blue, all mixed together to make up this perfect palette even Bravoure's greatest painters would envy.

Clarice cast a curious glance at the shrike. She looked at the flickers in his beautiful silver eyes. For a few seconds, her eyes followed the curve of his nose and rosy lips, which were half-open from this pure, enchanting moment. Of course, Jules had caught her looking.

"I'll get the wrong idea if you keep looking at me like this!" Jules teased, drawing inspiration from Ahna's remark of just a few days ago.

Clarice blushed and immediately headed down the hill. She sought to hide her face and avoid the shrike's gaze. Jules simply laughed with the euphoria he still felt from the view of the Eidolon Forest.

AHNA HAD to cut her sleeve wider to be able to reach her deep wound. She had not yet realized how deep the sharp branch had cut. It was hurting as if the blade of a flaming sword was lodged into her flesh. There was blood, lots of it, and it had soiled her linen shirt. She tore her sleeve open in frustration. It did not look good.

Luthan, Farooq, and her had reached another path with less thick trees, far away from the forest fire and the lycaonites. Ahna sat on a barkless log in the middle of the trail to tend to her wound. Farooq came to sit beside her while Luthan kept watch. It definitely did not look good. The young man frowned upon seeing her torn blue skin that had turned deep purple.

"It's inflamed," Ahna warned. "I hit some kind of branch while running. It happened so quickly..."

She soaked the piece of linen in her hand with the rest of the water in her canteen and began cleaning the wound. A small gasp escaped her lips. She winced in repressed pain as she rubbed carefully around the open wound. The elf cleaned it as best as she could, but she still had to stop the infection.

"Luthan," she called. The tall elf immediately came to her when he heard her trembling voice. "I'm going to need your healing fire."

Luthan frowned. This would hurt her, a lot, and he really did not want to do that right now. "Are you sure?"

"Yes, just do it," she almost begged. "I can take it."

He crouched in front of her, holding her left shoulder with one hand. He brought the other to the open wound on her right arm. Their eyes met, and she saw the burning flame in his eyes. He pressed his blazing palm against the wound. It was so hot, her skin felt as though it began to boil. There was even a sizzling sound between his fingers, and a faint smoke escaped into the air. Farooq had to look away and press his nose shut with two fingers to avoid the smell of burned flesh.

Ahna clenched her teeth together. She wanted to scream. Her free hand automatically latched onto Luthan's arm, and she gripped it with all her strength. His eyes had not left hers. He kept on staring into them with his flaming red gaze.

Once he was done, he abruptly let her go, and she almost fell. If he held her longer, he would have to pull her in his arms. To hold her. To tell her everything would be fine. But now was not the place. Now was not the time.

The open wound was closed, and around it was the pink imprint of skinless flesh. Ahna tore her other sleeve and wrapped it gently around her sensitive scar. The skin would grow over the wound in no time, but she needed to keep it protected.

To distract himself from everything else, Luthan flicked his chin to Ahna's bow, which he really had just noticed. Iedrias had told him about it, but he had not yet seen it from this close. From this close to Ahna.

"Nice bow," Luthan commented, a little inanely. "I can feel its power. It's not actually arcane…"

"It's ancient," the blue elf completed. "This weapon belonged to…the Resistance, to a Resistance soldier." There was a hint of hesitation in her voice. Why did the mention of the Cursed Bow's origin trouble her?

Luthan's eyes lit with the curiosity of an archmage. "I wonder how the Resistance got their hands on such an item…"

Ahna could not escape her thoughts as they whirled to the vision of Cedric, the weapon's rightful owner. She felt a pinch to the side of her chest, like she had just been running forever. Cedric's image as he had held the bow, proud. Cedric's image as he had stood on the Orgna battlefield, with bodies laid piled before him. Ahna had to shake her head to remain on track.

"We should keep moving," she declared, more to herself than to her friends. "Clarice said to continue east. We can meet at the ponds."

Luthan nodded, and Ahna rose to her feet. She motioned for Farooq to follow and they headed back onto the path.

. . .

THIS WALK WAS TAKING TOO LONG, and Jules was thirsty again. He and Clarice had sunk back into the thick trees that surrounded the thin trailed they walked. They thought they were headed the right way. They should have seen at least one pond by now!

"We've been walking for ages," Jules complained. "Still no water!"

"Patience, Jules!" Clarice jocularly said.

Jules expressed his disapproval with a deep sigh. The blond shrike passed his hand in his messy hair to distract himself. He then saw, in the corner of his eyes, a floating canteen. Clarice handed him the last of her water.

"Thanks! You're saving my life," Jules said with an honest smile.

He took the last bit of water in the palm of his hand and rubbed his neck. He was exhausted. They had walked for a full day by now, even if the sunlight appeared frozen in time.

"Have you reached the ponds yet?" Clarice asked her vox-ring.

Luthan's voice was quickly heard. *"We had a setback. Meriel was wounded, but she's fine now. We're approaching a clearing. I think I hear water in the distance."*

Clarice let out a sigh of relief. "Good. Let us know when you get there."

"Will do."

Jules stared blankly at the ring. "This mode of communication is very convenient. We would have made such great use of it with the shrikes!"

Clarice rounded her eyes. "The shrikes?" She wanted to hear more, once again.

"Ah, yes, the members of the Shrike Wing. We were the spies and assassins of the Resistance."

She caught a grip of his arm. "You were an assassin?"

"For a couple of Sols, yes."

Clarice gasped. "What..." she hesitated. "What did you do?"

Jules took a deep breath, letting it out slowly as he reminisced on the darkest corners of his past. "I stole intel, I killed enemy soldiers and envoys. I went on covert missions I don't even remember, and I got this"—he lifted the bottom of his leather cuirass slightly so she could see his abdomen.

There was a huge scar, like the imprint of a blade.

Jules did not wish to linger further on this memory. He had already forgotten about it. Why did he have to show her? She was just so...trustworthy. Jules simply felt at ease with her, almost like he did with Ahna. Clarice brought a finger to the erased wound. It made him flinch a little, as he did not really appreciate someone exploring his scars.

"What are you doing?" he asked as he adjusted his black leathers.

Clarice simply remained silent. *Jules, a killer.* The young sorceress had seen his ferocity during the fight against the lycaonite, but the idea of him being a cold-blooded assassin was something she found...frightening. Yet his eyes shone with such youth and joy.

"How many did you kill?" Clarice spontaneously asked.

Jules took a deep breath before answering. "I lost count."

His voice had turned to something darker, something that intrigued her. She looked to the shrike who passively looked ahead. She wanted to know what he had been through. The tales of the Resistance he told were glorious, but his eyes and his allure betrayed something that weighed heavy on his shoulders—the scars of war.

Jules's grip pulled out of her thoughts. He clenched his hand around Clarice's shoulders and slipped with her against a tree. He held his finger in front of her lips as a sign for her to stay silent.

Her eyes demanded answers.

"I heard something," he motioned with his lips.

Now she heard the distant crack of a branch. Surprised, she was about to gulp some extra air when Jules opened his palm and pressed it against her mouth. His grey eyes darkened as a stern warning. The shrike turned around to scan his surroundings. He stopped his breathing and only listened to the sounds around him.

Another crack.

Jules unsheathed his sword and readied his stance. In a short and steady breath, he threw his sword like a lance at whatever made the sound. The edge of the blade hit the ground at the feet of the source of the noise.

Jules looked straight at it...and saw nothing. He then lowered his eyes.

By the shortsword planted in the ground stood a small creature, not much bigger than the weapon itself. It was blue, perhaps slightly mauve, and looked at the two strangers with bulging eyes. Well, three wide eyes that trembled at the sight of the sword.

Clarice drew in her breath with exaggerated joy. She seized her mother's journal and searched through the pages.

There it was!

"Jules, don't attack it!" she urged quickly.

Jules approached the frightened creature and retrieved his sword. The sound the blade scared it off, and it hopped away on four feet.

Clarice scoffed. "No! You made it run away!"

Jules simply shrugged with confusion as a response.

Clarice went on. "My mother described these creatures. Look!" She showed him a page with a doodle of the mauve creature they had just seen. "She named them *ailunas*."

Jules turned around again, after hearing a small noise from behind a tree. He saw the thin contours of a pointy ear, like a cat's ear, that sprung from behind the trunk. Clarice saw it too. She clenched her staff, which began to glow. She came to her knees and crawled to the creature slowly.

"We are not here to harm you," she whispered to it.

The glow of her quarterstaff emitted a low buzzing sound. It seemed to relax the creature enough that it emerged from behind the barkless tree. It slowly walked to Clarice, on two paws. Jules could now wholly see it. It looked like a cat! A cat-like creature with three eyes, pointy ears tipped with long white tufts, and a rounded and fluffy tail, like a rabbit. The fur on its breast was thick, and the creature stuffed its features when Jules attempted to come closer, some kind of severe threat. The shrike simply laughed at it, and the ailuna rounded its three eyes. It tilted its head, tried to understand what the sound was that Jules made.

"It looks like a tiny sindur!" Jules exclaimed as he guffawed some more. "A tiny blue sindur with three eyes!" He kept on laughing uncontrollably.

A smile began to draw on the creature's face. It actually started to imitate Jules's joyous movements. It made little meowing sounds that resembled a chortle. All of this spurred Jules to laugh some more. He almost had tears in his eyes. The ailuna was so caught up in its meows that it fell on its back and rolled on the forest floor.

"Look, Clarie, he's also cracking up!" Jules could not stop laughing.

Clarice had joined their laughter as well. Once they regained their composure, the ailuna rose to its paws and waited expectantly.

"What do you want, little one?" Clarice asked the small creature with a soft mother-like voice.

The ailuna simply tilted its head again. Further among the trees, Clarice caught a glimpse of two more of its kind hopping toward them on four feet. Once they reached the two strangers, they stood and tilted their heads simultaneously. All three blinked one after the other.

"This is starting to be a little creepy," Jules admitted.

Clarice checked the journal. "Mother mentions they are very friendly. They only eat moonberries."

Speaking of the moon, Jules suddenly noticed the faint patterns on their fur. They had tiny blue spots on their arms and legs, but the most striking one was a silver crescent above their three eyes. Just like the crescent moon seen in the Terran night sky.

"I can't believe this," Jules said in marvel. "They have a moon on their foreheads!"

"A moon?" Clarice asked for clarification. Of course, she had never seen what a moon looked like in her life. She lived on one.

"This is how we sometimes see Luna from Terra," Jules eagerly clarified.

Clarice's brown eyes lit with joy. For a moment, she yearned to witness this silver crescent in a night sky she had wanted to see for all her life.

This little clowder of ailunas folded on all fours. They went on the path and hopped away. When they reached the top of the hill in the distance, one of them turned and meowed at Clarice and Jules.

"I think it wants us to follow," the young sorceress indicated.

"Should we?" Jules checked.

The ailuna meowed again. Clarice shrugged and took hold of Jules's wrist, leading him on the path to the small clowder. With a little hesitation, the blond shrike decided to trust and follow the young sorceress. This path slithered to the east, where the band of two needed to go. The three ailunas hopped by them, taking them up the hill and back down, following the trail until they reached a set of clearings at the foot of the low mounts. The two grew tired, and it felt as though night was near. They could hear the silent rustle of water in the distance. *Good!* Jules thought. He could finally gorge himself with the freshness of this mysterious forest.

12

FOLLOW THE RIVER

*T*he endless coils of purplish branches circled around a small clearing, close to the sound of a river. The golden light of the unending sunset rained over the tall silver grass. Ahna opened her eyes. They had made camp here, in this secluded glade, away from the dangers of the forest. She cast a quick glance at Farooq, who still slept soundly. She had no idea if it was morning or noon or evening on Terra—Ahna had officially lost track of time. Her pointy ears fluttered when she heard Luthan's footsteps behind her. He came to sit beside her, holding a handful of moonberries in his hand. He gobbled them, not laying eyes on her yet.

"Were you able to sleep?" he asked, distant.

Ahna simply nodded. She checked the wound on her right arm, underneath the soiled linen. It was fully healed. She discarded the piece of cloth that had served well as a bandage. When she turned back to the tall elf, he finally looked at her. He held his hand beside her, handing her a few berries. She thanked him and ate the delicious blue and sweet fruits.

"We should move," Luthan declared. "If we follow the river, we'll reach the ponds." He then clenched a fist around the vox-ring to activate it. It began to vibrate as he centered his thoughts. *"Is everything alright with you two?"* he asked in his mind.

Clarice's voice soon rang. *"We made camp up the hills, by a brook. You should meet the new friends we've made!"*

Luthan raised an eyebrow. *"Up the hills?"* He had not seen any hills.

"The low mounts further east—they border the ponds. We're headed to them as we speak. Let us know when you reach."

When Luthan was done, he lowered his hand, and his eyes landed on Ahna. She had her nose into the brown book Iedrias had given her, *On the Schillers of the Arc*, and the Cursed Bow on her lap. She still studied it, curious to grasp everything about the weapon the Ancients had created. She looked so beautiful doing it. The tall elf's gaze explored the Cursed Bow's upper limb, now that he could see it up close and had some time. He noticed the engravings, the same arcane glyphs he had seen appear in spirals and patterns on Ahna's dawn blue skin.

Unaware of what he was doing, Luthan mechanically brushed the markings with his fingertips, which immediately startled Ahna. She clenched the bow between her fingers and remained alert. She cautiously looked in Luthan's direction. He was too damned close.

Luthan followed a pattern closely with one of his fingers. "This one speaks of some kind of light," he murmured as he examined it. His finger followed the glyphs until it reached Ahna's hand. "I think it means *soul.*"

Ahna exhaled softly. Her hand could almost touch his. "I didn't know you spoke the language of the Ancients," she said, stuttering.

His finger found its way along hers, which he gently caressed. Ahna let a little sigh escape.

"Something about your heart," he whispered, leaning closer to her, closer to her lips.

Farooq awoke.

Ahna instantly jumped to her feet and strapped her satchel to her shoulder. She slipped the book through the opening and clutched the Cursed Bow.

"Let's follow the water," she declared in one instant.

Farooq murmured inaudible words, then gathered his things, brushed his wavy hair with his hands and went on the path with Ahna. Luthan stayed for a short moment behind, looking at the blue elf and the young man stroll away. He was caught by his own thoughts, by the sensation he felt underneath his fingertips from having touched his wife's skin. His eyes melted on the vision of Ahna's silver curls that swayed as she moved, which she had let loose for once. He had never forgotten this sight, and now, she was here. Oh, how he wanted to hold her, to take her lips, to tell her he loved her…and had never stopped loving her.

THE THREE REACHED a river of clear water. The stream slithered to the south then veered toward the east. They could now see the formation of hills to the north. They were convinced Clarice and Jules were somewhere in that direction. Farooq kneeled by the river and seized a large chunk of water in his palms. It was clear as glass and felt so fresh! He drank and drank until he could no longer breathe. Ahna and Luthan did precisely the same. They filled up their canteens in the process. Ahna passed her wet hand on her shoulders, arms, and neck to appease her stiff muscles. She cleaned her face and exhaled deeply as the cold of the water touched her skin. Some drops even ran underneath her shirt, giving her this intense and refreshing sensation.

"How long until we reach the waterfall?" Farooq asked Luthan.

The tall elf drank one more sip of water. He looked in the opposite direction of the river's flow. Judging by the strength of the torrent, they were close.

"We should be there soon," he replied.

Luthan began his march again, this time along the riverbed. Ahna and Farooq followed behind. They did not hear anything else than the sounds of water. No howls, no roars, no enraged lycaonites in proximity. Farooq felt a deep sense of relief, being so close to the source of life that water was. He contemplated the scenery to his left, the purplish trees and silver grass that carried a minty scent into the air. He breathed in deeply to invade his nose with this delicious fragrance.

Ahna's voice lured him out of his thoughts. "Do you have any regrets yet?" she asked the young man.

"Regrets?" he wondered. "Regrets for what?"

"For coming here, to this crazed forest," she replied, pointing at the odd-looking trees that surrounded them.

Farooq let out a sweet chuckle. "Ahna, the furthest I ever went from Drazul was Mokvar. This place is exactly where I should be! I want to learn all there is to it, all its mysteries, and I hope you can teach me some magic!"

Ahna smiled. She admired the young man for his courage and his eagerness to explore the world. She looked in front of them, at Luthan, the tall elf who was the best teacher she had known. That was something she could still admit.

"You should ask Luthan to teach you," Ahna said in favor of the high elf's academic prowess.

Farooq blushed slightly, and his eyes sparkled with a particular fascination for Archmage Hyehn.

"He sort of...intimidates me," the young man confessed with a secretive whisper. "I've never seen a ljosalfar before."

A burst of light laughter came out of Ahna's lips. "Speaking with high elves can indeed be very daunting!" Her laugh ended in a soft giggle. "But they have their ways with the arcane no other mortals have."

Farooq's blush faded, and he turned to Ahna. He hesitated for a moment, as though he wanted to ask her something inappropriate. His eyes bounced between her and the grass as he mustered the audacity to speak.

"He is your husband, isn't he?" Farooq asked softly. He knew the answer, of course, not that it was not obvious! But he had to ask out of politeness before saying anything else.

Ahna paused and exhaled deeply. Her lips curled up, but there was no smile. She looked to her feet and pondered on the young man's question for a minute.

"He was," she answered.

"You must have loved each other very much," Farooq inferred from observations Ahna grew curious about. She raised an eyebrow in wonder, so he continued. "I don't have many memories of my grandmother, but I will always remember how my *daadu* looked at her. It was different from a young heart's flame, something more...enduring. Luthan looks at you the same way."

Ahna remained silent. She did not want to hear more, because something in her heart ached too much. That idea made her stomach turn on itself. She felt torn. Torn between an old flame, passionate memories, and what she felt now. A part of her wanted to run back into her forgotten husband's arms. Another part wanted to slap him in the face, for abandoning her, Bravoure, for being a coward. A part of her wanted to feel safe. Another part wanted to move on and never look back.

The three walked along the river, silently, until the stream widened into a large, eye-stopping lake that stretched past their field of vision. There, in the distance, they saw the thick white cloud of a wild torrent flurrying into the lake. It was the waterfall, and in the light of the sunset, a rainbow of colors they had never seen adorned this place of paradise.

THEY HAD STARTED out with three, now there were five. Five ailunas of a shortsword's length hopped beside Clarice and Jules, who walked among the tall grass in the silver fields. To the south, they could hear the sound of a river. However, the ailuna seemed to be guided by something else than the melody of the stream. They hopped faster and faster upon reaching yet another large clearing.

"Something tells me we're not headed the right way," Jules observed with a frown.

He stopped his march and listened to the sounds around him. He suddenly caught a faint shriek, like the whistle of an arrow. The shrike immediately drew his sword and stepped in front of Clarice. The ailunas froze and turned to him, their three eyes wide open.

"What are you doing?" Clarice asked, startled by Jules's stance.

He hushed her with a motion of his hand. He heard another whistle.

Behind him!

He swiftly veered to the left and turned to whatever was making the noise.

What the...

"Duck!" he shouted.

He immediately bent forward, and a large, fast object flew over his head. It missed Clarice by one frizzy hair. Jules turned around to see what that thing was.

A flower?

He had to dodge a second flying projectile. As it dashed beside him, he could clearly see it. A floating flower—he was not crazy. It was indeed a bright white flower, with red sepals that extended behind its trajectory and oscillated like smooth hair in the wind. Jules blinked a few times to bring himself back to reality, but these flowers were very much real. Another bouquet of three or four flowers flew beside them, this time passively, and they could observe them a little longer. They headed in an unknown direction, away from the tall grass, and they disappeared back into the purplish trees. Jules and Clarice had simply no idea what to make of this. Awed by the sight of floating flowers, Clarice dived her nose into her mother's journal again. There were a few words about them, but no mention of how their existence was even possible. This was something she would definitely need to study once all of this is over.

Meanwhile, the ailunas hopped on the hill to their right. Jules and Clarice followed them until they reached the top. And then, as they rose above the trees again, they could clearly see where they were. They had gone further than planned. Downhill, beyond what appeared to be a silver gorge by one of the river's arms, they could see the largest of lakes, and the contours of a beautiful waterfall.

"We walked too far." Clarice sighed deeply as she spoke.

They noticed the color of the sunlight. The orange hue of the sunset had disappeared, and the night had almost fallen upon the low mounts.

Jules turned to the clowder that slipped away behind a large rock. He followed them, curious to see where they had gone, as he heard the meows of more ailunas. He peeked behind the rock.

"Clarice! Look at that!" he called to her with loud enthusiasm.

There must have been hundreds of burrows scattered around the crook of the hills! The ailunas that had accompanied them all slipped into their assigned hole. Some had rejoined other ailunas in the nearby pond for a bath. Some were cuddling with one another, as though they had not been together for a long while. Jules expressed his surprise with a fascinated note. Clarice immediately rushed to him and melted in front of this curious and adorable display.

"It's their home," she said in a soft voice.

A group of smaller ailunas of a pale mauve color came close to their shoes. One smelled the tip of Jules's boot and began rubbing its furry cheek against the leather. Another one started to climb on the shrike's leg. Jules was so overwhelmed by a set of three other ailunas that soared upon his legs, that he fell backwards and landed in the grass. They crawled on top of him and rolled all over his body. Clarice invited one in her arms. As soon as she touched it, it emitted a low drumming sound, like a kitten's purr.

"I think they're children!" she exclaimed.

"Get them off me!" Jules said with a cackle as he drowned underneath the balls of mauve fur.

The kittens had two tiny eyes. The third one was not yet fully developed. The imprint of the moon on their foreheads was, for now, a little silver spot. More of these small creatures found their way up Clarice's boots. She struggled to keep her balance, but fell in the grass beside Jules. She could not stop laughing. The thousand coils of her thick black mane folded as she turned to the shrike. She had the biggest smile on her face, and so did he. She looked at him dearly, succumbing to the euphoria this burst of cuteness had spurred in her heart. Jules kept on laughing, and his grey eyes that matched the silver grass sparkled with joy. Clarice searched for them, and she lost herself in his innocent gaze. Her laughter dimmed, and she remained still with a smile, looking at the handsome blond man.

"You fought an impossible war, yet you surrender to a clowder of ailuna cubs!" she teased him.

He remained joyous, shooing each kitten away if they got too close to his face. He was completely oblivious to the way Clarice looked at him. The fur balls began hopping away as the older ailunas meowed for their return.

Jules turned to his side to look at the young sorceress. Her brown eyes shone with a peculiar light, one that he did not know so well. She plunged her gaze into his, and her face came closer. Then, unexpectedly, she pressed her lips against his.

Jules froze.

His lips became rigid. He pulled his head back and looked at her with confused eyes.

Clarice gasped. "I am so sorry!" she said as she sat up straight. She noticed how Jules's entire body had stiffened. He had not been into this at all.

She immediately adjusted her robe and hair and rose to her feet. She was about to pace away when Jules caught her arm.

"Clarie," he began in a careful tone. He had to tell her it was not her fault. "I'm the one who should say sorry. I'm sorry if I gave the wrong impression."

Her eyes saddened. "The impression that you might...like me?" she asked hesitantly. "Is it because of Meriel? Are you and her…"

Jules had to laugh on that one. "No! No, no, no, Gods no! I really like you, Clarie, but that's not it." He spoke carefully. "I don't like you in a...*romantic* way."

Clarice chuckled, or was it a wryly scoff? "Yes, I got that part."

"No, I mean..." This was too awkward for the blond shrike. "I don't like any woman...in a romantic way."

The sorceress' mouth opened wide, and she let out a long, understanding note. She blushed and laughed a little at her silliness. Now, a lot of things began to make sense, how he was with Ahna, and perhaps how he spoke of his captain. He was not into Clarice. He was actually not into women at all. Clarice gave Jules another apology, which he swiftly dismissed, and they giggled together again from the awkwardness.

Once she regained her composure, Clarice activated the vox-ring to distract herself. "*We walked too far, but we see the waterfall. Where are you?*" the young sorceress asked through the ring.

Ahna's voice answered this time. "*We're at the waterfall. Where did you end up?*"

"*We're further east, on top of the valley,*" Clarice said with her thoughts. Her eyes then landed on the tender burrows of the ailunas. "*We can wait for you here. I think we're at a very safe place.*"

"*We'll make camp here and join you in the morning. We should be safe too.*"

Clarice lowered her hand and searched for the blond shrike. She still felt a little embarrassed and foolish for her action, but he did not seem too bothered by it. He was already fetching a handful of moonberries from the nearby shrubs close to the burrows. She observed him as he passed a hand in his blond hair, then she scolded herself for what she then realized. She was falling for him.

"Every magic-user has their own imprint," Luthan began. He sat next to Farooq by the lake's silver shore. "It's like a signature." He brought his hand above his own thigh and turned it around. "It is what determines where you draw your power from. Whether it's from the elements"—he drew an arc in the air, which turned to a soft wind—"or the mind, the soul, or even the different realms."

Farooq listened to the archmage with all ears. He wanted to ask so many questions but let him speak instead.

Luthan exhaled deeply, and in the palm of his hand, a cold blue flame formed. It rose above his palm and burned and flickered so bright, Farooq had to cover his eyes.

"The blue flame is what led me to Pyromancy," the high elf revealed. "You can try and do the same. Open your hand." As Farooq did what Luthan told him to, the archmage continued. "Focus your energy. Let the arcane flow through you."

Farooq concentrated as hard as he could. He gave it all he had, but nothing happened. He squinted, almost grimaced, the folds on his forehead began to curl. Still nothing. He let out a sigh of frustration.

"Be calm and focus again," Luthan told him with a didactic timbre.

Ahna observed them from behind the foliage of the trees. She had gone in search of some food while Luthan gave Farooq his first lesson in the Fine Arts of Arcanis. She carried a few moonberries and some mushrooms she thought could be edible. Bluecaps with black gills—Ahna remembered it from Clarice's journal. Between the barkless coils of the trees' branches, she saw the young man focus all the energy he had to manifest his arcane.

He tried it at least four times before Luthan gave him a break. Despite being young, Farooq had missed a significant part of his youth he could have used to train his magic.

"Focus again," Luthan requested a fifth time. "This time, don't try to conjure your arcane but be with it. Become your flow as it extends through your fingers." The tall elf then leaned closer to the young apprentice. "Think of something dear to you, like a joyful memory."

Farooq nodded furtively and made his final attempt. Luthan's request sparked but a single thought in his mind: the warm stew his grandfather made for his grandmother, his mother, and his even younger self. The memory of when they sat at the wooden table in his home, together, united as one family, before the Dark Lord's militia took all he had loved. Farooq focused on the smell of the stew, its colors, the eyes of his mother. The soft voice of his grandmother as she sang him songs of the Indus-Kali isles, even in a time of war. Farooq closed his eyes as a tear fell along his cheek. And when he opened them again, a green spark, a flicker of Bravoure's spring fields, grew in the palm of his hand. The young apprentice gasped. He drew a smile on his face, one that radiated with immense joy.

"I did it! I did it!" he exclaimed.

Luthan applauded. "That's a future geomancer right there!"

Ahna smiled dearly at the apprentice's glee. A geomancer he was meant to be, like his grandfather Mohindra. Farooq danced around by the lake's shore in pure happiness. Ahna was so caught in the young man's rapture that she had not seen Luthan's eyes on her. The tall elf had noticed her, peeking behind the trees. Now, she needed to run. To hide. Ahna blushed and paced away fast.

THE BLUE ELF stood beyond the trees, by another part of the lake's shore, away from the archmage and the apprentice. She stopped by the water to admire the waterfall in the distance. The light of the sunset gave this place the ethereal appearance of a divine dream. The sound of the heavy rain plunging into the lake masked the other abundant noises of the Eidolon Forest. While admiring Luna's nature, her thoughts drifted to her friends back home, and she let herself be taken by a stream of emotions.

In her mind, she saw Kairen's copper eyes and her sweet smile. The red-haired woman who had never lost faith in her. Ahna hoped dearly to be able to see her face again. She saw Thamias. A hint of worry settled in her heart. One more emotion to loathe. Here she was, on the moon, in a forest with dangers none could fathom, with a man she had lost and found again. She stood by the lake, still shaken by a resentful feeling. The thorn of abandonment. The feeling that Luthan had left her behind. *It was the right call to make.* That stupid mantra that she forcibly looped in her mind. But if she had to be honest with herself, with her heart, she was angry. They had kept this plan of escape hidden from her and had all left her behind. But despite this, despite her aimless efforts to clear Luthan out of her mind, he captured her thoughts like he had done her heart. Her heart that had loved him more than life. But did she love him now? She had mourned him, after all. She had been forced to move on, to deal with the loss, to heal. Could she ever love him again like fifty years ago? Should she even dare?

Tears began to fill her eyes. She clenched her jaw to repress her cries. She wanted to do anything else but cry, as she wished with all she had to remain stern and strong.

"The boy shows promise!" Luthan said behind her.

No! He was here. Ahna had not heard him approach. He walked to her until he was in an arm's reach. A tear had already escaped her eyes and flowed down her cheek, which she swiftly wiped away. She swallowed and sniffled a few times before turning to the tall elf.

"Luthan..." It was all she could say. His emerald eyes delved into hers. He was so close to her, she could almost feel his gentle breath on her face. She averted his gaze and looked in front of her, at his chest, never meeting his eyes.

Luthan cleared his throat. He saw her distress. He had to appease it, somehow. "I want you to know how sorry I am," he said. "I should have never left you behind." Was it an apology to her or himself? He was unsure, but he had to say it nonetheless.

Ahna shook her head. She could no longer feel angry. It was too much to bear for her. "Luthan, you had your reasons. You saved the magi. You saved them from my cursed brother." She wanted to hide from him again as tears had begun to flow. Tears of shame. Her brother, her own flesh and blood, the one who had caused all this...madness. "I'm glad you found a life here." Her voice broke in a faint whisper.

"I had to find a purpose again," Luthan preached. "Ellyra, she lost someone too. We found each other and helped each other through it."

His words had just cut through her heart. Ahna looked away and nervously pressed her lips together. "I understand," she whispered. She did not, though, but she knew she had to try. She wanted to say more, but the lump in her throat made it so hard. "You had to go on," she murmured. Then, she realized something. Among all this despair and pain was a faint spark. Something in her heart that still made it beat. The glimmer that had made her return to Bravoure, to the fight, two years ago. Yes, it was clear now. After all the grief, the shame, that moment, anchored in her history, was the moment of acceptance. "You moved on and—" *so did I.*

But that last part did not come to sound. Luthan stopped her right there. His body stiffened, and he took a step closer to her. His eyes lit with an old flame that caught Ahna by surprise. He seized her face between his hands, brushing the tears away with his thumbs.

"Don't say I moved on, *kyære.*" His eyes flickered, searching for something inside hers. "I had to go on. But don't you ever believe I moved on."

His hands slid to the nape of her neck. He clenched her silver curls between his fingers and pulled her in. He smiled gently, admiring the beauty of her purple eyes. He pressed his body against his wife's, feeling her warmth. Her palms came to rest on his chest, and he caught her trembling lips. He pressed her even closer, she almost lost balance. His hands made their way to the arch of her back as he kissed her with a passion he swore he had lost. His tongue slipped between her lips, and she let out a soft, uncontrolled moan. This sound set his body aflame. He let her go for a short moment to let her catch her breath, then he went for her lips again. He wanted for the world to stop, right here, in this moment with his wife. He wished for nothing more than to melt with her, to consume their love, lost in time.

Ahna gave into the kiss. This felt too good. A moment of comfort in this strange forest. Her hands climbed to Luthan's neck, and his skin burned upon her touch. He repressed a groan as she pulled him lower so she would not have to stand on her toes. He wanted her. He wanted to sink to the lake's shore and take her on the silver grass. This was wrong, twisted, justified, familiar...

But in the midst of this sweet embrace, Ahna's thoughts gathered one by one. Now was not the place nor the time. She took a step back, letting go of her husband. She did not say anything. She simply held his gaze with her luscious lips half open. She wanted to continue, they both did. Though, reality hauled them back. Ahna adjusted her hair and cleared her throat, to shoo the dangerous and lustful thoughts away.

THE GOLDEN LIGHT of the sunset beamed above the city of Bravoure. The people gathered for the declaration of their new leader. There he stood, proud, with his head held high above the platform of the central plaza. Charles Goshawk, Bravoure's new elected Regent, chosen by the Populi. Many applauded. Many cheered and raised their fists in the air. Charles Goshawk, one of Bravoure's favorite bankers, the one who promised to restore every citizen's wealth.

David stood in the back of the crowd. He wore the military garments of a Resistance commander, the green tunic with silver epaulettes, to honor Charles' *crowning* ceremony. But he did not feel like honoring this man. Next to him was his dear friend Diego Levireo and his lover Lynn, the Taz swordswoman. The three blankly started at the new Regent of Bravoure. They did not applaud. They did not cheer.

"What do you think is going to happen now, Commander?" Diego asked with concern laced in his voice.

David sighed and crossed his arms. "I honestly have no idea," he conceded. Goshawk and his promise of building a new army only worried him.

Lynn sighed deeply. "I have a bad feeling about this." She crossed her arms to mimic her commander. She worried too. This whole scene, Goshawk and his swarm of followers, it stunk. Stunk like a bad omen.

The three remained still until the crowd began to dissipate. Charles would move to the castle tonight. His chambers were ready, and many had already taken up work in the castle with golden towers. Kairen rejoined the group of three once everyone was gone.

"So, here we are," she began. "Charles Goshawk. Where does that leave us?"

The three had no answers. After the awkward silence, Thamias appeared from behind them. "It cannot be that bad," he said on a positive note. "He promised the people happiness and security." Thamias wanted to ease the mood, but he noticed his reassuring words had little to no effect.

"At what cost?" David immediately asked with a grim tone. "That is the mystery. How much will the restoration of our wealth cost us?"

Kairen shook her head. Enough. She was not going to let her husband sink further into desperation. "We should head home."

David nodded, and the two headed into the streets. Thamias remained here, together with Diego and Lynn. He did not know them that well, but his sister had told him so much about the two. Lynn had always been so kind to him. Diego, on the other hand, was ever slightly distant, as though something about the small dokkalfar made him cringe. Thamias knew very well what it was.

He looked too much like Sharr.

And he hated this. His resemblance with the Dark Lord, the man of his nightmares, he hated it all.

"Fancy a drink?" a voice from behind them said. It was Luk Ma.

"I could definitely use one," Diego immediately retorted to the sindur tom's offer.

Lynn refused politely. "I will head home."

"Me too," Thamias said.

Luk Ma and Diego made their way to the Gold Monk, to their usual table. It was not far from Castle Plaza, just a few minutes north. Luk Ma took a seat in front of his friend. The two sipped on a glass of goldrain rum, something more potent than ale. People were cheering at the back of the tavern, while some were drowning their disappointment at the bottom of a jar of rum.

"There are rumors, Levireo." Luk Ma emerged from their stillness. "Goshawk plans to fund our army. They say David will oversee our future as the new general."

Diego took a chug of rum. "Where are you getting at, Luk Ma?"

"They say Goshawk offered this opportunity to our commander before the elections," Luk Ma did not want to make it sound like a conspiracy, but it sure did. David had been bought, those were the rumors people spread.

The captain immediately put down his glass. He cast a severe glance at the ailuran tom. "Whatever you are implying, remember that David led us to victory."

"I know," Luk Ma reassured. Yes, he knew better. "That's why I think something else is going on." Because Diego's eyes turned curious, the tom continued. "Why would somebody spread rumors about the corruption of our dear commander?"

Diego had to think for a minute. "Divide and conquer?"

Luk Ma simply confirmed with an ample nod. "I am worried about David. Goshawk wants the military. With David in the way, that will never be possible. I fear efforts are made to remove David out of the picture, out of the people's hearts."

The captain pressed the heels of his palms against his eyes and let out a long sigh of exhaustion. "I have no time for this!" He exhaled deeply again, crossing his arms on the table. "What do we do, Councilor?"

Luk Ma chuckled. No one had referred to him as his Resistance title since the war. "We observe," he declared. "And in the meantime, we figure out how many people are playing Charles' game."

Diego shook his head. "I don't fiddle with politics!"

Luk Ma chuckled again. "We fought a war bigger than this banker. Bravoure doesn't deserve to sink in corruption after the fifty years we've lost."

Luk Ma was right, and Diego knew it. As so, the two elaborated on a plan that would become their next mission: uncover how Charles Goshawk had exactly gripped the crowd with his power of influence, and what he planned on doing with Commander David Falco.

13

THE PRIDE SYLVAN

*T*here was darkness. Absolute darkness. When Ahna opened her eyes, she was overwhelmed by an inexplicable weight of dread. Tears filled her eyes. She tried to move, to scan her surroundings, understand where she was, but to no avail. She took a step or two in a random direction. She heard screams, cries, laughter—noise that sounded horribly painful. Ahna stepped into the darkness until, up ahead, she distinguished the contours of a door. The handle was broken, but she was able to peek through the keyhole. There, in the next room, lit by a single torch on an invisible wall, Ahna saw a tall man, his back turned toward her. She could not recognize him, but she heard his voice. And her spine instantly froze.

"Where am I?" the man asked.

Ahna opened her mouth to speak. No sound. She tried to open the door, pushing her full bodyweight against it. Nothing, it would not budge. She called out to the man, still mute, only her lips moved in the darkness. Ahna took a step back. She focused her energy, the arcane, to blast that door out of existence. Not a single damned thing happened. She turned around, leaned against the door, and collapsed on the floor. She knew exactly who this man was, and it broke her heart not to be able to reach him.

She sat there, in the silence, hugging her knees and burying her face in tears. She remained lost in her desperate cries for a moment that seemed to halt in time. But then, as she dried her tears, she heard a sliding movement on the other side of the door and a thump of someone landing on the floor. At this point, Ahna knew the man in the room sat back to back with her, with only the door separating them.

"Where am I, Ahna?" the man asked again.

Ahna rested her head against the door and closed her eyes. This time, she realized she could speak. "Cedric..." she called his name.

She heard him gasp.

"I was hoping it was you," Cedric Rover said, with his voice she had not heard in two years. "Where am I?"

Ahna let a tear run down her cheek. "You're gone, Cedric. Your soul..." Her throat was too clogged to speak more.

Silence. Then he spoke again.

"How can I be gone?" he questioned. "How can I be gone when I'm here, with you?"

The blue elf, overtaken by this immense feeling of sadness, knocked her own head against the door. There was no pain, but it felt good.

"I failed you, Cedric. I let something happen to you that should never have been."

He hushed her. "Ahna, I made my own choice." He paused for a moment. "Now, will you tell me where I am?"

"I don't know." Ahna had no more words. She cried, silently, feeling the presence of the Resistance captain behind her.

"Of all things about you," he said with a voice that carried a smile. "Your lips were my favorite."

"This is a dream," Ahna whispered to herself, stating the obvious. Cedric was dead and his soul was gone. That was it. He was gone.

This realization made her weep more. That was something Ahna had not yet faced. She had not yet dealt with his death. This man's death. The captain of the Shrike Wing, whom she had spent so little time with yet who had meant so much to her. She focused on his presence, Cedric's presence, she did not want to let him go. Not again. What was she even doing here? What was she even doing on the moon, surrounded by ashes and ghosts, while she should have been on Terra, looking for a way to save him? But she could not save him. Cedric was gone. Ahna closed her eyes and warped into a sleep devoid of dreams.

———

AHNA'S DREAM of the previous night still had her shaken. She strolled the path without looking ahead, simply following Luthan and Farooq. She was silent, but her thoughts were racing. She felt guilty. Guilty of the kiss she and Luthan had shared, and guilty for letting her dreams sway her to the memory of Cedric Rover. The man she could not save.

She had to center her thoughts, to focus on something else so she would not feel this pain anymore. And so, she focused on the lake, which stretched east into the arm of a river that slithered into the silver valley. The band of three had walked since dawn, and they walked on until they reached the crook of a slope. By the myriad of burrows where a clowder of small cat-like creatures wandered, they finally rejoined Clarice and Jules. They immediately embraced each other with a loud sigh of relief. Jules wrapped his arms around Ahna's waist, pressing his dear friend close to him.

He turned to Farooq. "Rooqie, my man!" he exclaimed as he hopped multiple times. "Meet our friends!"

The blond shrike pointed at all the ailunas around them, who looked curiously at the newcomers. Ahna cast an intrigued glance at them, endeared by the adorable little creatures that populated the hills.

"They are ailunas," Clarice said. "They live in these burrows."

Luthan stared cautiously at the creatures. He checked if none would bite into Ahna's boots as she walked among them. They were very peaceful, and the blue elf's smile of admiration made him relax his stance.

"How do they live so calmly in this dangerous forest?" Ahna asked.

Jules shrugged. "Well, we haven't encountered more lycaonites so far, only bizarre flying plants..."

"Flying plants?" Farooq raised an eyebrow.

The shrike nodded furtively. "They went like...swoosh..." He mimicked the movements of the strange projectile flower that had shot like an arrow passed him.

Ahna looked to the horizon, below the valley and further to the east. A strange feeling began to manifest at the bottom of her stomach. She could not see clearly among the thick foliage, but the forest seemed to become darker the further she looked. The trees morphed far in the distance. The barks were no longer of this smooth purplish surface, but they clawed and spiked like stems with thorns shaped into eldritch visages. This sight brought a certain kind of chill down her spine. Where they stood, the light of the sunset had changed into the indigo hue of dusk. The longer they stayed, the darker the night became.

Clarice sauntered to Ahna, whose eyes still laid on the dark corners of the Eidolon.

"I think we'll only be in darkness from now on," she said.

Ahna squinted a little, as though to see better. "The darker the Eidolon becomes..."

"The more dangerous it gets," the young sorceress completed the elf's words.

The two turned to the men, who sat on a few rocks and began

to build a fire. A curious ailuna tom came to stand beside Farooq. It seemed attracted by the young apprentice's wavy hair. Farooq crouched to come closer to the small creature, and with its soft paw, it touched the tip of his nose.

"I think it likes you!" Jules noted with a smirk.

Farooq chuckled and touched the ailuna's nose in turn. Its three pupils followed the young man's finger until it crossed its eyes. Farooq let out a loud laugh. Another two ailunas came to sit with them by the fire and meowed at the small bush of flames.

"Nothing seems to scare them!" Ahna exclaimed in a light voice.

"Well, Jules's sword did," Clarice jocularly retorted.

Jules shrugged to express his innocence. He had not attacked it on purpose!

As they gathered around the fire, more of these little creatures came to sit beside them. Some rested on all fours, others rose to two paws and observed the band of strangers.

The night fell fast, and new sounds made their way to Ahna's ears. It sounded like chirps of nightingales or deep hoots of eagle-owls. Other, unidentified screeches, hid among the forest trees. When she turned her head to Jules, she saw him poke at the fire with a short purplish stick. He stared into the flames with wistful eyes, but he smiled as though he wished to hide something. Ahna sat close to him.

"Is there...something on your mind?" she asked.

Jules chuckled awkwardly. "I already miss the light of the sun," he murmured. He looked distantly at the fire. "Who knows what's out there..."

He stayed silent for a moment, observing the cracking flickers in front of him. In the corner of his eye, he noticed Luthan's gaze in his direction, but it did not rest on him.

"I see how he looks at you when he thinks you're not looking," Jules said to his dear friend who stared at the fire with him.

"I see how your eyes change when you think I'm not looking," she retorted, almost implying Jules hid a secret.

The shrike exhaled deeply. Ahna was right.

"Will you tell me why you decided to come on this mission?" the elf asked.

Jules did not reply and simply kept poking at the flames.

Ahna continued, "Did you hope to find something here?"

Jules motioned a no, but his eyes said it all. Something in his silver gaze revealed the emotions he dared not face. Perhaps they were the same emotions that gave him his nightmares, still to this day.

"What's going on?" Clarice's voice pulled the rest out of their thoughts. She looked left and right to the ailunas, who had all of a sudden become agitated. They curled up against each other. Their eyes were wide open, and they searched in all directions.

Ahna's ears flickered. "Ready your weapons."

They heard a loud roar from above the hill, followed by the drums of a stampede. Their heads turned to the source of the beat: two massive lycaonites were charging them at full speed. All ailunas sought cover and raced to their burrows.

"Clarice, hand me your staff!" Ahna shouted. The young sorceress heeded the order. "Stand back!"

Ahna clenched the wood of the silver staff. From the tip of the moonstone, a loud lightning bolt burst into the air and shattered against one of the lycaonite's hide. The beast caught its heels in its own claws and rolled to the ground. The other kept on charging. The tremor made the ailunas around them quiver in fear. Some expressed their distress with faint, trembling yowls. Jules brandished his shortsword and saw his blade catch fire again. He checked Luthan, whose eyes burned with a familiar redness. The lycaonite was about to launch itself into the air when, suddenly, another large creature emerged from the darkness and tackled the enraged wolf.

What in the Heavens was that? To the group of travelers, it

looked like a sumptuous white wave had surged from the trees and hit the lycaonite straight into its flank. The creature, much larger than the lycaonites, stood on four legs. Its three foxlike tails drew waves into the air. It faced the lycaonites with a fierce glare.

The band could now see the white creature clearly. Its enormous ears extended to the side of its head, and silver stripes adorned its soft back white as snow. Its muzzle resembled a cat's face. It had long, thin legs, and razor-sharp claws complemented its massive paws. They could not see its eyes, but they could definitely see the gigantic antlers that rested on its head, made of the same bark as the odd-looking trees. The creature howled a lion's roar at the lycaonites, who quickly hasted away from the burrows. They raced uphill, fearful of the legendary tiger that had come to the ailunas' rescue.

The white feline turned to the travelers. Its angered yellow eyes dimmed, and they could see the silver drawing of a moon beneath its antlers, the same crescent as on foreheads of ailunas. It relaxed its stance and walked graciously to Jules, who still held his sword high.

"Tell your friend to lower his sword," Clarice suddenly heard a soft voice sing to her in her mind.

Alarmed, her eyes snapped wide open, and she looked around her, searching for the source of the words. Farooq and Jules asked her what was going on, she did not reply.

"Tell your friend to lower his sword."

Clarice lay a hand on Jules's shoulder and made him put his flaming sword down. The creature sauntered to her and came to sit in front of the young sorceress.

The melodious voice, like the distant echo of a siren, chanted again between Clarice's ears. *"What brings you to our dwelling?"*

Her lips trembled. She did not know how to respond. "What are you?" she stuttered her question.

The four others looked at her, puzzled by the scene.

The white creature came closer. *"I am the Pride Sylvan. I guard the forest, and I protect my clowder."*

The creature's face did not move. It did not make any sound except for a low, humming noise that came from its throat, like a soft and gentle purr.

"What's happening, Clarice?" Jules asked.

The sorceress turned to him with mouth agape. "Don't you hear it?"

"Only you can hear me."

Clarice looked at her companions. "It is...speaking to me. It calls itself the *Pride Sylvan*. I think it protects the ailunas."

She swiftly scrutinized her mother's journal, looking for a clue as to what this animal was. Nothing.

"I protect my clowder."

"Tell it we're no danger," Ahna rushed.

Clarice was about to speak when the voice cut through her attempted words. *"I know you are not."*

"It can understand you," Clarice said, still looking at the Pride Sylvan.

Jules cleared his throat. "We come in peace!" he said as he bowed to the creature. "We can leave if you wish..."

"What brings you to our dwelling?" The creature interrupted Jules's voice in Clarice's head. It repeated its original question to her.

"It wants to know what we're doing here," Clarice whispered.

Luthan decided to take a step forward. "We are looking for something, further away from here."

"What brings you to our dwelling?" the creature asked again. It looked expectantly at Clarice.

She then understood what the creature wanted to know. It was just asking for their intentions, here, at the burrows. "We are just making camp here. We will be gone after we get some rest," she promised.

The Pride Sylvan folded its eyelids once. It turned to face

Ahna.

"One of you carries a power I have not seen in many, many skies."

It approached her. The elf was not sure what to expect, so she took a step back.

"I think it's talking about your bow, Ahna," Clarice informed her.

"What does it know about it?" the elf inquired, curious of what the creature knew of the Arc of Light.

Clarice wanted to repeat Ahna's question, but the Pride Sylvan's voice stopped her. *"Those who came before had the same power you wield, blue elf."*

The young sorceress divulged the creature's words to Ahna. The elf opened her mouth in surprise. This creature, this white and gracious animal, it knew the Ancients. She wanted to ask a thousand questions. She wanted to know what it knew.

"What do you know of them?" she dared to ask.

"They used to come here every now and then. Until they didn't anymore."

Clarice tilted her head to Ahna. "I think this creature had direct contact with the Ancients," she whispered.

Ahna whispered back. "This is the opportunity of a lifetime. The opportunity to learn about the one thing that has eluded us the most." She cleared her throat. "What did they look like?" she asked.

"Much like you. Some were tall, some shorter. They came to me and my clowder long before the forest moved."

"It says they looked like us," Clarice conceded.

Luthan took a step forward to speak. "Are we close to the Far Side?" he asked the creature.

The Pride Sylvan opened its eyes wide and tilted its head, as though Luthan had asked a confusing question.

"It doesn't know what you mean," Clarice informed the tall elf. She turned to the creature. "How far is the...darkness?" she asked.

"Nobody goes to the darkness."

"I mean..." she attempted to find the right words. "There is something we lost there, something very important to us."

"Nobody goes to the darkness."

"It belonged to..." Clarice hesitated. "To those who came before. They left something behind."

"If something was left behind, it has been eaten already."

Clarice did not quite get what the Pride Sylvan had implied. She raised an eyebrow and took a step toward the creature. "Eaten?"

The Pride Sylvan straightened its back. It looked to the travelers before rising to its four paws. Its three tails swirled around, and the white creature began to stroll away.

"Wait!" Clarice called. The creature curved its neck and looked at her, but she had nothing to say.

"Be wary out there, adventurers. The shadows always lurk in the corner of your eye."

It slipped through the tall silver grass. Ahna looked confused at Clarice, who shrugged to express her own uncertainty. The elf wanted to know more about what conversation had transpired in Clarice's mind.

"I am clueless, Meriel," the young sorceress confessed. "Something it said... The Far Side seemed to scare it."

Luthan came between the two. "We should make camp here," he declared. "We need to find something to eat."

Jules suddenly raised a hand in the air. "Well, I have an idea for that!" He smiled proudly, and the rest looked at him with expectant eyes. "We go fish."

The blond shrike pointed at the river below the hill. He motioned for Farooq to follow him down.

"I've never fished," the young apprentice admitted.

Jules dismissed him with a soft motion of the hand. "It's fine, I'll teach you."

The two disappeared beneath the silver grass. Ahna remained

here, with Luthan and Clarice, pondering on their encounter with the Pride Sylvan.

"The creature knew the Ancients," Ahna pressed. "There is so much we can learn from it." Ahna's curiosity had completely overwhelmed her. She wanted to run after this creature. Perhaps it had the answers she had been looking for. Perhaps it knew where the Ancients had gone.

Luthan raised a hand at the emptiness, where the creature had stood. "It's gone," he sternly said.

Ahna rolled her eyes. Luthan was right, the creature was gone. "I hope we get a chance to speak to it again."

The tall elf drew a smile. He contemplated Ahna's purple eyes that shimmered with the flickers of curiosity. He wanted to come close to her, to tell her how pretty she was when she looked that way, but he would not give into this urge, not again. Their kiss, last night, had been too intense. Too much. Hence, he went to tend to the fire instead. He needed to distance himself not to kiss her again.

AHNA WAS NOT sure what she was reading anymore. She still scried the thin brown book for answers. She sat by the fire on a barkless log, between Clarice and Luthan, while Jules and Farooq went down the hill to catch some fish in the river. If there were even any fish. What would lunar fish even taste like?

She stood, losing patience. She had to see this for herself. She needed to release the Arc to its full potential. Ahna clenched the bow's grip and closed her eyes, focusing on the energy she felt spread through the Item of Power and into her body. She had realized something as she had read *On the Schillers of the Arc*. She need not feel the urge to kill to activate the shimmer, just the simple will to fight would do. Perhaps not even the will to fight, but the intention to use the Arc of Light was exactly what she needed to spur. The glyphs danced from the Cursed Bow to her arm and latched onto her skin. The bow disappeared into the night, but nothing else happened. She felt the power. That, she certainly did. But she wanted to understand the meaning of ascension and chimaera and soul conduit and all! She tried to feel more, to activate *something*. Multiple times—nothing worked.

The elf sat back for a moment, thinking with long exhales. She was an archmage, and she knew everything about focus and concentration. Yet this power eluded her.

"Perhaps you need to do like our young apprentice," Luthan's voice shook her back to Luna.

Startled, Ahna veered to him. He had been observing her for quite a while. When their eyes met, she did her best not to think of their kiss from the previous night. He kept his gaze on her, which made the task even more difficult. The more he looked, the more she longed to kiss him again. It was an irresistible power he had over her.

"Think of a beautiful memory," he said again.

Ahna blushed. *A beautiful memory.* These words from his mouth could only bring her to one thing: their memory, together, of a long time ago. A time long gone. She closed her eyes.

It's just a blue winter moth. She heard Luthan's voice in her mind. She felt his touch, his lips locked with hers, and his fingers' soft caress along the arch of her back.

But nothing happened.

She fixed her thoughts with all she had, focusing on that one kiss. That one kiss. Yes! The blue winter moth. Blue…cerulean blue wings.

Cerulean eyes…

His eyes. Cedric Rover's eyes. His voice and his laugh. His touch.

And then, out of the blue, Ahna heard Luthan's voice of excitement and appraisal. She did not want to open her eyes. And she felt guilty for it. The thought of Cedric Rover—she was so caught in it that she had not noticed how the paintings on her arm glowed softly in the night. It was Luthan who flicked his head toward them to make her look.

Ahna gasped in surprise. "It worked!" she exclaimed, now focused on the light, letting the guilt rest.

Luthan chuckled sweetly. "You made it work. That doesn't surprise me."

Ahna's way with the arcane had always impressed him. It was only logical that she would make it work. She rose to her feet. The glyphs still shimmered. She felt calmer than she had ever been, something about this power seemed to soothe her soul. She could feel it radiate through her veins. Some of the book's words became clearer. The state of *chimaera*, becoming the Arc of Light itself and letting the weapon become her. Something about opening her soul to welcome the light. She could definitely feel it. This power was beyond anything she had sensed before. And it made her feel powerful, almost invincible.

But it scared her at the same time.

Ahna focused again. She had to let it go, for now. She let the glyphs gather into the palm of her hand, letting the Cursed Bow take form again.

"Let me in," Ahna heard. A sudden note between her pointy ears.

Who had said that? A distant, melodious voice, similar to a vox-ring's voice. It was in her mind. Definitely. It couldn't have been anywhere else. Ahna's head cocked left and right. Luthan still sat next to her, expectantly.

"Is there something wrong, *kyære?*" he asked, curious of Ahna's change in demeanor.

She carefully examined the bow, expecting to hear the voice again. Nothing. She waited a few seconds before she turned to Luthan. She had to come up with something to say.

"You know," Ahna began. "The old monks who studied the Items of Power, they were the same monks who wrote the scriptures of the dragon-gods."

Luthan scoffed with amusement. "Don't get started with religion, you know that's not my realm."

"I mean…" She hesitated. "This power feels so unreal." She swayed her eyes back to the Cursed Bow. "It almost feels divine." She pressed her lips together in contemplation of the glyphs as she held it. "Do you think the Ancients could have recreated the gods' power, somehow?"

Luthan rose to his feet in turn. "Meriel, did you ever wonder why the scriptures never mention the Ancients? We know they existed, so why wouldn't they be mentioned?"

"Well, everything from the time of the Ancients was lost. The old monks had to start over anew. Maybe they just didn't know what to say about them."

He pointed at the bow. "If they were able to create this, what else could they do?"

Ahna looked up to the sky. Her eyes were distant for a second, as though she searched for something far, far away. "I just wonder where they could be."

Who were the Ancients? And where had they gone? Terra's earliest mystery. The magi had begun the study of the Ancients, after the first traces of Items of Power were found by the old monks, centuries ago. However, not many results were obtained from their continuous research. Then there was the fact there was no trace whatsoever of the Ancients in the religious text describing the dragon-gods, the Scriptures of the Old, even though the monks had proof of their existence. This was one thing that did not make sense to a few magi. Why would the words of the Storms of Creation not mention an ancient civilization? Had the Ancients angered the monks? Then again, everything from the Ancients was lost. The monks would have had little to write about anyway. Still, some clerics, those who follow the scriptures to the letter, believed the Ancients had been cast away by the gods, for having crossed the line between the gods' domain and their own.

14

CASTAWAY

*J*ules and Farooq returned gloriously with their catch of the night. A big, lunar fish, or as Clarice's journal called it: a rose snapper. It looked exactly like a Terran snapper, though it was much larger and covered in sheening pink scales. Jules had shown Farooq how to prepare a fish down by the river. The young apprentice appeared disgusted at best, but he was hungry, so that motivated him enough to follow the blond shrike's instructions.

Jules had a fistful of silver grass in his hands. He had carefully picked the mintiest of blades. He turned to Clarice, just to check if he could use it as herbs for his fish.

"I think it will taste very good!" he pressed.

Ahna stepped between the two. "Since when can you cook?" she joked.

Jules gave her a proud smile. "I was the best in the Resistance!"

Ahna shook her head as she laughed lightly. *No, he really was not.* But the fish he then prepared turned out to be very good. The band of five sat on stones at the center of the burrows, eating the Jules snapper, munching like they had not had dinner in days. Which was true. Moonberries and canes were not as nourishing as a delicious minty fish fixed to wooden sticks. Jules had actually made skewers! How thoughtful of the shrike to plan two well-garnished skewers per person.

Farooq took the floor between bites. "My grandfather always said, the best sauce in a meal is hunger!"

Ahna and Luthan chuckled simultaneously, which reminded Farooq that both the elves had known his grandfather. He wondered for a moment what they remembered of him, and if Mohindra was as stubborn in his younger days as the young man was. And if the old wizard had been as odd as he was today.

Meanwhile, Luthan still heard Ahna's laugh in his mind. Being so close to her had become unbearable. He had to get away fast, or he would take her in his arms again. He would kiss her, would lead her somewhere they would be alone. He would— stop. Luthan rose to his feet. He wiped his hands on a larger leaf and was about to head down the hill when Ahna's voice stopped him.

"Where are you going?" she asked him.

He walked down without turning back. "I'm going to make myself clean at the river," he announced. Cold water in his face would do.

"Oh!" Jules raised his hand and talked as he ate. "The hot springs are down the river! You should see them, it's wonderful."

But Luthan had already disappeared below the slope.

Clarice, on the other hand, turned to Jules with eager eyes. "You said hot springs?" she asked, highly interested.

Jules nodded ferociously. "Yes, there are many pools! They shine with this light...I've never seen anything like it!"

Ahna laughed, joyful at the idea of a highly needed bath. Finally, she felt like she could relax. "Then we should get going as soon as we finish dinner."

The four finished their meal, making jokes and telling campfire stories. A good way to cope with the anxiety of what this forest still had to bring. They were eager to finish their fish and sink into the hot springs. Once they were done eating, they immediately stood and headed downhill toward the river.

THE RIVER RAN down the valley and ended in a series of small ponds that shimmered in the night. There was steam waving above the water, which radiated with a peculiar heat that gave it a blue glow. Scattered around these pools was the usual silver grass, but also tall canes with buds that opened in large purple blooms as the four walked past them. How strange, these plants bloomed in their presence and closed once they were away. Clarice and Farooq stopped for a moment to take a look at these interesting plants.

Ahna was too distracted by the glowing vapor above the ponds. "This is absolutely marvelous!" she exclaimed.

Then they heard a loud splash.

Jules had long taken his black leathers off and dived deep into one of the ponds. He sank underneath the water, passing his hands furiously in his blond mane. Not even a minute later, Farooq had joined him. They motioned for Clarice and Ahna to follow.

Clarice immediately rid herself of all her clothes. She had no care if the two men saw her naked. Farooq, of course, had instantly looked away. The amused Jules covered his eyes with his hand.

Ahna, on the other hand, refused to take off her now sleeve-less shirt. She was absolutely not going to take it off. Jules looked at her with curiosity in his eyes, probably because of the fact that she awkwardly stood by the pond without her breeches. Clarice had little trouble exposing herself as she had just done, but Ahna looked very concerned all of a sudden. Sure, Ahna was a bit odd sometimes, but nervous and shy were not the words he would ever use to describe her. No one else noticed, though, so Jules motioned for her to join him next to him. The elf complied and slipped into the hot spring, with her shirt floating around her like an engorged water lily. She reclined against the pond's wall and let her muscles finally relax from the tension of their travels and dangerous encounters.

"This feels so great," Clarice exhaled her words. "We can finally get ourselves clean."

Jules's nose sniffed at Ahna. "I can still smell you!" he exclaimed with a laugh.

Ahna slammed her hand against the water in Jules's direction, causing a warm wave to hit him in the face. The blond shrike kept on laughing. In the glow, they could distinguish each other's faces, but not much else beyond the walls of the pond.

As Jules observed the people around him, his gaze landed on Ahna. He had seen her fiddling with the Cursed Bow earlier, and he needed to ask her questions about it. His curiosity just had to take over.

"So, I saw you were busy with the Cursed Bow," he said with slight surprise.

Ahna gave him a nod. "I found out that the Cursed Bow wasn't so cursed after all." She took a deep breath, ready to explain. "Its true form is the Arc of Light. Iedrias's book mentions something about letting one's soul become the weapon."

Ahna chose not to mention the voice she had heard. She still had to figure it out for herself first before disclosing anything about it.

Jules gasped. "Can you merge with the weapon somehow?"

"The weapon can merge with me," the elf replied. "Though I don't think this is its final form just yet."

Farooq raised his hands, as though he wanted to ask a question. Ahna smiled and gave him the floor.

"The glyphs on the bow are not from our tongue," he said.

Ahna quickly answered. "They are in the Ancients' language."

Farooq rounded his eyes. "Who were the Ancients, and why does everyone keep talking about them?"

Ahna reclined in the water and let out a long sigh. "That's a story for another time," she said. She would need weeks to tell it! The idea of it just made her feel extremely tired. At this moment, she realized how exhausted she was. "We should get back soon. The Far Side is near, and we need to get some sleep!"

Clarice cleared her throat. She held the black booklet that had magically appeared in her hands above the water. "According to my mother's journal, there's a path they've dug over there"—she pointed down the series of ponds—"that leads to what she calls *the Shadows.*"

"That must be the darkness," Ahna inferred.

Clarice turned around and pushed herself up, out of the pond, with her palms on the ground. The rest followed quickly and dived back into their clothes. Ahna's hair and shirt were still soaking wet.

Jules giggled softly and smirked. "You're going to have to take your shirt off if you want it to dry," he declared as he stepped out of the water.

Ahna smirked back. "Wouldn't you like that, young shrike," she jocularly said. But no, she would not take it off. There was no way she would take it off.

Jules laughed and shook his head. Whatever Ahna's reasons were, they were probably good. Once they were all clothed and ready to head back, they gathered the last of their belongings and walked up toward the burrows.

THE FOUR OF them sat silently by the cracking fire. Ailunas had returned to the surface, and their curiosity brought them near the strangers again. Jules was already dozing off. Some kittens had curled up against his warm body. The softness of their fur appeased the blond shrike's dreams. Beside him, one of these large mushrooms gave light.

Clarice tended to the flames, while Ahna and Farooq sat

together on a large log. Luthan, on the other hand, had not yet returned.

"Here," Ahna showed the young apprentice a small sprout in the soil. "If you concentrate like you did last time with Luthan, you might be able to feel its growth."

Farooq did not hesitate once. He looked at the sprout, a thin stem with the mauve leaves, and focused his mind. The memories of his grandfather's stew passed behind his eyes. His heart slowed down, and his breathing stopped for a few seconds. He could hear it! He could not describe, at all, what sensation he exactly felt, but it was an intense wave of courage. As though the sprout gave it its everything to grow.

Farooq's brown eyes glowed green.

"What do you see?" Ahna asked.

The young apprentice fell to his knees by the sprout. He subconsciously planted his hands in the soil, no longer in control, he let his instinct guide him. He felt everything. The flora of Luna. He grasped it all.

"I can..." he stuttered. "There's so much."

He heard the movements of roots beneath the ground. The spur of growth of millions of sprouts like this one scattered around the Eidolon Forest. He felt their fears, their willpower, their emotions. All connected. He had no idea what to make of this. He began to hear the whispers of flowers, indistinguishable mutters he did not understand just yet. His eyes glowed brighter.

Ahna laid a hand on his shoulder, which brought him back to where he kneeled. He turned his head to her, and his eyes dimmed.

"You have great potential, Farooq, but be careful," she warned. "A geomancer's connection with nature can be overwhelming at times."

Farooq went to sit back on the log. "I want to learn everything!" he exclaimed.

Ahna smiled an archmage's smile, proud of her student. "You

will, once we go back to Terra, you will join the Academy of Bravoure."

Farooq's eyes searched their surroundings and landed on the campfire, where Clarice rested. He looked at the beautiful young sorceress and thought of the many other magi still here, in Skyshrine.

"I hope many will come back with us," he distantly said.

Ahna's body stiffened. She wished for the same, but the idea of bringing the magi back brought a pinch to her stomach. Would Luthan come back with them? She felt it again, the pain. It had dimmed, but she still felt it. She rose to her feet and began walking back to the fire.

"You should get some sleep," she advised the young man.

The elf went to sit by Clarice, by the flames, to finish drying her linen shirt. After a few minutes of silence, the young sorceress began to explore Ahna. Her father had mentioned the dokkalfar archmage of his past, never revealing too much about her. Clarice knew of her relationship with Archmage Hyehn, and she still wondered why he, at least, made it so difficult for himself. Clarice was a mysticist. After all, she could feel what they felt. Luthan still loved Ahna like he used to decades ago, there was no way in the stars he could deny that. Ahna, on the other hand, there was something about her that eluded Clarice. A complexity in her feelings that made the elf's so difficult to read. Clarice could have sworn Ahna was holding back. But why, was the question that remained.

Clarice pondered, for a moment, on elven love. Elves, who lived longer than six human lifetimes, felt emotions in ways humans could not. She turned to Jules, who slept silently by the glowing mushroom. She had to admit that she had feelings for the mysterious blond shrike. Feelings he could never return. And that made her sad.

Clarice wanted to stop thinking about all this, so she turned to the elf and spoke. "My mother never mentioned the Pride

Sylvan, but it was old. I could feel it. I think it came from a time before the Ancients..."

Ahna searched for an answer. "It protects the ailunas. There's something endearing to it," she retorted with a smile.

Clarice chuckled, but her gaze darkened again. "We are very close to the Far Side." She turned her gaze to the trees far off into the night. "This adventure is far from over."

Ahna gave her a nod. As she stared into the flames, she thought of the idea of going home. She knew Clarice and her father would join, but how many more? And what about Luthan? Images of their latest kiss raced through her mind. Again. All Ahna could think about was Luthan. The crook of his chest, the warmth of his arms, it all felt like home. Luthan had a duty. He had built a new life and needed to abide by it. He had a son! He had someone new. But screw this. Ahna wanted to be with him, to feel comfort for a brief moment. Even if this moment would end tomorrow.

Ahna rose to her feet. Her head was spinning like Terra on its axis. She needed her husband, right now, his touch, more than anything else. She longed to be close to him, no matter the circumstances. She needed his embrace, for just a moment of solace.

She needed to feel safe.

She left Clarice by the fire and headed toward the river.

STARS ILLUMINATED the sky with a thousand sparkles. Far into the night, Ahna saw the shimmers of faraway diamonds. *Tears of the gods, souls of the dead*, she thought. Underneath a large tree with raining opalescent leaves, she spotted the tall elf. His back faced her, but she could see him by the stream. He washed his face in the clear water. He had taken off the cuirass of his hardened robe, only his linen breeches and a thin shirt remained. Ahna observed him, unseen, as he unbuttoned his shirt and drenched his bare chest with the cold of the river. He eventually rose to his feet and noticed her. His blond hair by his chest was wet and stuck to his skin.

"Meriel, you startled me," Luthan said softly.

Ahna only looked at him, at the drops of water that ran along his chest. She came closer to him, and when she was within hand's reach, he straightened his posture and took a deep breath.

"I want to show you something," he whispered to the blue elf.

This caught her by surprise. She let out a small squeal and her eyes grew wide in an awkward expression. She had been just about to kiss him and had not expected him to speak. What was she even doing here? Luthan took a step back and, against all Ahna could have expected would happen next, he clapped loudly in his hand.

But then, it was simply wonderful.

A thousand little blue lights appeared around them, all scattered into the air underneath the large tree by the river. Ahna exclaimed her dazzlement with a single melodic laugh. She spun on her heels in wonder, laying her eyes on each shimmer. They surrounded them. She laughed again.

When she turned back to Luthan, he had a dear smile drawn upon his face. His eyes met her, and he contemplated them for a dear moment. The thousand glows reflected into Ahna's purple eyes, like the starry sky above Luna. The blue elf's laugh faded into an authentic smile.

"What's all this?" she wondered.

"I think it's the pollen from the tree," Luthan replied. "It reacts to sharp sounds."

Ahna laughed in amazement again. All this, all these little lights spurred a kind of warmth in her heart. She savored the moment as she contemplated the marvel that encircled them. Her eyes met Luthan's again. She could not contain herself, and she did not hesitate. She took a step forward, and her hands found their way behind his neck. She pulled him in and stole a gentle kiss from his soft lips. When she let him go, he kept on looking into her eyes. They remained close to each other for a short moment until the thousand little lights disappeared into the night.

In the sweet darkness, Ahna still caught the shimmers in her forgotten husband's emerald eyes. She delved deep into his gaze, which glowed with the kind of flare that made her lose all sense of reality. His breathing increased, and his heart began to race. She wanted to catch his lips again when she felt Luthan's curious hands in the arch of her back. He pulled her in, closer to his bare chest. Ahna touched his skin, first with her nose, then with her hesitant lips. She searched along his breast, kissing the soft surface. Bumps on his skin began to show as she ignited a spark deep in his heart.

With a low groan, Luthan caught her face in his hand. He could not hold it in anymore. The passion, the lust, it was all back. And it blazed like never before. He leaned in and made a move to take over her lips. She opened her mouth slightly, and his tongue intertwined with hers.

Ahna's hands slid beneath his open shirt and crept to his back. She pulled his chest closer to her. She let out a soft, repressed moan as Luthan ventured down her neck. She almost lost balance because of it. Immersed in this moment of rapture, she let Luthan's mouth explore the edge of her corset with his voracious lips and craving hands.

IT MUST HAVE LASTED AN ETERNITY, or maybe even longer, and her burning lips met his again. Only then did she realize he had rid her of her leather corset, her breeches, and her shirt was open.

Luthan straightened his body to look at her, his wife, the image of a blue muse that had conquered his dreams, all this time. Even if darkness reigned, he could still see the contours of her swollen lips and rosy cheeks. He made a move to kiss her again and slipped beneath her shirt once more. He wanted to release her from this piece of clothing, but she seemed to refuse. She wriggled as he tried to slide it off of her. Why did she not let him take it off? His hand slipped beneath her shirt despite her scuffle, and he made his way to the skin of her back.

That is when he felt it. Beneath his fingertips.

He felt the ridges of a hundred scars, sewn into her flesh. They were all over. The entire surface of her back had been torn. A cold, intense angst gripped Luthan by the throat. The angst for what had happened to his wife. That was what she had meant with torture. That was what had happened to her while he had left her and Bravoure behind.

How could you...

The blame crashed upon his shoulders. Luthan hated himself.

He stopped all he was doing. He retreated to catch her eyes.

She was crying. He had touched her where he should never have. He had touched her where no one should ever do so. Luthan made her turn around, and she let him. What could she do anyway? It was too late, he was about to see who she really had become. A victim of abuse. A body made of scar tissue. She squeezed her eyes closed, feeling ashamed, humiliated.

Luthan slid Ahna's shirt along her arms and body, delicately, careful not to upset her more. He examined the hundred scars. Seeing it for himself destroyed him a million times more than hearing about it. Her back, the smooth blanket of dawn-blue skin he remembered, had turned to this soiled, shredded tapestry.

It was ugly. The horrible result of what her brother had done to her.

Dread. Dread was all Luthan felt as he looked upon the part of his wife's past she had so desperately strived to forget. The past she wanted so desperately to scratch out of her memory. He brushed his finger between the scars, on the bit of blue skin that still remained. He could have fallen to his knees right there and begged her for forgiveness. He felt so guilty. He had left her there, at the hands of her brother. He needed to hold her, right now. He needed to make her feel safe. He needed to show her he would never leave again. He made her face him and pressed her close.

Luthan sank to the floor of silver grass and pulled her with him. She landed on his chest, and this time, she crawled up to take his burning lips. She wanted to forget what had just happened. What Luthan had just seen. She needed to. And she needed that bit of comfort that she more than deserved. She had cried enough, had suffered enough. She looked at him, her eyes demanded more.

"Make love to me, Luthan," she whispered.

That was it. That was all she needed to say. He seized her hips and adjusted her position on top of him. And in a soft movement of his pelvis, he—

"Wait," she murmured. Her palms pressed his abdomen as a signal to stop. "I haven't been with a man since..." She looked down, unable to finish her sentence.

Luthan gave her a brief kiss. "I'll be gentle," he promised.

He then made a slow move beneath her, carefully, and entered her. Ahna had to bite her tongue to repress a moan. The initial sensation, that alike love being released after decades of forced repression, erupted and turned into the utmost pleasure. Gods, it felt good. Gods, she had missed this. Her next moan, too loud, lit the whole place with a thousand blue lights again.

Luthan opened his eyes wide. He ran his fingers through her hair, pulling her face against his chest while he oscillated his pelvis in a slow, rhythmic pace. He just had to please her. His eyes glowed red. He needed her to feel it. He wanted to surrender to her, to honor her, to worship her.

The heat rose in her blood. She raised her body, arching her back and lifting her face to the starry sky. She let Luthan's fire take over. She felt a violent burst from between her thighs to her breasts, up until her fingertips and in all four corners of her mind.

Luthan now saw her clearly, in light of the stars and of the sparkling pollen. He saw his wife, the beautiful blue goddess that reached the pinnacle of her climax. It did not take a minute longer for him to succumb and join her in this burst of ecstasy.

Ahna fell back on her husband's chest. Her body writhed from the aftermath of this delicious blaze. She rested her head there, right in the crook, where everything was fine. Where she need not feel angry anymore. His fingers caressed the side of her face. His breathing had come to a calm and his heart synced with hers. They both remained silent, him contemplating the stars, her closing her eyes and letting his warmth take her to sleep.

15

POLITICS II

*T*he blue elf slept soundly, and her face rested on Luthan's chest. He could hear the soft whistles of her slowed breathing. He could feel its wind gently caress his bare skin in the night of the forest. He smelled her silver hair—the sweet scent he had missed in all his years away from her. It brought him back to the shards of his past, to the memory of their first kiss, and the first time she had said those three words that had changed his life.

When the blue elf had come to Bravoure, Luthan had discerned the hardship and pain she had endured in the Dwellunder, at the hands of an abusive father and brother. He had helped her go through it. He had given her the safety she had deserved. Luthan, a hundred Sols older than the blue elf, should have had the wisdom and patience of a high elf archmage, never to let his feelings guide his choices. But seeing Ahna this way, the weakness that made her so strong, had made him fall so hard for her. His family had most certainly not approved then, and they never had. Luthan Hyehn had become Fallvale's outcast, but none of that had ever mattered. His wife's serene and sincere love had been everything to him, the only truth, the only thing he had ever wanted to treasure forever.

Yet in the tremors of war, when the threat of extinction clutched the magi, Luthan had been fooled to leave her behind, to save his people from hers. The magi, the protectors of Bravoure, had chosen to protect themselves.

He let his hand slide behind her shoulder, touching with the tip of his fingers the crest of a scar.

Is this what I've done? He couldn't help but let his thoughts wander. He shut his eyes to hold in the tears.

He tightened his embrace but made sure she would not wake. In this moment, he did not think. He solely felt love, the reason his heart beat as it did. He felt in a way only elves could feel. Emotions of the soul, tailored and polished by centuries of walking the world.

The sound of the river slowly brought him back to reality. He could have lost himself in the smoothness of his wife's hair, but the sudden image of his son shocked his core. And the image of Ellyra, the woman he cherished but had never loved. The one that had helped lift him back to his feet after he had collapsed deeper than Luna's ground. The one that had always known Luthan's deep infatuation for his wife had never faded. He felt a slight ache in his heart. The guilt, for never having been able to return the good Ellyra had done him.

But that guilt, it was appeased by the love he felt for the woman he held in his arms. Did this make him evil? He, a powerful and gifted archmage, and an outcast at the same time. But he could not care less about that last part. He had never ever seen the choice of his past as failure. Yet that one, foolish deed, the one that had torn him away from his wife, that was the failure he should never have made. He hated himself for it. It had driven him to near insanity—the countless days and nights he had tried to get back. He had almost killed himself.

Luthan gazed into the night, following the appeasing movements of the stream with his eyes. He only thought of Ahna. Everything she had been to him. Everything she still was. Ahna, the dark elf that had shaken his world, the love of his almost eternal life. She must have been pursued by dreams because he heard a small sound escape her nostrils. He held tighter. He would hold her for the rest of her slumber, and he would never let go.

CLARICE STILL SAT QUIETLY by the fire, unable to sleep. She gazed upon the flames, fiddling with the vox-ring on her finger. The sorceress could still feel its magic, though it would not be long before the enchantment would fade.

Behind her, Jules exhaled a particularly long sigh, and she caught notice of some movements approaching her.

"Can't sleep?" she asked the shrike softly, who came to sit beside her.

He took a seat, legs crossed, by the dying flames. "I sleep like a baby," he whispered.

Clarice chuckled. She did not want to disclose it, but she knew why Jules had trouble sleeping. A mysticist knew these things.

"How long have you had nightmares for?" she asked the handsome blond shrike, who looked at her as though she had posed a forbidden question. "Come on, you can tell me." She used her mother-like voice to soothe Jules.

He laid his blue eyes on her. She thought she was about to melt, and she remembered he could never be hers. But that did not make her so sad anymore, after hours staring at the fire, setting her thoughts straight.

"I've fought a war, Clarice," he said with a slight smile. "Nightmares are part of it."

She looked to the distance through the flames, feeling what the blond shrike felt. She, who had grown up in a castle of glass, had never even thought of the idea of war. Safe, in this high tower she almost resented, while Bravoure crumbled under the oppression of the false king.

"I wish I could turn back time, Jules, I mean it," she assured. "I honestly wish the magi had never left Terra. Maybe we could have made a difference."

Jules took a deep breath and let it out as though the world depended on it. He did not want to get angry—that was not him.

He leaned back and looked into Clarice's eyes. "It's too late now, anyway," he said and sighed at the same time.

His eyes had darkened, and there was a dim note in his voice that still alarmed Clarice. She searched for a light in his gaze but could not find any shred of gleam.

"Your nightmares will stop one day," she told him. "Whatever haunts you, it will pass with time."

"Oh, that, I'm sure of. Time is my absolution," Jules said as he yawned.

One final flame cracked and disappeared into the night. The fire burned no more, and the two remained still in the darkness that surrounded the burrows. Clarice was unsure what to say. She felt his pain through his aura. She felt the insecurities of a renegade lieutenant without a captain, a man he had obviously held dear in his heart.

"Go to sleep, Clarice," Jules's voice pulled her back. "I'll stand watch."

The young sorceress looked over her shoulder, toward the river. "I wonder where the two elves went," she said with a dim smirk.

Jules shrugged, emotionless. "I bet they had a lot to talk about." He did not know what Ahna was doing. He did not want to know. But he most certainly did not trust Luthan, and he did not like the idea of his friend losing herself to him.

Clarice stood and went to rest in the silver grass by the mushroom that gave light. Farooq still slept soundly, surrounded by small ailuna kittens that had curled up to him. Jules looked in the direction of the two, calming his heart that still paced fast from the monsters of his dreams.

What Clarice had just said, expressing the buried guilt she felt for the magi having abandoned the fight, it rang inside the walls of Jules's mind. Of course, he felt anger! He was not showing it now, since they had other things to worry about. He did his best to empathize and practice compassion like Mother Divine had taught the rebels to, but come on, he had the right to be angry. He did not want to blame Clarice nor her father, Iedrias, who had been so kind to him, but still. Jules was angry. And he could not imagine what Ahna was going through either. He just hoped she would not lose herself to the charms of the man who had...abandoned her.

He dared not admit it. He dared not face it. Jules's nightmares of the war were not all that crept in the darkness of his mind. There was something else. Something he could not explain, and something he could most certainly not tell Ahna. The fear that had gripped him when the terrifying shadow had been cast over the valley at the Battle of Orgna, two years ago. He, fallen on the battlefield, had seen the beast of war that screeched between his ears at night. The void dragon, the oozing darkness that had consumed his captain, Cedric Rover. Ahna never talked about it. She had not spoken of it since that day, the last day of the battle. It was who she was—never speaking of the things that hurt her the most. Jules knew it, that was why he had never pried. But his nightmares still pulled him down, and part of him blamed Ahna for it. A part he shut out and silenced every time it called to him.

In the night of the Eidolon Forest, Jules returned to his place of rest and went to silently lie on the grass. Before he closed his eyes, he took one last look at the sky, which seemed slightly different than on Terra. And speaking of his home, he searched for it in the infinite Domain of Stars but could see it nowhere, alas.

It was dark and damp in the Bravan streets after the rain. The paved road Luk Ma walked split in two, and he took a left. His tail swayed cautiously behind him, and his ears remained alert during his evening stroll. Was it not for the dim lantern he carried that allowed for his eyes to gorge with light, he would not be able to see in this alley to the tavern's square. For a moment, he remembered the last time he had roamed these quiet streets at night, from a time before the failed Uprising.

He saw them in the distance, his two friends, who waited for him by the stone wall in the back of the street.

"Deja-vu," Diego said as he shook Luk Ma's paw firmly.

The Ailuran tom chuckled a little. "Indeed. I thought night escapades were of the Oppression." He shook Lynn's hand as he spoke.

"What have you learned?" she asked, getting straight to the point of this secret meeting.

Luk Ma's shoulders relaxed, and he lowered his lantern. He took a deep breath, curved the tip of his muzzle, and his whiskers followed.

"Goshawk has plans to expand the city into multiple barracks. He wants an arsenal. He wants new weapons to be built."

Lynn let out a long sigh. "David's not happy with what the people are saying about him. Those who didn't vote for Goshawk believe the commander to be corrupt."

"David is going to quit, which is exactly what Goshawk wanted, all along," Diego said in a grave tone.

He knew what his dear commander and friend was going through. The talks of him being *dirty*. Those who opposed Goshawk blamed David to have had a hand in getting the man the many votes he had gained. Because Goshawk or perhaps one of his pawns had spread rumors about his appointment with David before the elections. How he had divulged his plan of making Bravoure's army the greatest of all. The rumors said David had used his influence to subdue his entire army to support the new Regent. It had all been an elaborate plan to force David out of the way.

"There's Kairen," Lynn said as she looked in the darkness.

The Taz swordswoman saw the red flickers in the night of her friend's hair as she emerged out of the alley lit with torches. Kairen made her way to the group of seeming dissidents who leaned against the tavern's stone wall. When she was in a whisper's reach, she laid her furious copper eyes on the three rebels.

"Well, they've done it," she said, stern and bitter. "People look at David like he's some kind of deceiver. They've discredited him. David is losing his confidence, and I fear"—she inhaled deeply, a lump in her throat—"that he'll give up."

Luk Ma brought his gentle paw to her shoulder. Lynn looked at her like she wanted her friend to know she would do everything to resolve this.

"What's it going to be?" Diego asked them, desperately hoping for a plan.

Lynn crossed her swordswoman arms, and she turned her face to her lover. "If David quits, another will be chosen to bear the title of General. None of ours, but one of Goshawk' own men.

"A banker with his own militia," Luk Ma snickered. "Whoever thought that was a good idea!"

"Sharr did," Kairen declared, her voice as somber as how she felt.

The four remained still at the red-haired woman's last, piercing words. The comparison drawn with the Dark Lord was a grim one, and they did not dare to think of Bravoure's fate in the hands of yet another threat. In the hands of Charles Goshawk. What could possibly become of the golden kingdom?

Lynn's voice abolished the dismal silence. "Fifty years we fought for our freedom," she said. "And this is what we get?"

Kairen simply stared at an invisible point. Diego shrugged and looked to Luk Ma, who seemed dazed by Lynn's last words. The Taz warrior was right, this is what they got, and they were most certainly apprehensive of what would come next.

The four rebels remained here, in the dark alley of the golden city, discussing on what mission they would lay out next. However, as much as they wished it to be otherwise, there was nothing they could do at this point. Goshawk had promised a new era greater than dreams could fathom. He had cast David aside, most probably to place his own men in command of the new Bravan army. What were to be his following steps? Something was definitely wrong. To what dark fate would Bravoure succumb?

"Some of my scouts have come to work close with Goshawk," Luk Ma emerged out of the silence. "But they're still faithful to me."

"Have them be our ears," Kairen said, and Luk Ma acknowledged.

Later that night, Kairen returned to her husband, who still sat at the wooden table once she came home. He had his face pressed against the heels of his hands. He had been crying, she could see it. David Falco, the bravest man she knew, had slowly begun to lose hope in himself. Kairen hugged him with all the love she could give and led him to their bed. He needed to sleep. They would meet with the rest tomorrow and see what could be done to save the kingdom from the danger that preyed within.

AT THE HEART of Bravoure's City of Gold was the tall edifice of the Congregation. A cathedral of stones and glass that would let the rays of Sol rain during the day, into the large nave where services were held. The tall spire at the back of the building surged into the night sky, like a holy beacon that let the moon drench it in light. The two towers that encompassed the sturdy wooden gate were the many clerics' quarters, and Mother Divine's chambers were at the top of the southern tower. At the square, there was the majestic circle of golden statues of the five Deities of Light. The Bravan Pantheon, with the God-king Varko facing the gates.

Thamias walked the halls of the Congregation at night. He did not like it much during the day—too busy. Too crowded with souls who were obviously afraid of him. Yet he was now Mother Divine's protégé, and she had insisted on teaching him her clerical ways. As Dragonborn, he was gifted with the divine, a special kind of energy that could almost resemble magic. Thamias had never learned to master this holy force, and Astea had begun to teach him.

She wanted him to feel at ease in the city that resented his kind. Most people kept it to themselves, but Thamias, despite being terrible at reading people, could feel the stares of fear and apprehension that rested on his back when he walked away. He did his best to understand them. After all, his own brother had tormented the kingdom for fifty years. But for fifty years, Thamias had endured nothing but pain.

There was no one in the nave. The flickers of candles on the altar of the transept caught Thamias' eyes. They reflected in his amber gaze like distant mirrors of gold. He approached them silently. The wooden floor creaked beneath his sandals, and his pale, salmon-colored alb followed with him. He had his long curly hair loose, but uncombed, which made him look like a silver mountain lion, he thought. He enjoyed that idea. Turning into a dragon was one thing, but a lion—that was mighty!

He walked along the long corridor that encircled the main hall of the Congregation's cathedral. He wanted to do one more round before heading back to his chambers, and take one last look at each painting, statue, or sculpted mosaic that decorated the inner walls. Most were representations of the good deeds of the Mother Divine and the ones before her. There was a depiction of the Red Cardinals, above the altar, past the candles. The five priests and priestesses who guided the Deities of Light's disciples.

During the elections, Mother Divine had wished for none of her Red Cardinals to endorse any party. It was not of the Congregation's responsibility to intertwine with politics. Yet, as Goshawk wanted the people's unconditional devotion, there were reports of foul play, even here, in the cathedral's halls. And more worrisome for the protégé were the rumors of the fate of the remaining dark elves in the city. His own fate—for Goshawk had to appease the people and promise them safety and security from the dokkalfar kin.

Thamias was anxious. He feared for what would happen to him, should his sister not return in time. And speaking of Meriel, she had been gone for too long already. He worried again. Thamias loved his sister like she was his everything. She had been with him all his life, protecting him when their brother seized every chance to inflict him pain, caring for him when Karlus, their cursed father, forced him to do horrible things he still hated himself for. He was frightened by the idea of losing her, perhaps his last hope at acceptance in Bravoure City. Highly regarded as she was, people respected her. They recognized her assistance in the city's revival. They acknowledged her terrific efforts to rebuild the Magi Academy of Bravoure. Yet the longer she stayed away, the more of these austere looks Thamias received. He was Mother Divine's protégé, but he was nonetheless the emblem of a failed prophecy, and his similarity with Xandor Kun Sharr could never be denied.

16

FAR SIDE OF THE MOON

*A*hna awoke from the touch of Luthan's lips lingering at the nape of her neck. It was still dark, and she realized she had spent this whole time in his arms. She straightened her body and glanced around, checking uphill on the rest of the band. She was light-headed, woozy, still inebriated from the night she had just spent. As Ahna looked to the hill, she felt Luthan nibble softly on her pointy ear. A sweet smile appeared on her face, and she giggled a little. She let out a soft moan before turning to him.

"If you don't stop, I'm going to climb on you again," she warned in a sly whisper.

"I want nothing more, *kyære*," he said, matching her tone. "But I'd prefer our next time to be in a proper bed."

His husky voice in her ear sent sweet shivers down her spine. But the shivers, as they crept to her back, slowly brought her back to reality. The warmth began to dissipate and gave place to a cold feeling of uncertainty. There she was, on the moon, torn between comfort and bitterness. The comfort of her husband's arms. The thorn of abandonment lodged deep beneath her skin. Torn between a lost love and the new life she had learned to live.

Ahna turned her face to him. "Our next time? Luthan, I'm not sure what we're even doing," she confessed.

Luthan chuckled. Two faint dimples appeared at the corners of his smile. "It's a bit late to say that," he said. Still swayed by the night they had just spent, he felt more certain than ever.

"I'm serious," she reinforced. Unlike Luthan, she was far from certain. She wanted Luthan to face her and tell her what this night had meant. "What's going to happen to us?"

The high elf looked away instead. It was now his turn to get pulled back to reality. As much as he wanted this moment to last forever, his life had changed. He had a duty. He had a son. "We find the Planar Mask," he said, stern again. The mission was his scapegoat.

Ahna shook her head. "And then what?"

He exhaled deeply and locked eyes with hers. "Then we go back to Terra."

This answer brought nothing useful to Ahna. What had just happened? They had spent a night of dreams. Two seconds ago, she could have made love to him again! Yet now, he was more distant than he had ever been, avoiding her questions. What did she want as an answer anyway? Did she want him back? Would she even want him back? Things could definitely not go back the way they had been. And his evasive behavior made her doubt he even wanted that. Ellyra, Tiberius—Luthan had a life here. But last night…

Last night had been so real.

They heard footsteps marching downhill. Ahna quickly rose to her feet. Her linen shirt was on the ground, her breeches were hiding somewhere, along with her boots. She immediately gathered her things, dived into garments and tied her hair in a knot. When she turned to Luthan, he was just finishing to strap his robe. He swept his long hair behind his shoulders and did not even lay eyes on her.

"Ah, that's where you're hiding!" Jules's voice echoed against the tree beneath which they had slept.

The sharp noise of the shrike's words immediately lit the pollen around them. Jules expressed his surprise and astonishment with a full note.

Clarice and Farooq followed behind him, dragging something behind them. Actually, that something was floating beside them in the river. It was some sort of raft.

"Look at what we've built while you two were snoozing!" Jules exclaimed, pointing over his shoulder at the raft.

"This will make the journey much shorter," Clarice added. "The river is calm enough for us to travel it into the Far Side."

Ahna was both startled and impressed. Apparently, these three had been busy with barkless logs and sturdy vines for the last couple of hours, and they were now ready to venture deeper into the Eidolon Forest. As Jules passed Ahna to board the raft and begin their journey again, he smirked and winked at her, knowing well what sorts of events had transpired here. Ahna followed him, mute, and boarded the raft in turn.

"You forgot your satchel by the burrows!" he remarked with a grin as he handed her the cloth bag. At least his sense of humor had not left him! He just hoped his friend was being careful. Careful not to get hurt again.

Ahna blushed. She wanted to hide her embarrassment, so she twirled on her heels and placed herself next to Farooq. She would let all this be, for now. They had more important things to do. They had a mission—she could focus on that instead of feeling lost.

LITTLE BY LITTLE, the forest grew darker. No more sunset hues from west of the burrows to the waterfall. No more twilight blue skies that reigned over the hot springs. Darkness. Solely pitch-black darkness. The group must have been traveling for a long time because the forest was as black as the sky, and there were no stars to be seen. The river stood as still as a blank sheet of linen. Yet what struck them the most was the total absence of sound. No more birds chirped, no more howls or yowls of distant creatures—only silence. The barkless trees coiled and twirled like large brambles that stretched above them with giant thorns. They could only see the shadows of said hedges that bordered the river.

A couple of yards further, the raft eventually collided with the ground. The river had ended. They had to start walking again.

"This place," Clarice began, carefully getting off the raft first, followed by the rest. "It gives me chills." She gave it her best to remain brave, but she took each next step with more hesitation than the previous one. "Remember what my mother's journal says," she said, to the group and maybe to herself. "Once you reach the Far Side, you begin to lose your mind."

She knocked her staff against the cold ground, twice, and the core of the annealed moonstone began to glow. This brought some sort of comfort to the band of five, as it gave them enough light to see into the forest. The radiance of her quarterstaff emitted a low hum, the same buzz that had rung to soothe the frightened ailunas.

As they had just begun picking up the pace, something moved in the corner of their eye, up ahead in the darkness. Far in the distance, beyond the reach of Clarice's light, Farooq saw something, a shadow, and it stared back at him.

He froze. An incomprehensible sense of fear clutched his spine.

"Farooq, what's wrong?" Clarice asked, feeling his distress.

The young apprentice only stuttered. He raised a trembling finger at the forest ahead. He swallowed to speak. "There's something there."

Clarice pointed her staff at the darkness. Nothing to be seen. She raised an eyebrow at Farooq.

"I swear it was there!" he assured.

Ahna also thought she had seen something. The trees by their side had thicker trunks, with hollow relief that looked like a screaming mouth. The branches formed arms that squirmed in fear. One of them had moved. She dashed to the side, bumping into Jules, who had to stop himself not to swing his sword at the elf.

"We need to keep our calm," Luthan urged, looking at the two. "Let's keep on moving."

The group of five walked further and plunged deep into the far east of the dark forest. The more steps they took, the thicker the trees became. They had flashbacks of their first encounter with the lycaonites, who also preferred the denser foliage. However, this place did not cry wolf. The darkness inspired something more bizarre than eight-eyed wolves with horns. Something more dangerous, yet more quiet, more...patient.

"This place begins to look like where we found ourselves, after we used the Planar Mask," Luthan declared. He continued to explore the darkness with careful eyes.

"How did you even activate it?" Ahna asked out of the blue. The question had popped in her mind. She realized she had not yet asked how in Hell the magi had activated this Item of Power she had researched herself.

"Are you really asking now, *kyære?*" This place did not seem like one to discuss arcane research, but because Ahna nodded, Luthan proceeded to explain, with as little words as possible. "Very well, we made a tear through the Fabric of Realms, with stellar fire."

Ahna gasped. "Of course! The Planar Mask drew energy directly from the tear." Of course, stellar fire. Luthan's fire. As an archmage in Pyromancy, his fire was definitely powerful enough to create a hole through the Fabric.

Luthan smiled as his wife had the fascinated eyes of the

hunger for knowledge. But his smile vanished as soon as the idea hit him, again, that he should worry about other things, for now.

A crack of a branch.

Jules abruptly turned to what he thought to be the source of the sound.

"Seriously, I have no time for this!" he barked, annoyed, and a little freaked out.

Clarice's light still lit the space ahead, but nothing had changed. It was still dark. The trees still seemed to scream and run statically for their lives. The ground beneath them had become ice cold.

Ahna spotted a yellow glimmer on the horizon. She stopped the group with her arm. There was not one yellow light, but two, which oscillated in the distance like a wobbly head. She held in her breath, alarmed by this strange sight.

"There's a creature over there," she said and pointed. "And it's looking at us."

As her arm reached before her, the two bright glimmers shot through the air straight at the group, racing through the absent wind. All of them had to duck one by one.

"Those white flowers again!" Jules exclaimed. He glanced over his shoulder to observe them head back into the woods behind them. He had no idea what they had been doing here, in the darkness so cold. "This doesn't seem like a place for them."

Ahna slowly shook her head. The lights she had seen were definitely different from two floating flowers. Or were they? They had looked like eyes, eyes of a creature that had been watching them. Or had they? She turned back. She still felt as though they were being watched. Her heart pounded in her chest like the beating of a rolling drum. Her flickering ears matched the cadence of the beats.

Luthan caught her arm by surprise. He had long noticed her distress. "Your ears, *kyære*," he remarked. "What do you think you saw?"

Ahna frowned and curved her lip in concern. "Something with yellow eyes." Her voice ended in the silence.

"We need to be careful," Clarice reinforced. She walked past Ahna and tilted her head to her. She began whispering. "Especially Jules, he's no magic-user."

The elf nodded. There was some truth to Clarice's words. Jules was no mage. He was at a distinct disadvantage, with a weakness to the illusions of the Far Side. He was much more susceptible to believing the lies of this dark and mysterious forest.

THE COLD GROUND liquified into lifeless mud. Their steps sunk slightly into the softened soil, and they felt as though they walked on molten rock. Clarice's light illuminated their surroundings at a body's length. Their pace was slow, careful, but frankly, they were a bit lost.

"How will we find this item if we cannot see further than ourselves?" Jules asked, concerned for the mission.

Luthan's staff knocked the ground in turn. A flame rose from the crystal and lit the trees further in front of them. But when the fire reached its highest, Ahna caught a glimpse of a monstrosity that stood above the staff. A horror. A shadow with claws. When the light touched it, it screeched loudly and disappeared.

Ahna screamed in fright.

The other four shrieked when they saw the creature vanish.

"What in Hell was that?" Jules shouted.

Farooq shouted with him.

Their eyes scried Ahna for an answer. The elf slowly regained her calm. She panted for a moment, attempting to piece together what she had seen.

"I'm not sure," she uttered with a lump in her throat.

Despite the unsettling thoughts that crept in their minds, they now had a better view of their surroundings, thanks to Luthan's flame. They moved further, alert, deeper into the soft ground and farther into the darkness.

When they finally began to relax, Jules heard another crack. He was not sure what had then taken him over, but he dashed away from the group, impulsively, and went after the source of the noise. The blond shrike frantically cut through the foliage, in the darkness, as he moved deeper among the trees. He had officially lost his sense of control, and he was obsessively swinging his sword.

Clarice immediately ran behind him. "Jules, stop!" she yelled. "You're going to get lost!"

The shrike did not reply, he had already vanished out of reach.

Jules jumped through the barkless woods, avoiding the few branches he could see until he reached what he believed to be the source of the sound. Luckily, Clarice was able to trace him and rejoined him soon after. She swept her staff in the air to scan their surroundings.

"There's nothing here!" the sorceress exclaimed, alarmed and out of breath.

Jules groaned softly. "Well, there's something here alright."

A flame appeared in the corner of his eye. The shrike immediately veered to it with a slash of his sword.

Luthan blocked the blade just in time.

He held his palm in the air, an invisible force prevented Jules from swinging his shortsword further. The high elf's eyes glowed with a dim, crimson light.

"Calm down!" Luthan roared, his voice distorted. Jules really needed to get himself straight. "It's just me."

Luthan let go of his arcane grasp on Jules's sword and the two relaxed their posture.

"What in Hell is going on?" Jules asked with a stern voice. He quickly bounced his head left to right. "Where are Ahna and Farooq?"

Luthan looked behind him. He could have sworn they had followed him. Clarice opened her eyes wide when the fear that the band was separated again gripped her throat. Jules let out a loud shout, and he planted his sword in the ground in frustration.

"Get your mind straight!" Luthan ordered the angered shrike.

But Jules did not respond. His heart stopped when he felt his sword pierce through something that was no ground. It was softer, more fragile, and most of all, wet. He motioned carefully for Clarice to light whatever his blade had struck. And so, she moved her staff, slowly, apprehensive of what she would see.

What in Hell?...

Luthan aimed his quarterstaff at Jules's victim and burned it to the ground with a feral howl of fire. Jules toppled backwards and landed on his back in the cold mud. Clarice attempted to keep everyone calm with the hums of her moonstone staff.

"What was that?" Jules yelled, stammering as he attempted to get back on his feet.

"It looked like a dead lycaonite," Clarice replied. "One that has been dead for days."

The creature's bones melted from Luthan's flare. The putrid stench was horrid. Jules felt this retching feeling clench his stomach together. He finally managed to stand, pulled out his sword, and made a disgusted face.

"We need to find Ahna and Farooq," he declared. That was the only thing he cared about right now.

The three traced their steps back until they reached familiar trees. But there was no Ahna or Farooq. Jules shouted again and quickly turned to Luthan.

"Why did you leave them behind?" he asked the tall elf, pointing an aggressive finger at him. He was so angry at Luthan. All this buried resentment of the past few days was about to lash out.

Luthan raised an eyebrow. He did not get why the shrike was

so furious. "Why did you race into the darkness like that?" he retorted with a low voice.

Jules wanted to step into the archmage's comfort zone, to punch him in the face, but Clarice dashed in between the two.

"Keep your calm," she directed. She then turned to Luthan. "Both of you."

Jules spun on his axis and called Ahna's name. He raised his voice even louder. Clarice wanted to shut him up, but Jules had now become uncontrollable.

"Jules!" They heard an echo through the forest. Ahna's voice. "Jules, where are you?"

The echo came from very near. Jules, Luthan, and Clarice rushed to its source. They only found a crooked tree with a hollow face. The echo came from inside the trunk.

"Jules! Jules! Jules!" it kept on calling, then it started laughing.

It repeated words in Ahna's voice over and over again.

The blond shrike was in complete shocked disbelief. When he turned around, Clarice was missing.

Only Luthan stood behind him.

"Where is Clarice?" Jules urged.

Luthan only now noticed as well that she was gone. They looked around, called her name like they had called Ahna's.

No response.

Jules raised his sword in the air, making compulsive movements in frustration. "She can't just be gone!"

Luthan brought his vox-ring closer to him. "*Meriel, Clarice, can you hear me?*" he urged with racing thoughts. He could hear the wind whistle as he waited for a response.

"Damn this place!" the tall elf shouted.

He searched the woods. He paced around in circles, checking each corner, growing more and more impatient. He worried about his companions. He feared what could possibly have happened to Ahna. He could not lose her. No, not again. Not after the night they had just spent. Not after being reunited with her. He had not even gotten the chance to tell her how much he still…felt for her.

He scanned his surroundings with the flame of his staff. Nothing.

Then they heard a distant laugh.

It sounded like a crazed soul choked on its own burst of laughter. Something grew out of the tree's hollow mouth, something like a dark shadow. They could not see what it was, but something most definitely moved. It swirled behind the shrike like an invisible silk veil in the wind.

Jules felt a cold hand on his shoulder.

He immediately swung his sword at whatever had touched him. Luthan turned his staff to the shadow, and they heard the same shriek they had heard just moments ago. Whatever creature it was, it had quickly run off into the darkness again.

"How many more of these will we see?" Jules asked, panicked.

"They seem to be afraid of the light," Luthan observed. "Stay close to my staff, and don't you run off again!"

"Speak for yourself," Jules snickered. Oh, his anger had just burst.

"Excuse me?"

"Running off—that's what magi do, right?" Jules no longer could control himself.

Luthan had no idea where this scorn had come from, but Jules stared at him with smoldering eyes. The tall elf veered to the shrike and pointed a warning finger.

"Have I offended you in some way, human?" Luthan asked sternly.

Jules scoffed. *Elven arrogance, much?* "No, not at all!" He shouted and flapped his arms around. "Maybe we wouldn't have had to suffer for fifty years had you not run off, Archmage."

Enough. Luthan was about to rebuke and put the shrike back in his place, when they heard a voice behind them.

A strident shriek followed. "You damned mortals and your hatred," the darkness rattled.

Jules turned to the voice with his shortsword, but the weapon vaporized into the air.

The darkness raised its pitch, chuckling and chortling at its own words. "What takes you here, shrike? Searching for something you don't even understand? She dragged you here, didn't she? The one that took your captain away!"

What? How... Who was speaking? Jules cast a fist at the shadows and fell face-first on the ground.

"Jules, keep your composure!" Luthan ordered, swinging his staff to illuminate the place.

When Jules raised his head, he was faced with something that startled him to cower back to his feet. He let out a loud scream of fright and needed a minute to regain his calm. Luthan checked what the blond shrike had seen, and his own eyes snapped wide open.

It was a corpse. The rotten human flesh and a broken skull with hollow eyes. The bottom of its jaw was missing, as though it had been eaten by whatever crept in this damned forest. The stench... Luthan swept the staff around the corpse.

Then it hit him. Its garments. The robe it was wearing. His heart stopped, and he almost choked on his breath.

"It's a mage," he stammered.

Jules panted in horror. "What the fuck..."

Luthan flicked his staff left and right, there were two more corpses. He saw their robes, the insignia on their right shoulder. The Magi Academy's symbol. Everything became clear. They had just found the dead bodies of three magi explorers, from Clarice's mother team. Luthan was in absolute shock. Clarice should not see this. Not ever.

A sudden, dreadful melody pulled him out of his stupor.

"Luthan, coward, traitor," a voice recited in an undertone. It began to sing in Luthan's own son's voice. *"Fifty years in hiding,*

Luthan lost his meaning. Running to save his life, Luthan abandoned his wife."

Luthan almost thought he had lost his mind. He heard his own son's cries.

"Bad, bad father," the voice repeated over and over again. But it turned to maniacal rasp. "You couldn't even stop yourself from fucking the scourge on the dirty floor! How will your son feel, Luthan? How will Fallvale feel? Oh wait, Fallvale cast you away—and for good reasons. The whore you love is an abomination."

Luthan roared with a thousand flames by knocking his staff on the mud. They heard a shriek again. Whatever creature that was, it had rushed away from the fire that began to consume the trees. The tall elf helped Jules stand, and they both ran away from the blaze in an arbitrary direction. The more they ran, the more observed they felt. A thousand eyes staring at them. Jules ended up dashing past Luthan and hitting something with full force.

Both bodies collided and were thrown opposite from each other. When Jules recovered his stance, he noticed a silver staff that lit the floor and the young sorceress sprawled out next to it.

"Clarice!" he exclaimed.

He came to check on her and gasped when he saw the state she was in. Her eyes were white. He tried to shake her back to her senses but to no avail.

"What is happening to her?" Jules asked Luthan in angst.

Luthan kept his calm. He knew what was going on. "She's in a mind prison," he explained. "I think she used that on herself as a protection from whatever these creatures are. The light of her staff kept her safe from their reach."

"We need to get her out!" Jules pressed, but Luthan shook his head.

"Only she can stop it."

Jules crouched beside Clarice with his back to the shadows. And that is when he felt it again. The grasp of an invisible claw that pierced through his shoulder. He jumped to his feet, holding the young sorceress' glowing staff in both his hands. He distinguished more of these shadows in the glow's penumbra. He instantly took a step back, closer to Luthan, and the two faced a dozen of these monsters.

Jules swung the quarterstaff. First at the shadow in front of him, then with full force at the others, that screeched away in exaggerated fear. The shrike now stood back to back with Luthan, whose eyes glowed red, and both staffs caught flame. With a loud battle cry, they both slashed through the air with all strength they had, cutting through the shadows with rapid blazing swings.

In this moment, Jules felt the intense power of the burning weapon he clenched. When the blond shrike caught a glimpse of a taller shadow about to strike Luthan, he made a circle with the quarterstaff so the moonstone would face the monster. Then, in an instinctive squeeze, he cast a cone of flames toward the beast. The shadow instantly vanished into the air in a ghastly shriek.

That was cool.

"First time using a magic weapon?" Luthan asked with a smile as he repelled the shadows away from him and Jules.

Jules nodded. It was definitely the first time. He wanted to use the staff's fire again when another of these monsters caught a violent grip of his shoulder. Jules felt his blood turn to ice.

But then, out of the darkness, he saw a bright light shoot through the forest and land on the cold ground with a hammering thunder. The shadow creatures were scattered around, shrieking for their lives, screaming with rattling voices that disappeared into the silence of the Far Side. Another beam of light emerged from the darkness and ripped the forest apart. Jules and Luthan had to press their ears close shut not to be deafened by the roar.

When they turned their heads, they saw Ahna, who brandished the Cursed Bow, which created a radiant aura of light around her and Farooq. One last monster moved in the dark and raced toward the blue elf, who raised her arm into the air, pulled a simple arrow from her quiver, and shot another ray of light, completely destroying whatever creature she faced.

A burst of relief overcame Luthan. "Meriel!" he exclaimed. She was alive.

Jules joined him, and they hurried to her, carrying Clarice with her arms on their shoulders. Once they reached her, Luthan immediately took his wife in his arms, not thinking, just immensely glad to see her again.

Ahna let him, at first, but then she carefully escaped his grasp. They had to leave this wretched place! She went to retrieve the sorceress' staff from Jules and pointed it where the shadows had stood, making sure it was gone for good.

"These are not normal creatures, I fear," she warned. She knew damned well what they were. She had figured it out just a few minutes ago.

"What do you mean?" Luthan asked.

"I have met them before."

She wanted to elaborate, but they suddenly heard the seeping sounds of moving liquid. From the fragments of the dispatched monsters, a new form was born. It twirled and whirled on itself like oozing flesh. Right beside them, they saw a body's shape appear in the darkness, and it stared them down, with a scowling grin from a child's nightmare. Then, it laughed with its shrill voice.

Ahna recognized the twisted laughter. It could not be, but she had to make sure. She had to make sure it was really him.

"Ahna!" Jules called to stop the elf.

The creature's skin hardened into the features of a ghost.

Ahna's heart finally stopped. It was him. He was back.

"Xandor…" she murmured.

The monster had turned into a man, but his eyes glowed dark, and his skin was grey. There were veins that crept from his chest to his jaw. Beneath his throat, his body was covered in the same black liquid that submerged the ground.

His husky voice clawed through the silence. "Have you never seen a ghost, dear sister?" the revenant asked.

The man simply looked at Ahna with a disconcerting glare. He had a vicious glow in his dead eyes. He looked exactly like Xandor, but his flesh was transformed, and it all felt so wrong.

"How long has it been?" he penetrated the silence deep.

Ahna's lips trembled, and Jules froze into place once he recognized the Dark Lord.

"You're not Xandor," the elf blurted.

The man, whoever he was, screeched with a peal of macabre laughter. "You dare not face me, Meriel?"

Ahna brandished the blazing Cursed Bow in the air. Startled she had been, but now, she was more determined than ever. The bow formed an arc of light that spread from her fist toward both the ground and the sky. She raised it, pulled an arrow from her quiver, stretched the string and shot a beam fast. It hit the revenant with full force. The creature disintegrated into a thousand shreds. The sound it made as it vanished was incomprehensible. For a piercing minute, it was all she could hear.

Ahna exhaled with relief once it was gone, and she turned to Luthan and Jules, who held an unconscious Clarice.

"I've seen these creatures before," she conceded. "Luthan, where are we exactly?"

The tall elf raised an eyebrow, unsure of where she was getting at. "The Far Side?"

Ahna shook her head. His answer was not right. "This is more than just the Far Side, and I think you know it."

However, Luthan did not. His eyes remained wide open and demanded an explanation. But before she could continue, Clarice snapped her eyes wide open and awoke. She gasped loudly, as though she had been in a bad dream.

"You found me!" she exclaimed as she jumped in Jules's arms.

The blond shrike awkwardly accepted her hug. He returned her glowing staff and looked to Ahna, also expectant of the arch-mage's explanation.

The blue elf took a deep breath, cautious of even speaking the name of...

"The Shadows," she said.

Luthan looked confused. "*The* Shadows?" He needed to make sure Ahna had meant the Shadows he was now thinking of.

Ahna gave him an ample nod. "I think we're near a breach of the Shadow Realm."

Luthan inhaled abruptly, and his eyes rolled back. He understood, and everything began to make sense. The illusions, the twisted laughter, the madness... But how did his wife know about this? She was a ritualist, after all, but the Shadow Realm? That was something unspoken. Like a secret. An abstruse mystery. Something magi did not linger on anymore. The magi in Bravoure, at least.

"How do you know the Shadows?" he asked. He had to ask. *The* Shadows had not been studied in centuries! Not since the Equilibrium Order, at least.

Ahna shrugged. She curled her lip up, perplexed. "Well, it's still practiced in the Dwellunder. It wasn't my favorite subject, but I still learned it. And I damned well remember. It's not really something you can forget."

This was one thing about Ritualism—she knew it was not appreciated by everybody. Especially Shadow Realm studies! But she shrugged it off, as she had always done.

"The darkness is what they're made of," Ahna continued. She looked off into the distance where the creature had stood. "We need to find the Planar Mask fast, and we need to get out of this place."

17

INTO THE SHADOW REALM

*A*hna's grip on the Cursed Bow now radiated through the pitch-black forest. She no longer needed to brandish it, no longer needed the will to wield it. Despite what she had experienced before, she felt no pain. She was not sure what more to expect from the weapon, but at least now, they had three sources of light. Eventually, they were able to find the way again that led deeper into the dark forest. Jules walked by Ahna, still and silent. He had significantly calmed down, for now. Luthan tailed the group as he was the best fit to protect Clarice and Farooq from any more danger. In these woods, there was only silence. Not even their steps in the cold mud made a sound.

"You could have told me he was your brother," Jules whispered to Ahna out of the silence. He had made an educated guess before. He had heard Mohindra mention something about it. Hearing the Shadow's words had only confirmed it. But he would not let that matter. He loved Ahna for who she was, not for who she was related to. "It wouldn't have changed how I see you."

Ahna swallowed something in her throat. Jules knew the Dark Lord to be her brother. Of course, he knew, as perspicacious as he was. But it hurt her to hear it in his voice. "I'm sorry," she uttered.

"I think it's in your habit to silence the things that really hurt you," he said, ignoring her apology.

"My brother was responsible for the fall of an entire kingdom," Ahna continued nevertheless. "I just wish I had done something earlier."

"Nonsense!" Jules exclaimed. "Lord Sharr was a tyrant. You couldn't have done more than you already have. Your little brother Sonny may be the Savior, but you are our guardian." He forced a smile to show the love for his friend. "Because that's who you are—the Guardian of Bravoure."

Ahna smiled back. She felt tears glaze her eyes. Jules's words had hit her at her core. "That's a good title," she wistfully said. She did not know if she deserved it, but it sounded glorious.

In the silence of the Far Side, Luthan abruptly halted his march. His posture ordered the rest to remain silent, even with no words.

"What's wrong?" Ahna queried.

"This whole place is wrong," Luthan declared. He recognized the musky scent that lurked in the air. "We've passed here before. I smell fire."

The odor of burned wood. Luthan's unleashed fire when they had been attacked by the shadows. It made them realize that they had walked here already, not even a few hours ago.

"How can we be walking in circles?" Clarice asked with a worried note.

Farooq looked left and right at Ahna or Luthan, in search of an explanation.

As a cackle through the night, they heard the crazed laughter again.

Ahna immediately raised her bow, ready to shoot another beam arrow. Luthan seized his quarterstaff in his two hands, and the flames burned brighter. Jules had lost his shortsword, so he pulled Farooq's baton out of the young man's hand. The three formed a circle around Clarice and Farooq, to protect them. Clarice's staff hummed again with the soul-soothing vibration. They really could not afford to lose their heads right now.

"Stay close to me," the young sorceress said. "The staff will keep your mind still."

"Let's not run off again, shall we?" Luthan requested of Jules with an almost passive-aggressive tone.

Jules scoffed at the tall elf's arrogance, but before he could speak, a loud screech shook the earth beneath them. They felt the cold wave of a gust of wind sweep the air back and forth above their heads. Ahna and Jules ducked mechanically. They did not dare move anymore. Whatever creature this was again, it raced and dashed above and around them. When it brushed against Ahna's skin, her entire spine locked and froze. At this point, it was fight or flee.

Ahna chose *fight*. She raised the Cursed Bow in the air, which lit even brighter, and shot a beam at where she expected the creature to be. The shadow monster shrieked and disappeared into the darkness. Its screams turned to this uncontrollable laughter they had heard before.

"This sound is absolutely daunting," Jules admitted and shuddered exaggeratedly.

He felt something brush down his neck. In fright, he swung the baton and hit Luthan straight in the jaw. Luthan dashed back, losing focus of his staff. The flames disappeared.

The high elf wiped the blood off his mouth. Jules had hit him with full force. He felt a surge of anger beat in his ribcage.

"Are you deranged?" he shouted at the shrike. "You need to seriously keep your grip on reality, or you'll put us all in danger!"

Jules began to stutter. He had not meant to do this. Despite all, he really felt bad about his actions. "I'm sorry. I thought—"

"Manage your impulses, human!" Luthan roared.

That last word made Jules forget his regret. He wanted to strike again!

Ahna immediately cast a scowling glare at them. "You both need to keep your calm," she ordered, but her eyes relaxed once she saw the cut on Luthan's lip. She let out a long exhale to calm herself.

Clarice and Farooq looked at each other, unsure of what to say or do. Jules had officially begun to lose his mind. The noises, the creeping sounds and shadows of the Far Side, the mind games and hallucinations, all of this had become too much.

Clarice attempted to soothe Jules. "We're here together," she said with her familiar mother-like voice. She laid a gentle hand on his arm and caressed it.

"I didn't vote for this elf to join us," Jules spat at Luthan, who could have spat back with his fiery scowl. "And I most certainly did not vote to see the Dark Lord again."

Ahna intervened. "Jules!" she shouted to bring him back from wherever he was in his mind. She came closer to him and took his face in her hands, looking deep in his eyes. "Stay with us," she whispered to him.

"You want me to stay? We've been walking in circles!" Jules exclaimed. He released himself from Ahna's claws and veered back to the main subject of concern. "All I smell is burned wood!"

But Ahna remained still. Her eyes had caught something far in the distance. They had definitely not been walking in circles. She motioned for them to look in the direction. Her eyes stayed fixed on what she was looking at, as though she examined it with her entire devotion.

She pointed at it.

"The Shadows were toying with us," she declared. "We've been walking in the right direction all along."

Above the horizon, at the end of an ancient stone path that still laid ahead, were a series of bright, red lights that illuminated the sky. The lights were not static. They flickered one by one and tore through the air like lightning bolts of a raging storm. There was not the sound of thunder, just the silence of the Far Side.

"Does this look familiar?" Ahna asked Luthan.

He took a step forward to examine the red storm in the distance. He squinted and dug into his memory of fifty years ago. Yes, it definitely looked familiar.

"The red flashes…" he pensively murmured. "I remember them."

"Then we should keep going," Ahna said, resolute.

They set on their march again, pawing the wet ground underneath their boots. The Cursed Bow's light blazed brighter than ever before. Ahna's entire arm was now engulfed in the radiance, like a white flame that graciously enveloped her limb from fingertips to shoulder.

THE CLOSER THE group of five got to the raging storm, the brighter the place seemed. A red glow covered the trees and fields around them, and they noticed the same silver grass, except that it was tainted by a black substance. They could now see each other clearly. Luthan swept his quarterstaff in the air, and the black diamond lost its fire. They raised their heads to the hundred red cracks in the sky. They were surrounded in a circle of whirling clouds that fractured in flashes upon collision with the invisible wind. Up ahead, they spotted the contours of a geometric structure. They could distinguish a tall edifice, like the square edge of a claymore, erected on a higher platform, a hill, and a long set of stairs that led to the top. The structure touched the red sky. Luthan now finally recognized it.

"That's the vault where the Planar Mask was when we arrived," he disclosed, his voice more confident than before. "Nothing has changed here in fifty years." He was flabbergasted by how this place looked exactly as it did in his memory.

Ahna signed for the group to hurry to the stairs. She led the way, but when she got to the foot of the hill, she noticed who stood at the top, underneath the vault's roof. The figure of a revenant.

"Xandor," the elf stuttered in disbelief.

The man, covered in a black veil of darkness, turned to Ahna and stared her down. It was the same man they had seen in the dark wood. Though this time, his skin was as blue as Ahna's, and his eyes burned with the embers of rage.

Xandor Kun Sharr, the defeated despot who had brought Bravoure to its knees. Her brother, who had ordered for the magi's extinction, imprisoned Thamias, killed her mother, and enslaved the rest of the kingdom.

Ahna, speechless and voiceless, carried a burden too heavy on her shoulders. Seeing him once had shaken her, but a second time... She wanted to collapse to her knees.

Luthan, noticing her anguish, came to stand beside her and scowled at the figure. "I heard you died, Sharr," he sneered.

Xandor's shadow scoffed. The dokkalfar prince sat on the highest step, his legs were open, and he handled a sword rested on his thigh with care. It was a black sword, which he thoroughly filed with a piece of moonrock in his hand.

"Have you finally moved on from the shame of abandoning my sister, Luthan Hyehn?" Xandor snickered. "Wouldn't you care to know how many times she desperately screamed your name while you were running away with a flock of magi?"

Ice-cold shackles gripped Luthan's spine. He checked Ahna, who simply stared at Xandor in horrific spite.

The Prince of Mal continued. "It was more than I'd ever heard. She screamed so much, I honestly thought she'd lose her voice for good," he rasped as he laughed.

Luthan's eyes lit red. Enough. He would not let this monster spew words as such. Words that cut like knives. He roared a fireball from his free hand that crashed at Xandor's feet. A stern warning for the dark elf to shut his maw.

But Xandor stood. He took a few steps down the staircase and cast a dangerous glare at Ahna. "Care to catch?" he asked as he launched the black sword in the air.

Ahna, startled, reached for the sword, catching it by the blade that cut through the skin of her palm. She let out a repressed sigh of slight pain. She gripped the sword by the pommel and took a step forward.

"I sincerely hope you slice better than you catch!" Xandor mocked as he took a final step toward Ahna and swung a second sword.

The two blades clashed with a shattering sound. Luthan had to dash back, toward the three others who could not do anything else than blankly stare at the fight. Xandor roared and pushed his weight forward, pressing against Ahna's blade. But the elf had expected this move. She hauled him in by pulling her sword toward her chest and slinked to the side. Xandor lost his balance and almost fell.

"What are you doing here?" Ahna asked the burning question.

Xandor raised his body up and anchored his feet. "I thought the Shadows were a better fit for me!"

The prince spun on his heels and sliced through Ahna's blade. He commenced a series of powerful cuts. She was forced to cower back, not to be sliced herself. With all the strength she had, she locked on to his last slash and thrust him backwards. He almost forsook his balance again.

"No, you are not Xandor!" she shouted. Ahna was convinced as much. She did now know how she knew, but she did, and to her, that truth was undeniable.

The eldritch man simply laughed. He sank his sword in the mud and leaned on it, for a moment, panting from mere exhaustion.

"Congratulations, Meriel," he praised in an undertone. "I am not your brother, but where is he? Where is Xandor the unkillable?" He paused, as if to answer his own question. "Because

Meriel, Xandor never made it to Hell, and your dear brother refused our offer. So, where could he be?"

Ahna most certainly did not have the time to linger on these dark thoughts. Xandor was deep in Hell and deep in Hell he should stay! She charged. She was going for the man's head when he raised it and spoke his final words.

"The Dark Lord still roams the Underworld. Do you think he'll find a way to crawl out of it?"

In a furious screech, Ahna swung her blade and cut the man's head clean. *Lies*, she thought, yet the unknown man's words had now planted a tiny, frail seed of doubt in her gut. Would her brother have attempted to escape the torments of the infernal maw? No, nothing escaped the Underworld. She kicked the lifeless body so it would fall to the cold ground.

Ahna turned back to the group. She exhaled deeply, exhausted and angry. But then, when she heard that disgusting sound of oozing flesh, she mustered the courage to look.

The figure began to morph into something darker. It grew out of the ground and reassembled itself in a tall monster-like shape. Its flesh rippled from its head and its eyes, oh its eyes, they leaked out of their orbit in green, glowing sludge. It had messy teeth that even pierced through its own jaw and lips. They were aligned and misaligned all together, and they bled this black, leaching liquid that smelled of death. It lowered its head and seemed to smile. It growled deeply, like a starving lion.

"Welcome to the Shadows, mortals."

Its voice was nothing any of them had ever heard before. Its shredded lips did not move, yet the sound of its words tore through their minds.

This creature stood on two legs. Its body was covered in a veil that swirled in the darkness. The rags coiled behind it like tentacles of an eldritch monstrosity.

Ahna's rage took complete control, and she threatened the beast with a stretch of the Cursed Bow.

It laughed in response.

"Why don't we talk first before we fight?" it asked.

Back to the group—Jules did not dare move. Clarice and Farooq were frozen, gaping at this unknown creature. Luthan did everything to keep his composure, and he raised his eyes to the shadow, which pointed an oozing arm to the ancient vault up the hill.

"If you want this, we can make a deal." None gave a response, so the monster went on. "One of you must give me their soul!"

Ahna looked over her shoulder. Her eyes searched for Luthan's. A flaming sword, now! She tilted the weapon she still held upward and gave him a firm nod.

He understood. He set the blade on fire with his glowing red eyes.

Ahna did not wait. She dashed forward and swung the sword at the beast, taking it by surprise. The creature had no time to dodge the flaming sword that cut it in half. It screeched loudly, the sound piercing through Ahna's pointy ears. She had to cover them rapidly and let go of the sword not to be deafened.

The shrieks turned into laughter again. A hoarse, sequential series of maniacal gasps and cries. The beast retook form. The black liquid rejoined together, and Ahna saw the figure sink to its knees in front of her. Its glare never left her.

The flesh solidified into a face she damned well recognized. At the last second of transformation, Jules saw it too, and he froze more than he had frozen before.

Ahna could not believe what she saw. Who she saw. It was impossible. It ripped through her like a thousand sharp needles. She brandished the Cursed Bow. Her arm quivered. The man she faced chuckled upon seeing the weapon engulfed in arcane light.

"That's mine, *dokka*," he declared.

Ahna cringed.

The elf trembled, even more than when the image of Xandor had faced her. She felt the tears climb in her eyes. It was not him.

Let it not be him. She could not face him, not now, not after the rollercoaster this damned adventure had been. Too many spasms in her arm, and she let the Cursed Bow fall onto the mud.

"Can't face the one you couldn't save, Ahna?" he asked, his pulsating voice ringing in their minds. It was just like in her dreams.

The blue elf felt herself lose sense of reality. There he stood, Cedric Rover, in front of her, like a ghost from a treacherous past. Ahna, unaware of herself, reached out to him, to the man who sneered at her.

"Meriel, stop!" Luthan called.

But Ahna could not stop. She was drawn to him, beyond anything comprehensible. The man laughed again. He looked in the direction of the others. His eyes met Jules's, who stared at him like he stared at death herself.

"It is good to see you, Lieutenant."

Jules did not respond. He could not respond. His lips were frozen, and it was like his vocal chords had been ripped apart. He knew very well this figure was not his captain, yet he felt so drawn to it. He was incapable to do anything else than to walk to it.

"Jules!" Luthan yelled and pulled him out of his thoughts. "Whoever this is, it's not real!"

The ghost veered to Ahna again. "Do you still hate yourself, *dokka*? Do you still hate your own existence for what you did to me?" it asked in Cedric's voice. "Do you hate yourself for killing me?"

No, Cedric would never say this. His lieutenant could never say this. Not to Ahna. Lies. Deceit. His grim fate had never been Ahna's fault. This realisation hit Jules and made him snap out of his thoughts. "Get your fucking face away from my friend!" he roared.

The impersonator laughed some more. "And how would you know? Did you know me so well?" His voice rang louder. "All you are is a sad veteran who lost the man he loved and wets the bed at night!"

That was it, the last straw. Jules dashed to the flaming sword that sprung from the ground. He seized it in both his hands and charged the memory of his captain. Without hesitation, he raised the blade in the air above his head and prepared to plunge it deep into the nameless man's chest.

Not so fast.

In a burst, the ghost had discarded the blade, and Jules with it.

Ahna still reached out to the creature, hypnotised, with the sole purpose of touching it. Luthan figured he needed to act fast, before his wife could reach this man, whoever he was. But he needed something more powerful than whatever fire he had left. He went for the Cursed Bow. He rushed to it, seized it in his hand, then hurried to Ahna. The bow radiated with arcane light, but before Luthan could take one of Ahna's arrows, the dirge of pain, strident and shrill, sang beneath his pores. It screamed so loud, his own blood could pierce through his skin. It was too much to endure. Luthan had to release the weapon in a loud grunt, but he picked himself up quickly and aimed at his staff, which lit with the brilliance of a thousand blue flames. He pushed Ahna to the side and launched a cone of flames. The creature, amused by this fire show, let out an exaggerated dying scream. Once the flames were gone, it feigned the sounds and movement of a dying soldier on the battlefield. It caught Ahna's arm and forced its glare into her soul.

"I'll tell you a secret," it whispered. Then it raised its voice and laughed. "There's been a change of plans. The Rover was not to be touched."

And it dissolved into the ground.

Ahna fixed an empty point in space. She was in shock—tears flowed like a torrent out of her eyes. Luthan rushed to her and took her face in his hands. He made her look at him.

"*Kyære*, whoever this was, it was not real," he said to her with a soothing voice.

Jules, who stood behind them, snapped—he had enough of this place. "Not real? This monster looks pretty fucking real to me!" Maybe it was not Cedric, but it was definitely a physical creature that could probably cause serious damage!

"*Hol skeft!*" Luthan flicked his head to the shrike and silenced him in Ljosalfari. "If you keep going like this, I'll have Clarice cage your mind, how's that?"

Clarice scoffed as a retort to come to Jules's defense. She stepped between the two and denied Luthan's vain request with a loud *no*.

Little by little, Ahna regained control over her whirling thoughts. Seeing Cedric, the man she could not save. She cast a broken glance at the blond shrike. "Jules... Cedric's soul..." She thought she was able to talk but could not do better than a stammer. "If there's any chance a part of him still remains..." She could not speak more, something clogged her throat.

Ahna was frozen. Not physically, but her heart had stopped beating. Seeing Cedric's face, his cerulean eyes—it brought memories of her short bit of time with him. The pain they went through, the things they shared... If there was a chance, any chance, that Cedric's soul still existed, Ahna could maybe find it. Where would she even start? Why was she even thinking about that? Why was it the only thing she thought about right now, while there was a Planar Mask to retrieve and an academy of magi to bring back to Bravoure? But Ahna could maybe save Cedric. The thought had latched on to her aching mind, and remained there, fixed like her gaze into the emptiness.

"Guys..." Farooq's voice interrupted Ahna's spiral of unending thoughts. The young man was looking up to the sky. "What's happening?" His voice shivered with dense worry.

The band looked up. The clouds shattered by red bolts of lightning had accelerated their swirling motion. On the cold soil, the sound of oozing liquid caught Jules's attention. The putrid substance expanded and spread into arms of black fluid that stretched all the way to the vault's stairway.

"That's not good," Jules said.

Luthan seized his staff firmly, picked up the Cursed Bow and handed it to Ahna. She mechanically grasped it, still recovering from her haze. He then motioned for the rest to follow. "Let's get up the hill before it's too late."

Ahna followed, her mind forced to return to the mission, but her heart eager to save the man she had lost once this was all over.

18

INTO THE SHADOW REALM II

*T*hey ran up the staircase that led to the vault up the hill. First Luthan, then Ahna, Jules, and the rest followed. The sound of the brooding storm echoed in their ears and beat in synchrony with their pounding hearts. A hammering thunder followed each rapid burst of red lightning. The oozing darkness behind them sunk into the soil. Farooq took one last look at it, cautious of what was to come next. He was more than dead afraid, but he could not stop now, not when they were so close.

Luthan and Ahna quickly reached the vault grounds when, suddenly, the black liquid surged from beneath their feet and rose to form a newborn monster. The creature resembled the one they had just fought, but somehow, it appeared to be different. Larger, darker, it growled as it came into existence. It was the four horns on its head that made Ahna realize she was looking at another, perhaps more powerful being. A much more terrifying being. It stood between her and Jules who rushed behind.

It faced her.

"Lesser Shadows use tricks; I prefer to settle disputes more quietly." Its voice was deep and whole. It did not sound like an animal that attempted to speak but more like a person who had survived death for centuries.

Its glowing green eyes were now fixing Ahna with no expression. Her entire body was gripped with fear. Her heart pounded inside her throat, and she had to force herself with the greatest effort to be able to speak. "What are you?" she uttered with tremors in her vocal cords.

The creature laughed first before answering. "I am exactly what you think I am."

This was no shadow monster afraid of the light. This was no trickster who used illusions to toy with their minds. This creature was something even darker, something more frightening.

Ahna took a glance over her shoulder and saw Luthan. His back was toward her, standing in front of what looked like a small altar. She instantly knew what he was looking at. She could not see it, but she intrinsically sensed that it was the piece of the puzzle they needed to get home. Her entire being felt for it. It was as though she was connected to it.

"Keep your eyes on me, dokkalfar," the creature ordered Ahna.

She instantly veered her chin back to the Shade. It observed her. Analyzed her.

Until it spoke again.

"That power you wield," it said in a voice close to that of a demon. "Do you even understand it?"

Ahna clenched a warning fist, and the Cursed Bow she held lit brighter than it already had. "I don't have to," she assured.

The horned monster laughed. It laughed with that kind of laughter from the deepest bowels of Hell. But it was no demon or infernal being. It was something older—much, much older.

"You may take the Item if that is your wish, mortals," it said in a low, raucous voice, then it faced Ahna. "But you, the runaway elf, will have to stay behind."

At the strike of the creature's words, Luthan turned back,

holding the Planar Mask in his hands, in its original form. An orb of whirling blackness that fit in a crook of a palm. He saw how Ahna's weapon lit even brighter as he brought the item closer to her, like an ethereal power surge. The Cursed Bow lit fully and engulfed her arm in radiance.

Ahna felt the strange power connect her to the Planar Mask. Something spurred this energy beyond anything coherent. She recognized it, and the synergy with her soul could not be denied.

"Let me in," she heard, that same voice again, the same one as back near the river.

This time, Ahna was not afraid. She knew she could fully trust this voice, this call, the call of the Arc of Light itself. There was no longer any doubt that this was meant to be.

She turned her eyes to the Shade before speaking once again. "You know I can't stay behind," she declared, anchoring her feet in the ground to prepare to strike.

But what she saw next stopped her from making a crushing move. The darkness that had leaked to the vault rose at each corner of her and her friends' eyes combined. It formed a dozen of these monsters they had seen before, except that these were not affected by the red flashes of the raging storm. Ahna and the rest were surrounded.

The Shade with four horns grinned.

Ahna saw its teeth, more organized, but sharper than a blade.

"You have no idea what you are," it rasped. "You carry the Arc like it's some kind of ordinary tool, but dark elf, you have no idea what that makes you."

Ahna raised her voice to hush the creature's words. "We won't leave without a fight." She would not let this creature taunt her with futile words.

She flicked her head to Luthan, who already had brandished his staff. The diamond at the tip of the weapon lit with the blue flame of his own arcane imprint. His eyes glowed red, and Jules, who stood behind the Shade, saw his sword be set ablaze.

Yet the creature only laughed more.

"Very well," it whispered the sort of whisper one hears in their worst nightmares.

The others of his kind folded onto vault grounds. Luthan swiped his quarterstaff around and launched a scorching wave of fire. Jules swung his blade at those who targeted him. The fire burned their flesh without leaving a mark, just the putrid smell of the black liquid. There were screams, screeches louder than the thunderstorm. But the shrieks quickly turned into laughter again. The Shadows whirled around them to match the movements of the rolling clouds beyond the platform. It felt as though the sky fell on them, and the Shadows followed with it.

Ahna raised the Cursed Bow and plucked the last arrow out of her quiver. She stretched the string, aiming the weapon at the Shade. She cast a fierce glare at the monster, who simply stared back, static, with its leaching green eyes.

"Let me in." That melody, yet again.

That was when Ahna felt it, as Luthan came even closer to her, the orb he had slipped in his belt satchel. She could feel its power, almost as strongly as she could sense the Arc of Light in the weapon she held. A flow that connected the two Items through the Fabric of Realms. She felt it. And she understood what it meant to wield the Arc of Light. A connection, beyond the tangible world, not only with all Items of Powers, but with the Ancients themselves. A conduit of souls, a tunnel through space and time that linked her to Them. And so, she focused her mind. She halted the time between her thoughts and let the arcane stream from her core to her fingertips.

The elf lowered the Cursed Bow. She closed her eyes and exhaled deeply.

WHEN AHNA OPENED her eyes again, the Shade still stared. But the bow she held had disappeared, only the flames of its radiance remained. And they had grown. Her arm was no longer hers. It had become the blinding conflagration of the weapon's unleashed potential. Her entire limb was immersed in a raging blaze that did not even make her flinch once. She knew this power. She had complete control over it, as though it had always been with her soul, before her birth and perhaps even before Terra's creation. The waves almost reached the Shade that faced her with an atrocious grin.

"The light welcomes the darkness, runaway elf," it declared in a somber, rhythmic tone. "And you are ours to feed on."

"You'll have to fight me first," Ahna retorted effortlessly. No more time for games, now was the time to strike.

She pushed her heels away from the ground and dashed toward the black creature. She clenched a fist she did not need, because her arm had become a distorted blade of light.

The Shade countered her attack with an overgrowth that spiked from its leaking flesh. The liquid of its body solidified into the edge of a blade that clashed with Ahna's light razor. Ahna dodged one of its arms and rolled to the side, then cut through the creature's flank. A loud, shattering roar emerged from its mouth.

The elf finally turned back to her companions, who observed the fight, immobile, caged by the set of whirling Shadows around them. Luthan still stood by the altar, his quarterstaff with flames as blue as his robe. He blasted with scorching fire any creature that came close to him.

Ahna had to think fast. She had to get them out of the Shade's reach. The others did not attack the unarmed Farooq and Clarice, so she suspected they had different plans.

And she was right.

In a swipe of its tenebrous limbs, the Shade absorbed the essence of one of the lesser creatures that flew into it. Then more followed. Each flowed inside the Shadow's veil of gloom and formed an even larger monstrosity. Ahna could not keep her eyes on the growing body of darkness, she needed to get the rest out of here, and fast.

The archmage, with all the arcane power she had left, cast the three others out of the vault in a controlled gust of wind. The wave brought them to the feet of the staircase that led uphill. They landed on their backs, shaken by the draft, but softly enough that they quickly rose to their feet and rushed out of this forsaken place!

The Lesser Shadows in front of Ahna, dazzled by this unexpected move, swirled on each other to get to the elf, but she sent a destructive blast of light in their direction. She quickly spun on her feet, raised a fist in the air and smashed the vault grounds with full force. The burst of arcane light and power shattered the platform beneath her. Everything that surrounded her shot in the air from the shockwave of her crushing fist. All the Shadows around her screeched from the blast and vanished away from a dome of light that expanded until the sky.

Luthan was launched over the staircase into the mud where they had stood before. His staff shot in the air and landed too far away. He staggered to his feet, disoriented from the crash. He checked himself—he still wore the satchel that carried the Item they had come all this way for. Ahna was rushing to him soon after. Behind them, the Shade appeared to recover from her explosive force, much too quickly.

She looked to Luthan, urged him to follow her.

The two ran.

They hasted on the path whence they came, but they were chased by a giant, crawling behemoth with sharp teeth and stiff dead eyes. The stench that followed, that odor of a rotten mass grave, developed with the sounds of the creature creeping on the cold ground.

Ahna halted her escape. She cast a worried glance over her shoulder, calculating at how much time she had until the creature would reach them. Among the red flashes of the whirling storm, she saw hundreds of these creatures surging out of the clouds to meet the expanding behemoth's flesh.

Luthan took her hand. "*Kyære*, we need to run!" he shouted as he touched her. They had to save themselves. They had to, now!

Their eyes made four. Ahna looked at him with a certain light he did not want to recognize. A resolute glow. She was going to save them, but she might not follow.

"We'll never be fast enough," she murmured. She looked over her shoulder again—the monster had almost caught up to them. "Luthan," she turned back to him and looked deep into the emerald of his eyes. "I can save you."

Luthan never left her gaze. He was not going to let her do whatever she planned to do. He would not leave her here, yet the light in her eyes begged him to listen.

"We need to run," he pressed instead.

Ahna pulled her hand out of his. She began to pace away from the monstrosity that slithered behind. Her eyes landed on Jules, Clarice, and Farooq, who rushed away in the distance. But she knew they would never make it in time. They were soon to be chased by an army of Shadows that would only consume them one by one.

It took Ahna a tremendous amount of energy to focus the blast of the Arc of Light. She was not sure what she was doing, or if she was even in control. Her instinct had taken over. She had to save them. Her subconscious thoughts guided the flash of bright, white light in the direction of her three companions who ran for their lives. When the radiance hit, she realized herself what she had just done. The blast propelled the three into a blinding tunnel of light that matched its speed. They were shot into the event horizon, as though they had become the light themselves. When the darkness regained terrain, Jules, Clarice, and Farooq were gone.

. . .

LUTHAN CAUGHT UP TO AHNA, and the light had faded from her arm. He did not have time to address her, she swirled to him and gripped his arms, and pulled him in in front of her.

"Your turn, Luthan, I can save you," she ordered and assured him once more. She was not going to let him contest.

Luthan still leaned forward to come closer to her. He did not want to leave. His gaze beseeched that he would never leave without her, ever again.

The monster behind them hammered a loud and decimating roar. It had grown larger than the hill where the vault had stood.

Ahna's purple eyes lit with a resolute spark. "I'm not giving you a choice," she declared.

The crawling creature roared again.

Luthan wanted to speak, but the radiance engulfed Ahna's arm again.

She stepped away from him and looked deep into his eyes, the green eyes she had never forgotten.

"I'm saving you," she said like there was no choice left to be given. There never was.

Luthan held her gaze for a fraction of a second, his mouth half-open and the glaze of tears in his eyes. He wished to tell her how much he wanted to stay, how much he wanted her to follow. He wanted to say words unsaid for fifty years without her. He wished to tell her he loved her, and that he had never stopped loving her.

But she did not give him the chance to respond. When the Arc of Light immersed Ahna's arm completely, she slammed her hand against his chest. Luthan was thrust back. His entire being merged with a tunnel of light and disappeared with it.

The Shade, which had now turned into an oozing beast larger than a dragon, caught up with Ahna and clutched her in its clawed hand. Its jaw came to her face, and she saw its leaking eyes stare deep into her soul.

"Welcome to the Shadow Realm, runaway elf," the creature howled.

There, she felt it. She felt the biting cold liquid of its molten hand slither along her arms and shoulders until it gripped her neck. The closer its maw approached her, the better she could see the slime that straightened and pointed at her. It made its way to her mouth, nose, eyes and ears and penetrated her to possess her whole.

The pain she felt was excruciating. She screamed a scream that could not be heard. The burning liquid slid underneath her eyes, pierced through the drum of her ears, and sank deep into her throat. Part of it slinked underneath her clothes and boots and ripped her bare flesh open. She begged for it to stop. It was agonizing. Her voice broke as too much of this liquid had torn the tissue of her lungs. The fists she clenched slowly loosened, and her head fell back to hang on her spinal cord.

LEGENDS SAY that passerine birds sing the melodies of prophecy.

It was the voice of a goldfinch that awoke Ahna. Her eyes snapped open. She blinked a few times to haul her consciousness back. There was no more pain.

She looked around. A stone house, a crude wooden table, a few empty chairs beside the one upon which she sat. Behind her, a bedroom with a small bed. It was all simple. She did not feel anything but curiosity and confusion. Where in Hell was she?

A man suddenly opened the door. The loud creak caught Ahna's attention away from this house she swore she recognized. The man entered the little stone house.

He wore a long, white robe. An alb covered by a tabard of the same color. His waist was girded with a red cincture. That man, she also knew him. But she couldn't dig deep enough to find his name on the graves of her mind.

His voice startled her. "There's nothing more delightful than a jolly morning walk! Isn't it right, Ahna?"

That voice sounded so familiar. Ahna simply nodded, waiting for the man to say more so she could get a hold of his name.

"What have you got yourself into, now, Ahna?" he asked, and his question made her heart leap.

The elf did her best to utter a question, but she could barely speak. "I'm not so sure. Where am I?" She really did not know.

The old man with nut-colored eyes and a bald head chuckled with joy. "You tell me, Archmage. This is where you spent a lot of your days!"

Ahna could not believe it. The elf had no idea where she was, or even who this old man in a clerical alb was, yet she was definitely sure she knew. *Wait a minute...* A clerical alb?

"Who are you?" she managed to ask.

The old man chuckled again. "Have you forgotten about me already? I was your favorite old coot!"

Ahna shook her head. She had his name on the tip of her tongue.

"Alright," he said as he motioned for her to stand up and follow him. He stood by the open door again. "It's time, Ahna." The elf rounded her eyes, and the old man continued. "You must come with me."

She let her own words take over. "And go where, Gideon?"

Gideon! That was his name. It was him! The wise Resistance cleric who handcrafted statuettes for the souls in need. He was here. Gideon was alive! Ahna felt tears rise in her eyes as she realized in whose presence she was. Everything came back to her. Then fewer things made sense. This place...it was her little stone house back in the village of the north.

"Why are we in Miggdra?" she eventually asked. "Why are you here?"

Gideon straightened his posture and gave her a soft smile. His eyes lit with kindness and compassion, the compassion he had shown her many times two years ago.

"You must come with me," he declared. "The Domain of Stars awaits."

Ahna lowered her eyes. Her lips could no longer move, as though Gideon's words had struck her at heart. She realized what they meant.

"The Heavens await," she inferred. "Is it my time to die?"

"That is only up to you," Gideon answered with peace.

She needed to make a choice: life...or death. She rose to her feet and came closer to the old cleric. She paused once she stood in front of him and gazed into his eyes.

"What am I supposed to do?" she murmured her question, the tears had reached her pupils. She did not want to die. Not now, after all she had been through. After she was this close to completing her quest.

Gideon took her left hand in his. He turned it over, and a dim light began to shine in the crook of her hand.

"You have a power that impressed even the gods themselves," he said.

Ahna fixed the light with her worried eyes. So, the gods were aware... "What do the gods know of the Arc of Light?" she asked, distant.

"Ahna," Gideon began in a different tone. "Do you know why the gods and the Ancients never really got along?"

One quick guess. "Because the Ancients didn't believe in the gods?"

Gideon chuckled a third time. "Because the Ancients found a power that could match the gods'."

Ahna remained still as he spoke, looking at him with incredulous eyes.

"But *Gods* and *Ancients* found a common accord. They allied on the same ideal, the same goal, for mortals to live in peace through Balance and Harmony." As he explained, Gideon had a smile of a proud child. "There is something in you, Archmage," Gideon pursued. "A power that now flows through your veins. The power of Balance between light and darkness. You can unleash its true potential."

Ahna had no other words but her question: "So, what am I supposed to do?" Was she to follow him to the Heavens? Leave her pain behind and head to a place where she could forever be safe? How was she supposed to honor the power she had been given then? Was she to stay in the tangible world and restore order to a torn Bravoure?

"You can come with me, and we pass the threshold together," Gideon said. "Or you use that power and bring the magi home and Bravoure back on its feet."

"Wouldn't the use of the Ancients' power anger the gods?" she asked with a tint of humor in her voice.

A warm smile simply drew on Gideon's aged face. "The gods have a place for you in the Heavens, Guardian of Bravoure. And they always will. But ultimately, it is your choice to make."

Guardian of Bravoure...

"You are the second one who calls me that," Ahna said with a faraway simper.

The light in her eyes changed. It muted to something more certain, more resolute. She had made her decision. She was staying. Gideon saw it and knew. The cleric gracefully turned around. His white alb swayed behind him as he spun on his heels. He was about to leave the house when he turned to Ahna one last time.

"Bring them home," he said. "It was good to see you again."

Ahna gave him a dear smile. "Indeed, it was." There were tears in her eyes, but not of sadness. Tears of seeing an old friend again and knowing he was more than just fine. Gideon was safe and sound in the Domain of Stars.

When the cleric disappeared through the door, Ahna remained silent for a moment. She looked in the distance, to the golden fields in the light of a bright sun she was eager to see again. The elf brought her hand to the doorknob and pushed it passed her so the door would fall shut.

A BLAST BRIGHTER than the Storms of Creation slashed through the soil and sky, sending bits and pieces of black, bleeding flesh into the cold air. The behemoth shrunk on itself, blinded and petrified by the radiance that now submerged its victim whole.

"My power flows inside you. I am by your side, and I will never leave you."

The voice of Balance.

Ahna rose above the ground.

She faced the giant creature of horrors, almost gracefully, illuminating the entire area around her, submerged by a power she had never felt before. There were shrieks and screeches of the other, less powerful pawns that crawled and cowered away in fear, attempting to find some kind of shade to protect themselves. But all effort was in vain.

Ahna soared into the sky of the whirling red storm. A halo on her back, piercing through the skin above her shoulder blades, vibrated through the air as she faced the beast. Her eyes were no more. Her face was too bright to stare. She cast one last glance at the monstrosity before vanishing into a powerful shockwave of dazzling light.

IN A BRIEF MOMENT OF STILLNESS, a split second of silence, Ahna felt the presence of a ghost, a man from her past. The shrike's presence. She was certain of it. She heard his indistinguishable voice call to her. She wanted to keep her eyes closed, to remain in this instant, close to Cedric Rover. *I'm coming for you, Cedric. Once I'm done here, I'm coming to save you.* This was her resolve.

. . .

"SHE'S NOT BREATHING!" Luthan shouted as he held his wife in his arms.

He looked around. Jules and Clarice hasted with canteens full of water from the nearby stream. The sunset lit their surroundings with a dim golden light. They felt so relieved to be able to see and think for themselves again.

Yet Farooq still stared with the eyes of someone lost. Ahna, who had appeared in a flash at the foot of the hills behind them, laid lifeless on the silver grass. Her eyes had lost their color. Her heart had stopped beating. The young apprentice was so panicked that he paced around her in extreme worry.

Jules rushed to his dearest friend. He collapsed to the ground next to Luthan and drenched Ahna's face in the fresh water. Her skin was burning. Jules felt so desperate. His friend was dying, and he could not do anything about it!

"What's going on, Luthan?" he urged with dread in his voice.

The tall elf simply clutched his wife close. He held her face in his hands and spoke to her softly. "*Kyære*, my love, please, I can't lose you again." He really could not. He felt the sorrow of decades completely grip his mind.

Clarice came to kneel beside them. She no longer had her staff, the magic that could maybe stabilize the blue elf, but right now, she helped Jules with attempting to shake Ahna awake.

After a few waves of cold water and the voices of her companions begging her back to life, her eyes regained their purple color, and her breathing slowly recommenced. Her heart beat anew, under Luthan's hand, who had not let her go.

And who swore he would never do so again.

Ahna rushed her body back up in a nauseous burst. She spat out a pool of black goo from the depths of her upset stomach that dissolved into the silver grass. She had to cough most of it out.

She disgorged the rest out of her throat in violent spasms before looking around.

Ahna called for Luthan before meeting his green eyes. Once he made sure she was stable again, he hauled her in his arms. He did not give her the chance to resist.

Jules had his eyes wide open in concern. He could have thanked the gods that his friend still lived, but what in Hell had happened out there?

Ahna's thoughts were slowly materializing again. She was safe, and so were they. She saw Clarice and Farooq with the biggest smile on their faces.

A thought suddenly rushed through her mind. "The Planar Mask?" the elf prompted.

Luthan gave her a smiling nod as a response. He fetched the small spherical artefact from his belt satchel and held it in his hand to show his wife.

"We have it. We can go home."

Ahna smiled. Her eyes sparkled with the success of an ending quest. They were going home. Luthan helped her rise to her feet. They gathered their belongings and headed onto the path. They were close to the edge of the Eidolon Forest. They just needed to walk the trail west for a day, and they would make it back to Skyshrine before the fall of the night.

19

HOME

The band of five made their way back to the citadel of glass, carrying the Item of Power they had gone to the Shadows and back for. The small, black orb that could expand to form a gateway through space and time. Luthan carried it close, in his belt satchel, afraid of losing it when they were so near to ending this fifty-year-old chapter away from Terra.

Once inside the dome, they headed to Iedrias, who rejoiced upon seeing his precious daughter and friends. After a good and long-awaited rest, Archmage Dallor proceeded to gather the people in Skyshrine's great hall, underneath the Taraxacum. He gave his speech, announcing to his adepts and apprentices that they could return home. Most had been born in Skyshrine. Only the elders and elves remembered. To the youngest, Terra had always sounded like a long, distant dream place with forests of trees and mountains that could touch the sky.

They placed the Planar Mask on the pedestal outside, by the gates of the citadel. Many had already gathered their belongings. Some discussed among themselves what the Great Return meant for the fate of the magi. Iedrias and his associates went to set everything up to activate the Item of Power, but before that, Luthan had a duty to fulfil. He had to come clean.

The tall elf went to find Ellyra, who had told him to meet her by the lake, away from the citadel of glass and away from the crowd. She sat on a bench, looking at the still waters, as though her eyes were longing for something, but Luthan could not quite discern what. He felt a lump inside his throat and a guilty pinch in his stomach. He was not sure at all what to do, but he knew one thing: he needed to tell her about Ahna, that was the least he could do. He sat beside Ellyra, calmly, first waiting for her to speak. She did not. Instead, she still fixed the water with her brown eyes. The silence rhymed with the movements of her chest as she breathed in and out as though a heavy weight rested on her shoulders. Or at least that was what Luthan thought. He had to speak. He could not hurt her any longer.

"Ellyra," he tried to say, his voice failing him.

But she raised a hand in the air as a motion for him to stop talking. To his surprise, she smiled at him. But when he analyzed her smile, he saw it was fake, and there was sadness hiding in her eyes.

"I'm sorry," he simply said, yet she held her smile. He had absolutely no clue what else to say.

She responded with a slight titter, still looking upon the man who had never loved her. "I know," she retorted and let the silence sink in again. A minute passed, and she looked at Luthan again. "So, what will you do?" she asked.

Luthan sighed and looked away. Her question took him by surprise. What would he do? He did not love her. He held her dear, but he had never loved her, but he had a son with her. "I'm unsure," he replied. "She's my wife but... you are—"

Ellyra immediately interrupted him. "Have you gone mad, Luthan?" She let a laugh escape her lips. Or was it a scoff? Her vague amusement confused him, but she spoke again before he could ask her what had transpired inside her head. "You can't make me believe you want to stay after you've dedicated the first thirty-five years of your life in Skyshrine hopelessly trying to get back to *her*!"

"That's a fair point," he responded. He did not know what else to say.

Ellyra turned to face him completely. She brought her hand to his face and looked at him dearly, while she caressed his cheek with her thumb. "Luthan, I know I've always been in her shadow."

Luthan's eyes darkened. So Ellyra had always been aware of the love he could not return. It hurt him to think he had never been what she had deserved. "I'm sorry, Ellyra, I really am."

Ellyra laughed. This time, her laugh sounded real. "Something has happened to you, my dear. Something even the most fortunate could only hope for." She lowered her hand and took a deep breath, and her eyes flew back to the lake. "The love of your life was returned to you, Luthan."

Her last words made Luthan's heart skip a beat. He really had no idea what to respond to all this. Ellyra, on the other hand, held her serene gaze upon the lake for a moment, and turned back to him.

"My dear, if my husband came back to me, I would leave you in a heartbeat," she said with that jocular smile. "You are the luckiest person alive—don't let her go like you did fifty Sols ago."

"But..." Luthan pleaded. "What about Tiberius?" He had to think of his son, after all.

"You will always be there for him, I know you will. Because that's who you are. You don't have to worry about him; he'll still be around, and so will you."

The tall elf felt that pinch in his heart again. He had to apologize once more. "I'm sorry I couldn't be more to you," he said. Ten Sols of feeling guilt about never returning her kindness.

She silenced him with a finger to his lips. Then, she took his face in her hands and gave him a long, soft kiss, which he did not return. It looked like something she needed to do, to be able to move on herself. When she released him, she plunged her eyes into his and smiled once more. "Luthan, there was never any love between us. Just...partnership. And you have given me everything I could ever wish for. You gave me a son."

Luthan took one of her hands in his and kissed it softly. This gesture was his way to express his recognition for her deeds, for her support and help in healing his wounds of war. Ellyra had been his savior and the best friend he could have ever wished for.

The ljosalfar with copper hair rose to her feet. She took one last look at the lake and at Luthan before she headed into the streets and walked toward the citadel of glass.

BACK IN IEDRIAS'S humble home, Ahna seized the Resistance cloak Jules handed her. She thanked the blond shrike and gathered her things. She had dived back into her Terran clothes, ready to go home, resolute.

"Excited?" she asked Jules and Farooq as she strapped her empty quiver around her body.

The two nodded, also determined to finally get out of this place.

Iedrias came downstairs. He carried a large bag in his left hand and a staff in his right. A staff Ahna had not seen in years. His old Bravan quarterstaff—made of a dark oak that matched his skin and golden-green engravings that did his mossy eyes. He smiled at the elf and his daughter, who had just stepped through the door.

"The first few people have gathered," she announced to the group. "They're ready."

Iedrias nodded. His eyes met Ahna's, who smiled as she gazed upon him. "We're going home," he said.

"I have enough room for you to live in the Academy," she told him.

"Let's first see how this goes. I have no idea what will happen next once we're back on Terra," Iedrias conceded, his heart pounding from excitement and apprehension together.

"One step at a time," Ahna said and nodded.

Ahna took a moment as the rest followed Clarice outside. She glanced upon her arm—the glyphs had definitely disappeared. She was unsure why, but she still felt the imprint of this unknown power that flowed inside her. It still called out to her, but in a much dimmer voice. It was something she would definitely study once back in Bravoure. After making that mental note, she headed outside and joined the group.

Farooq's cloak swayed behind him as Ahna's did. They walked next to each other gloriously and head held high, as though the world belonged to them. Jules tailed and looked at his two dear friends march in front of him. His thoughts lingered on his return. He dreamed of the mines of Orgna that had become his home, but he also wished he could find another in the golden city.

A familiar voice reached them.

"Meriel," Luthan called.

Jules turned to Luthan, who did not seem to see him and only had eyes for Ahna. Before the tall elf passed him, Jules caught his attention for a brief moment with a hand to his arm.

"I hope things between us are...alright," the shrike said, hesitantly.

Luthan halted his march and looked to him. "We're good, Jules."

They both smiled and nodded respectfully at each other, and Jules kept on walking. When he passed Ahna, she turned to Luthan. Jules laid a supportive hand on her shoulder. He took an educated guess at what the two wished to discuss and gave them some privacy. He still worried about his friend, about the decision she would make with regards to Luthan. He did not want her to move too fast, but if it was what she wanted, if she wanted to get back with him, then Jules had no say in the matter. He signed to Ahna that he would be waiting for her at Skyshrine. After all, this was none of his business, but he still cared about his friend.

Luthan stood in front of her in his black archmage robe embroidered with green threads. He had a light in his eyes that Ahna was unsure she recognized. Something that made him look like he was about to kneel before her and surrender. He seemed so candid when she got closer to him. He breathed softly, as though he, for the first time in decades, had a calm feeling of home.

"*Kyære…*" he dragged out. He wanted to continue, but she was too close, so he pulled her in and kissed her instead.

He heard a small sound that came out of her lips and brought little bumps to his skin. But she quickly released herself from his embrace. That was not what he had expected. That was not what he wanted. Her eyes begged for something that worried him, namely for him to stop. He gazed upon her with a frown, questioning what had caused this distress.

"Luthan, what are you doing?" she asked as she shook her head.

"I'm coming home with you," he declared.

Ahna was simply confused. "What about your son? And what about Ellyra?" Those were the logical things she could say while she pondered on why exactly she held back. She became silent for a minute. A smile that was no smile was drawn upon her face.

The blue of his wife's skin almost shimmered as a tear passed over her cheek. Luthan could not stop himself, he had to hold his wife, who was obviously still shaken. He smiled dearly at her and stepped in to take her in his arms. "I'll make it work with Tiberius. Please, Meriel, let me hold you."

Her hands landed on his chest to stop him from getting

closer. She felt drawn to him, yet there was definitely something holding her back. This whole journey, this time she had spent with her fears, her spite, her anger, her joy to see him again, her doubts that things could never be the same, it all fell crashing on her shoulders, right now, in this moment.

"I'm not ready for this, Luthan."

Her voice echoed in his mind. He thought he had misheard— he wanted to have misheard. He wanted to take her lips, bewitched by the amethysts of her eyes. He made a move despite her cautious glare.

But she took a step back.

"Please," she implored. "I wish it was as simple. I want you"— she made a tender face; she really did want him—"so bad. B- but... But I still need to process the fact that you left, Luthan."

His heart broke. She was not going to take him back. His hands felt numb; he was frozen, petrified.

"Even though you thought I was coming with you," she continued. "You still left. You left Bravoure, and I don't know if I can deal with that yet. I'm going to need time." Ahna saw the tears fill his eyes. "Please, give me some time."

Luthan simply wanted to hold her, but Ahna's stance implored him not to. And so, the tall elf found the strength to take a step back and let go of the idea.

"What can I do to help?" he asked, tears in his voice, wanting nothing more than to be there for his wife.

She delved into his emerald eyes. She did not have an answer for that. As much as she searched through her mind, she had no idea how Luthan could help her process the fact that she had lost him, mourned him, witnessed the squalor and mystery in Bravoure after the magi had gone, fought a war without him, then found him again.

"I'm still angry, disoriented," she said as tears now flowed freely. "I need some time to figure things out and let them rest."

"Whatever you need." Luthan could not stand still. He stepped toward her and took her in his arms. He did not want her to cry. He had to comfort her, to make her feel better, to make her feel safe. "I love you, Meriel. I have never stopped loving you."

Why did that sentence coming from her husband's lips hurt so much? Ahna felt confused. His last words echoed in her mind. *I have never stopped loving you.* Had she stopped loving him? The idea seemed inconceivable, and yet here it was. She could no longer deny it. As much as she wanted to latch onto his memory, to clench it close to her heart, to grasp it and not let it go, Luthan, the man of her life, had truly become the man of her past.

She took a deep breath, forcing her thoughts to retreat to the final step of the mission at hand. Luthan's blue flame was required to use the Planar Mask, so they had to keep moving on. "They'll need your stellar fire," she said with a slight smile.

Luthan smiled back, unaware of her struggle and simply mesmerized by her beauty. He walked with her to the staircase that led to Skyshrine, where Iedrias and a dozen of magi waited for them.

IEDRIAS MOTIONED for Luthan to commence the spell. The Planar Mask was placed on the pedestal, and four of the adept magi stood by it to monitor the arcane fluctuations around the Item of Power. Luthan and Iedrias were the only ones left who had activated the Mask in the past, and so, they stood by the pedestal, ready to work their magic.

The Tazman-elf turned to his old friend Ahna and addressed her in a cautious voice. "The four adepts here are geomancers. In case we arrive six-feet deep under Gurdal, they'll be there to dig us out."

Ahna gave him a nod of acknowledgement. "Farooq can learn a thing or two," she said with a didactic smile aimed at the young apprentice who stood beside her.

Iedrias took a deep breath. "Here we go," he said, prepared to return home.

His daughter stood beside him, eager to see the Terran sky her father had told her about countless times. The young sorceress observed him as he prepared to activate the Planar Mask.

"It is a mysticist's power to wield the arcane as we do," Iedrias told Clarice. "This allows us to feel the arcane shifts caused by an Item of Power." He then took a step forward, and the golden stone encrusted in the claw of his staff began to glow. "I am channeling the energy into my staff," he explained. "Observe." He knocked his quarterstaff once on the pavement of Skyshrine's plaza.

The orb of whirling darkness rose into the air. It came to levitate away from the pedestal and toward Iedrias, slowly, emitting this buzzing sound that matched his staff's frequency. As it moved through the windless air, Luthan paced closer to it. In a flicker of his eyes turned red, his arms became engulfed in flames bluer than deep oceans. He needed no staff—his magic had to roar freely in the chaos of stellar fire.

He brought his curved hands to face each other, almost touching. In the hollow of his burning palms, a stranger blaze formed. It grew from an unseen point at the center of what he clutched into a black halo that ruptured through space. The blue flames dissipated into this crack, and it took him all his energy to tear the Fabric of Realms.

Once Luthan stabilized the blackness between his hands, he cautiously approached the Planar Mask. The latter descended, like a veil that came to rest upon him. It morphed into a thin layer, untouched by light, and formed a mask on Luthan's elven face.

Luthan opened his red eyes through the mask.

"I can see it," he uttered in a distorted voice. "I can see the cave..."

The Planar Mask began to drain into the tear between Luthan's hands, which the tall elf lowered not a moment later. A circle of pitch-black ripples took shape before him, and it grew wider as it absorbed the mask's power. It expanded and stopped once the mask was entirely consumed.

Everyone opened their eyes in bewilderment at the formation of a gateway through the Fabric of Realms. Iedrias smiled—he recognized this portal that had brought him here in the first place. He turned to his daughter once again.

"Call the rest of those who want to follow and tell them the gateway is open."

Clarice stared at the portal in awe. "Is it a one-time thing?" she queried, as she had observed the Planar Mask being sucked into the stellar rift.

"Once the portal closes," Iedrias proceeded to explain. "The Planar Mask will be reborn. From orb undone to orb anew."

Clarice then stepped away and headed down the moonrock stairs to fetch the rest of the magi who had expressed their wish to return to Terra. Iedrias prepared the first few travelers, who now stood beside him.

The portal spread tall by the gates of Skyshrine. It had grown larger than the gates themselves and extended into what looked like a circle of black water with motions across the air. Luthan gazed upon it for a minute, then paced calmly toward Ahna, who stood near Jules, behind Iedrias and Clarice. He motioned for his wife to step through the portal with the first group.

Ahna slowly shook her head, still dazed by the sight of the portal, but she wanted to wait for now. "Let's make sure everyone gets through first," she suggested.

Luthan acknowledged. He came at a standstill near the three Terrans who had come all this way to rescue the lost magi. He looked upon them, wistful, perhaps regretful that it had taken this long to find a way home.

He then turned to Iedrias. "Go, my friend," the tall elf insisted. "You've been waiting for this moment for a lifetime."

Iedrias's eyes lit with hope. "Make sure you follow," he said.

"I will. Now, go!"

Iedrias took his daughter's hand. He strolled behind the travelers that disappeared through the portal one by one. Once he stood by the shadowy circle, he gazed upon it with nostalgia in his eyes. Home—the concept he had long forgotten, was just within his reach. Clarice noticed her father's hesitation, and she led him through the gateway.

From the group of magi that reached the high of the steps, surged a little elven boy with pointy ears that flickered in the absence of wind. The boy went to hug his father, the tall elf much bigger than he, who held him in his arms for a minute. Ellyra followed behind. She cast a glance at Ahna and walked toward her. Ahna felt a slight tremor in her chest, anxious of what Ellyra would say to her. After all, Ahna's return had ruptured whatever they had. But Ellyra smiled at Ahna dearly instead and leaned forward.

"I kept him safe, *dryaa*," she said with her melodious, elven voice. "Now it's time I return him to where his heart has always belonged."

Ahna mirrored the ljosalfar's smile. "Thank you," she said with a thin bow of the head and her lips awkwardly pursed. She was unsure what else she could say. She was not even sure Ellyra had been sincere.

Luthan kissed his son on the cheek and put him down. He motioned for him to follow his mother, who was about to step through the gateway with the rest of the group. Tiberius turned to his father and waved with as much enthusiasm as he felt from the idea of stellar travel. The two were tailed by other apprentices eager to see this new world of legends. They stepped into the portal and disappeared in the swoosh of a cold wave.

Another group of magi followed, and only a few remained.

Ahna turned to Farooq. "Go with them; we'll make sure everyone's through."

The young apprentice gave her a nod and headed to the gateway. He stepped into the portal with no hesitation. After his adventures in the Eidolon Forest and on the Far Side, this mere portal did not scare him one bit!

Jules looked around him and Ahna. Only Luthan and a few others were ready to embark. The tall elf turned to one mage who had decided to stay for now.

"Once the Planar Mask on Terra's end is secured, we'll make our way back," Luthan declared. "We'll find a way to have a permanent gateway as the Ancients did."

The mage nodded furtively and bid the travelers goodbye, for now.

The remaining three magi were first to enter the gateway. Luthan looked one last time at Ahna and followed. Then, as Jules and Ahna walked together and faced the black, pulsating portal, the blond shrike thought he saw something in the shadows of the Planar Mask. It looked like a swirling glimmer. He wondered, for a fraction of a second, whether Ahna had seen it too. He stepped through, knowing that Ahna would soon follow.

THE COLD SENSATION that spread through Ahna's body made her open her eyes. It was dark and dry in the stone room she appeared in. Ahna's head cocked from side to side, but her eyes were still covered with a dark veil, and she could not see further than her hand. She heard no voice, no one beside her footsteps. She called for Jules, Luthan, Farooq—anybody! Only the silence responded.

She searched through the dark. Nothing. Confused, she roamed the darkness, touching a cold stone wall with the palm of her hand. Finally, with the flicker of her hand, she wished so loud to light the place with a flare.

Nothing.

She tried again. Failure.

Her magic was not working. Fear gripped her throat. Her heart began to race.

She then realized more that did not make any sense. She was not underground. She moved back to where she had first appeared. Her eyes slowly grew more accustomed to the darkness, and she was able to distinguish a pedestal erected at the center of the room, upon which the black orb encasing the Planar Mask rested. She was definitely not underground.

She stood in the middle of a vault-like structure. The more she looked around, the better she could see.

She was in the Academy.

Ahna gasped. Now she was terrified.

"The Academy's vault..." she mumbled to herself. But that was impossible. That was simply impossible.

A door shot open, and the light of a hallway beyond the vault loomed into the room. It cast a multitude of rays that illuminated the entire chamber. Ahna was briefly blinded. By the light stood a man, a human who wore a long, black robe. The fact that someone stood alone in the vault startled him, but what truly frightened him to the bone was the sight of what Ahna was. He pointed at her, his brittle hand trembling, then he began to scream.

"Dokkalfar! Dokkalfar!"

The broken shreds of his voice shattered Ahna's eardrums. The man ran back through the door into a hallway, and ignoring her own gut feeling, Ahna raced behind him. She recognized it all. The long corridor, the main hall where the man almost fell to his face, all the people in robes who stared and gave her these disgusted looks. This was the Magi Academy of Bravoure, but something was different.

Something was very wrong.

The running man cried for help, but people simply stared. He made his way to the main entrance, passed the two statues of phoenixes that stood proud and tall, and caught his feet in his robe as he rushed down the outside staircase. He fell on the pavement of the wet Bravan road, and Ahna caught up to him.

"Help!" he shouted into the rain. "Dokkalfar!"

Everything next happened so fast. Someone grabbed Ahna's arms. Another man seized her by the waist and immobilized her. She struggled to anchor her feet to the wet ground. She attempted to shout something when a flat hand muted her lips. She met their eyes, angry stares of dismay, but when her gaze landed on the road, her heart took the highest of leaps.

It was all different. Ahna had no idea what she glimpsed at. The houses had grown. The buildings had grown. The road was paved in different stones, and the carriages looked so much more...different. There were so many guards. They wore an armor Ahna had never seen before. Black armors. Made of black-steel, for sure—the stronger iron of the north. They marched in square formation toward the Academy, toward her.

"Take her!" one of them ordered.

Another one relieved the two citizens of their duty and seized Ahna by her wrists. She sought to defend herself. She struggled against the guard as hard as she could. He almost fell.

Another three blacksteel guards dashed toward her and held her paralyzed when the blade of a sword met the blue skin of her neck.

Ahna called for help, for someone to come. For Jules. For Luthan.

No one. No one came.

It became harder to move, harder to breathe. As she fought against the grasp of angry guards, she felt her energy slowly slip away through her fingers. She tried to focus, to call upon a thud, a throb, a pulse of power through her veins—anything! She had no more time.

A kick in the back of her leg and Ahna was pinned to the floor, on her knees, helpless.

All the guards brandished their swords at her.

She wanted to defend herself. She focused again, screamed in her mind for something to happen.

Nothing.

Ahna attempted yet again. And again and again. She desperately called for the arcane, one more time. Absolutely nothing. She felt powerless. Helpless, and all alone. Like the time after the war had been lost. Like the time she had found Antaris in ruins in search for magi survivors. Like the time she had thought she had lost everything.

A boot clashed against her jaw. Her head jolted back. She found herself thrown in the soaked mud, pinned down on the ground, an excruciating pain taking over half of her face.

Then, as she gazed upon the dirty fingers of her left hand, something unexpected, unprecedented happened. That surge of energy manifested. But it was different. Not the arcane, no, something much older.

"I'm still here," that same voice spoke to Ahna with the purest of calm.

A flash, brighter than a thousand Sols, burst from her hand to her arm to the rest of her body. The radiance, too bright, blinded the guards and people around her, and in the blink of an eye, Ahna was gone.

FAR BEYOND THE plains of Bravoure rested an unholy creature darker than nightmares. His cold lifeless eyes had not seen the light in decades—or was it centuries? He had lost count long ago.

The night had engulfed the sky above him, never to let a day rise again.

His mind stained by decay reached out to that one shred of sanity he had left, doomed to let it go. He heard a distant scream that, for a brief moment, awoke him from his fated slumber. A voice, an echo of a past long forgotten. Did he remember that voice? How could he? The creature had forgotten his own name. It was just a matter of time before he would truly lose himself.

This was to be his resting place. These ruins would be his tomb. He had buried himself, deep beneath the ground, so that no more soul would suffer the curse that followed him. The ground was where he would sleep for eternity. The ground was where the dead belonged.

AFTERWORD

That was a hell of a journey, wasn't it? What is Ahna going to do now? Where did she even end up?

I hope you enjoyed this adventure. I am aware that this story is very different from the first one. Kingdom Ascent was about hope and unity, while Castaway is much more about moving on, inner conflict, finding a way back home and all the challenges that come with it. There is a stronger focus on the characters and what they have to deal with after the end of a war that tore thousands apart.

I would like to thank you, dear reader, for traveling to the moon and back with me. Sit tight, because *City of the Dead* is coming for the final showdown.

Did you like this book? As I mentioned long ago, honest reviews go a very long way for us authors. I'd be ever so grateful if you left some words about this second story, on your favorite retailer.

Prepare yourself for the next ride.

May your life be filled with dreams and your dreams be filled with love,

Valena

ACKNOWLEDGMENTS

I would like to thank some precious people who were part of this wonderful journey:

My mind-twin, developmental editor, and best friend, Janina, who taught me how to really feel things.

Yuliya, who's been here from Day One and has traveled with me far beyond Bravoure.

Shen and Elise, who came back for more.

Vincent, my listener and first-round proofreader.

My awesome review team, and all of you, who supported me and believed I could do this again.

ABOUT THE AUTHOR

Valena might be into computers, but programming is most certainly not her only passion. Born in France, she moved to the Netherlands in 2006. She started writing short stories at a young age, first in French, then she quickly switched to English in her teenage years. Her dream has always been to publish an epic fantasy novel, so she kicked off with Kingdom Ascent in 2020, the first book of the Tempest of Bravoure series. By doing so, she fulfilled the promise she made to her child-self. As an avid gamer, Dungeon and Dragons player, Star Trek/Wars/gate fan, and metalhead, she's had all the sources she needed to invent alternate realms that derive from all we know about life, the universe, and everything.

facebook.com/authorlenagelis
twitter.com/lenagelis
instagram.com/authorlenagelis